HUNTED

OTHER BOOKS AND AUDIO BOOKS
BY CLAIR M. POULSON:

I'll Find You

Relentless

Lost and Found

Conflict of Interest

Runaway

Coverup

Mirror Image

Blind Side

Evidence

Don't Cry Wolf

Dead Wrong

Deadline

Vengeance

HUNTED

A NOVEL

CLAIR M. POULSON

Covenant Communications, Inc.

Cover images: *Alpine chalet* © Maica; *Footprints in Snow Leading to Tree* © diane39, courtesy iStockphoto.com.

Published by Covenant Communications, Inc.
American Fork, Utah

Printed in the United States of America
First Printing: August 2011

17 16 15 14 13 12 11 10 9 8 7 6 5 4 3 2 1

ISBN-13: 978-1-60861-202-4

To the brave men and women of law enforcement, who put their lives on the line each day to protect the rest of us

ACKNOWLEDGMENTS

My family are a great help with each book I write. I thank them for the time they take to read and critique each of my manuscripts. I couldn't do this without them.

I would also like to pay tribute to my editor, Kirk Shaw, for his hard work, his patience, and his efforts in seeing to it that each of my books is the best that it can be. I feel fortunate in having such a capable and dedicated man as Kirk assisting me.

PROLOGUE

When the top officials of the Apex Coal Company in western Pennsylvania came to work that Monday morning in May, there was a broken window in the main office. Inside they found a brick with a note attached. The note read, *Shut the mine down by Friday night, or you will pay the consequences.* There was no signature.

The officials were perplexed. What was this about? they wondered. What consequences?

The police responded, but they were as baffled as the company officials. It wasn't until the police were getting ready to leave that the general manager booted up the computer in his office. He drummed his fingers on the desk as he waited for his e-mail account to pull up. His back suddenly stiffened, and he leaned forward when he saw an e-mail titled "Earth Militia." After a moment's hesitation, he opened the message, his eyes scanning it quickly, and then he sat back and groaned. It was a chilling warning, more specific than the note attached to the brick. He called the cops to come in and take a look.

The pollution from your coal production is destroying the planet. You must stop your operation, or we will stop it for you. You are killing people, destroying the environment, and facilitating global warming. If you fail to cease operations by this coming Friday, you and your kind will face the penalty of death. It's better for some to die than for an entire planet to suffer so needlessly. We are the Earth Militia, and we will not be ignored.

At about that same time, a similar message appeared at the company headquarters of a large coal-fired power plant in West

Virginia. As in Pennsylvania, the group calling themselves Earth Militia claimed to have delivered the message.

A third threatening message was also delivered to the company headquarters of one of the largest rail lines in America—a railroad that hauled millions of tons of coal from mines to customers each year.

All three companies took the threats seriously, as did each of the local police departments involved in the various investigations. By noon that Monday morning, the top officials in each state were in communication with each other. By early afternoon, the Department of Homeland Security had been notified.

The threats were not treated seriously there. No one had heard of the Earth Militia before, so it was reasoned that it could not be a large enough organization to carry out its unspecified threats. Some officials even joked at what they considered a feeble attempt by a handful of lunatics to frighten people.

In an attempt at a response to something they did not take seriously, Homeland Security simply instructed the companies to be alert. No further action was taken. Sometime during the course of that Friday night, an explosion at the Apex mine killed several miners and forced closure of the mine.

Another explosion occurred at the large power plant in West Virginia. Some of the night crew died, and the damage to the facility was extensive enough to force its closure for two to three weeks. The families of the dead and injured employees at both facilities were devastated and innocent lives forever changed.

The destruction and death didn't stop there. Two trains collided in the Nevada desert. One was carrying coal, and the other was a fully loaded passenger train. The accident derailed many coal cars, and a couple dozen passengers were killed or injured on the passenger train. The investigation soon revealed that someone had intentionally sent the trains onto the same track. The person responsible for those tracks was found dead a few feet from his building.

The morning editions of a dozen major newspapers reported that they had received anonymous e-mails stating that all three disasters had been orchestrated by the Earth Militia. Each of the major TV networks in the country received similar statements.

The federal authorities, when contacted, said they were shocked—that the attacks had come out of nowhere and without warning. Considerable controversy arose when the affected companies countered the claims of the Department of Homeland Security. Members of the Senate demanded that heads roll, and Homeland Security promised to take immediate action to find those responsible. But as far as the public knew, nothing ever happened, and many companies from coast to coast implemented, at considerable expense, enhanced security procedures.

A month passed before another message from the same mysterious organization was sent directly to the White House. It stated,

You haven't seen anything yet. Coal mining and the commercial use of coal will *be eradicated. We will not allow such destructive practices to continue. Take heed or this country will be brought to its knees.*

Homeland Security finally took the matter seriously and went to work. However, months passed without further incident, and so public and top government officials relaxed, much as they had in the years following 9-11.

Chapter One

One year later

The water was smooth, the day warm for early May, and the lake only had a few boats on it. Rich Phillips fished from a small yellow boat far from shore, when a second boat approached. The lone occupant, wearing a jacket and with a cap pulled low over his eyes, was hunched over the steering wheel at the front of the boat. Rich signaled for him to slow down and steer clear, but the driver didn't appear to notice Rich or his boat. Two men and a woman in a third boat noticed the danger and waved their arms and shouted at the operator, trying to warn him of the danger, but he didn't appear to hear them and continued on. He seemed to be drunk or suffering from a medical condition.

They continued futilely shouting for the second boat, an old vessel with flaking, faded blue paint, to turn its course. At the last moment, the operator looked up, and it appeared that he attempted to swing the boat around. But he was too close at that point, and his boat collided with Rich's little fishing vessel.

Rich's boat rolled far to the side, and he was thrown from his seat into the water. He didn't have a life jacket on and disappeared beneath the surface almost instantly. The larger and older boat that had struck him continued on, seemingly undamaged. The operator was still hunched over, but the boat gained speed as it fled the scene. Rich's boat righted itself as the third boat sped toward it. The woman on board covered her mouth in shock as her male companions shed their life preservers and dove in to rescue the missing boater. The operator of the old blue boat didn't look back once as his boat disappeared around a peninsula.

After diving in and frantically searching for several moments, the men gave up and reentered their boat. While they were swimming, the woman called for help on her cell phone, promising the operator that she and her friends would stay there until authorities arrived.

Shortly after the call, the authorities conducted a thorough search of the surrounding waters and checked the land for the possibility that the man had made it to shore. And despite their best efforts, they failed to locate the old blue boat or its negligent operator. The two boaters seemed to have vanished.

* * *

When the doorbell rang early that same May afternoon, Patty Phillips stopped her contented humming and answered it. The man standing there identified himself as a deputy sheriff. "Ma'am," he said, "there's been an accident at the reservoir."

Patty gasped as the deputy continued. "Was your husband fishing this morning in a yellow boat?"

Her body shaking, Patty stumbled for the nearest chair and sank into it. "Yes," she confirmed in a trembling voice, her head spinning. "He was planning to spend the day at Strawberry. Why? He's okay, isn't he?"

She grew pale when the deputy said, "The state registry indicates the boat was your husband's. I'm very sorry, but divers have been looking for him without success.

"Would you mind going out to the resorvoir to answer a few questions for us?"

Patty felt sick to her stomach, and a wave of dizziness washed over her. She gripped the arm of her chair. "I don't know. I'm so shook up I don't dare drive."

"We'll have someone pick you up in a few minutes," the officer promised. "Unfortunately, it won't be me as I have to stay in town and patrol. I'm really sorry, Mrs. Phillips."

As soon as he'd left, Patty brushed her short blonde hair, almost unable to maintain her grip on the brush because of her shaking hands. A few minutes later, another knock came on the door, and

Patty answered it. She didn't say ten words to Detective Andrew Wakefield from the Duchesne County Sheriff's office as they drove west from Duchesne. The officer tried to talk to her, but she had a hard time doing anything but rubbing her eyes with a white hanky. Even though the drive took only forty-five minutes, it seemed like hours before Andrew pulled up and parked near a host of cop cars.

The authorities there were subdued and businesslike. Patty answered their questions in a quiet voice, periodically wiping at her red eyes. Yes, she was sure Rich had taken the little yellow boat out this morning. No, she didn't know of anyone who had a boat described as old with worn blue paint. No, she didn't know of anyone who would want to hurt her husband. Yes, he fished here from time to time. No, he hadn't ever had a boating accident before. Yes, he was a good swimmer. No, she didn't know why he wasn't wearing a life jacket.

She kept her emotions in check while inside she was dying. Not until Detective Wakefield delivered her home did she break down.

"He's dead, isn't he?" she cried, leaning into him for support.

He gently took her by the arm and directed her toward her front door. "We don't know that yet," he said, but she wasn't comforted. Once she was inside, Andrew left and Patty collapsed on her sofa and cried while she waited for the authorities to bring her children home. She hoped to get herself under control before they arrived. She needed to be strong for them.

* * *

The last period of the school day was in its final ten minutes when Bria Phillips was called to the principal's office. Sheriff Lee Rutger greeted her with a solemn face.

"Hello, Bria," he said.

Her heart sped up in her chest, and she nervously brushed at her short brown hair. Something was terribly wrong. When she and her family had moved to Duchesne four years earlier, the sheriff had been their bishop. She knew him as a loving and compassionate man. But she also knew from what others had told her that he could be a tough and unbending lawman. What was he doing here?

"Hello, Bishop," she greeted him using the title she knew him by. She began to wring her hands. She locked eyes with the sheriff, feeling that if she looked away, the news he had to share would get worse somehow.

"I'm afraid I have some bad news," he said, his voice breaking. "Your father has been in an accident on Strawberry Reservoir. We're pretty sure he's drowned. I'm so sorry."

"What do you mean 'pretty sure'?"

"We've conducted an extensive search of the lake and surrounding area and found nothing."

Bria stared at him. She couldn't speak. Sheriff Rutger put his arm around her.

Finally, she was able to ask in a shaky voice, "Where's my mother?" Tears suddenly rushed down Bria's cheeks as the impact of what he'd told her became a reality.

"She's at home waiting for you and your brother," he said gently as he took her by the elbow and helped her to a nearby chair.

Her tears flowed freely now, and he sat next to her, just letting her grieve for a couple of minutes.

She finally asked, "How did it happen?"

"According to witnesses, your father's boat was struck by another boat operated by someone who seemed to be drunk. Your father was knocked out of the boat and went under. He never came up."

"Are you sure?" she asked again in a tiny voice, hoping for a miracle.

"The witnesses called the accident in on a cell phone. They stayed right there until the authorities arrived."

"What about the guy who hit him?" she asked.

"He fled. His boat hasn't been seen since," the sheriff said with anger in his eyes. "No one can find it on the lake, and no one saw it leave the lake. Roadblocks were set up, but somehow the man and his boat have vanished."

"Just like my dad," Bria whispered, and she broke down again.

"Come on, I'll take you home," Sheriff Rutger said. "Your mother is waiting for you."

"What about my little brother?" she asked, worry in her voice.

"My chief deputy and his wife are with him right now. They'll take him to your house too. Bria, I can't express how sorry I am."

Heartbroken, she got to her feet and left the principal's office, her eyes red and her shoulders slumped. The final bell had rung, and the halls were full of students.

Walt Hinshaw, a boy who'd taken her to the senior prom before and a good friend, saw her with the sheriff and ran over. "Bria, what's wrong?" he asked.

When Bria looked into Walt's concerned eyes, her tears spilled out anew, and she couldn't answer.

"Sheriff Rutger, what's going on?" Walt asked.

The sheriff shook his head as he steered Bria to the front door. "Her father has been in an accident," he said. "I need to get her home to her family now."

Walt stood and watched Bria, a look of shock on his face. She wanted to say something, but she couldn't. Their eyes locked for a moment, and then she walked to the front doors with the sheriff.

* * *

For the next several hours, a continual flow of people stopped by the house with food and condolences. Several of Bria's friends came, including Walt Hinshaw and his older sister, Sage. The last of the visitors left around eight o'clock that night. After closing the door behind them, Patty slumped onto the sofa. Her heart was breaking for her daughter and son. She didn't know what they would ever do. After a few minutes, the phone rang, snapping her out of her daze.

"Hello," she said uneasily after she put the phone to her ear.

"Hello, Patty." The voice on the other end was unfamiliar, yet he seemed to know her. He relayed a short message and then said, "Don't breathe a word of this phone call to anyone—not even your kids, but you'd better watch your back." The line went dead. Patty stared at the wall in shock, and the room seemed to spin around her. She didn't sleep much that night.

* * *

Authorities searched the lake for several more days, but the body of Rich Phillips was never recovered. The boat that had struck Rich's was finally located in a shallow inlet just about a mile from where the accident had happened. The boat had sunk to the lake floor, about twenty feet from the surface at that point, and seemed to be in fairly good shape except for a large crack in the hull—which had most likely sunk it. The recovered boat offered no clues and had no numbers or identifying evidence inside.

The police couldn't find the man who had been driving the boat. The site was close enough to shore that officers assumed he might have succeeded in swimming away from his sinking vessel. They assumed he must have left in the vehicle he had used to tow the boat to the lake before they'd set up the roadblocks.

Rich Phillips's disappearance was ruled an accidental drowning, and the case was closed.

Chapter Two

A strange sound drifted from the forest to the south. One young hunter suggested that it seemed like someone playing a harmonica, and the others agreed. The music continued for several minutes. At times it was clear, and at other times it faded away, sort of like an AM radio station that was a little too far away to pick up clearly.

The group of eight young hunters huddled around a blazing fire. The crackle of the burning wood added a percussive effect to the bizarre sound. The wind picked up, and the sound faded away again. When the wind slowed once more, they thought they could hear it again until eventually it stopped for good.

Bria was nervous and said, “There is someone out there.”

One of the guys, Caden, roared with laughter, “Bria, you have a vivid imagination. It’s just the wind.”

“It doesn’t sound like the wind to me,” she retorted.

“It’s probably a murderer,” Caden said sarcastically. “Someone wants to kill all of us.”

“Caden, that’s enough,” Zach, who’d invited them all on the trip, said firmly. “I’ve spent a lot of time in these mountains and I’ve never heard a sound like that before. It’s probably the wind, but it sure sounded like music.”

Caden ignored him and spoke to Bria again. “Hey, I have an idea. Why don’t you go out there and see if you can find whoever it is. Then bring him back and introduce him to the rest of us. But you better take your rifle. I’m sure it’s someone dangerous.”

“Why don’t you go?” Janie, one of the other girls, said with a snicker. “You seem to think you’re all that.”

"I am, actually," he said. "I know about things that really *are* dangerous—things you have no idea about."

"What are you talking about, Caden?" Janie said, rolling her eyes.

"I'm serious. You all seem to enjoy being up here in the mountains, but this won't last long if things continue as they are."

"What?" Zach said, wondering where this had come from.

"The coal mining industry and other forms of pollution around the country are destroying our environment to the point that we won't have anything left to enjoy. There are other alternative energy sources out there, but certain idiots refuse to open their eyes to it. It's time to shut those mines down and educate people."

Zach, surprised by Caden's passionate outburst, asked, "Surely you don't believe that it was okay to kill miners in order to save the earth. That's insane."

"How else do you get the point across when others won't listen? It makes sense to get rid of a few causing major problems for the rest of us. Kind of like exterminating termites."

"So you condone what terrorists did to the coal industry?"

"Sometimes it takes something big to get things changed. You should be able to see that."

Bria jumped in then. "All I see is that you are deluded, Caden. That's way too extreme." The look he gave Bria across the campfire chilled her to the bone.

"*You* are deluded, Bria. You have no idea how this type of pollution will change your life, or how dangerous and effective those who are trying to make the world a better place for you are."

Bria looked at Caden as if he had lost it and, without another word, went into her tent.

"You're ignorant, Bria, just like your dad was," he called after her.

Zach told Caden to knock it off again, and when the others banded together in telling him to shut up, he eventually did. Later, when all but Bria were still gathered around the fire, Walt mentioned the sound again. "I swear it sounded like someone playing a harmonica or a violin or something. Weird."

"You're as stupid as Bria," Caden said.

Sage, Walt's sister, looked at Zach before she broke in. "It didn't sound like the wind."

"Yeah, it seemed like music to me," Janie agreed. "Could have come from another camper somewhere out there. I think I'll go to bed too."

"Good idea," Zach said. "We want to start early in the morning."

One by one, they headed to their tents, the strange sound soon forgotten.

But Bria didn't forget it. After everyone else was asleep, she awoke, tossing and turning in her sleeping bag. Then, to her dismay, she heard the sound again. It seemed closer, and she shuddered, pulling the sleeping bag over her head and putting her hands over her ears to shut out the sound. When she eventually eased her head back out of the bag, all she could hear was the gentle wind stirring the branches overhead. It reminded her of happier times.

She missed her father so much that she ached. She'd never hunted with anyone but her father, and now the tragic boating accident had robbed her of his companionship. She wept silently and finally fell into a restless sleep.

"Did you hear the music again?" was the first thing Caden asked when he crawled from his tent the next morning and saw Bria sitting by a newly started fire. He was grinning and watching her with what she interpreted as lustful eyes.

She shivered and turned away. She'd decided not to go with the others when they left to hunt again. "I'll stay and watch the camp," she said.

"Good idea," Caden said. "That way if Harmonica Man comes around and tries to steal our stuff, you can frighten him away."

"That's enough, Caden," Zach Barlow said angrily. Then he turned to Bria, his face softening. "Are you sure you want to stay here?"

She nodded. In a few minutes, the group left and she was alone.

* * *

Shots to the north of the High Uintas hunting camp two or three hours later brought Bria off the log she'd been sitting on and to her feet. She didn't care if she got a deer or not, but she hoped the others soon did so they could all go home. This had turned out to be anything but a fun experience. It wasn't at all like hunting with her father. She had always looked forward to spending time with Dad when he was home from his work trips. She got along well with her mother and little brother, but her relationship with her father was something wonderful, and the time she spent with him when he was home had always been the best times of her life. He took her hunting, fishing, and camping a lot. This wasn't the same.

Bria threw a couple of branches on the fire and stirred the embers until they started to flame. As she worked, she thought about why she was even here. Zach Barlow had invited her to hunt deer with this group of friends. They had at first driven to the trailhead at Moon Lake and then ridden on horseback several miles into the High Uintas Wilderness Area. Zach, the oldest of the group, was particularly kind to Bria, and she liked his attention, even though she carefully guarded her feelings. Bria was eighteen—one of the youngest of the group—and now in her first semester of college.

Zach had brought a couple of packhorses to carry their gear and food. All of the horses they had ridden into the mountains but one belonged to his family, who owned a cattle ranch near Duchesne.

She and her dad had ridden horses a few times, but she didn't consider herself much of a rider, although she liked horses a lot. She and her father had always hiked when they hunted and camped. She preferred hiking to horseback riding any day.

Bria let her thoughts drift to the others in her hunting party, three girls and five guys, who ranged in age from eighteen to twenty-two. The other girls in the group were not part of her small circle of close friends, and she was somewhat puzzled as to why she'd been invited. She guessed it was because of Walt Hinshaw or Jay Kilpatrick. She'd gone out with Walt several times over the past year and rode with him most days to classes in Roosevelt, where she was attending the Utah State University–Uinta Basin campus. He was a nice guy and probably the only one in the group she considered a close friend.

She'd dated Jay, too. He and Walt were both good to her, but they didn't seem to care a lot for each other. She wondered if Jay was a little jealous that Walt and Bria were the same age and had graduated from high school together. Jay was nineteen and worked at a garage in town when he wasn't working on his father's farm. She could feel the friction on this trip between them, and she couldn't help but think that she was at least part of the reason, although she didn't really care for Jay and had only gone out with him because her mother reminded her she needed to give every guy at least one chance. Now, Zach—Bria wouldn't mind a date with him. What girl wouldn't? She had noticed, though, that Sage seemed pretty interested in Zach too.

Sage was a year older than Bria, and although she was kind to Bria, she had seemed a little jealous of her ever since Jay Kilpatrick had taken her out. Walt told her that Sage had once had a crush on Jay.

The other gal in their group, Janie, had mostly ignored Bria both on this trip and before, and Bria was certain that if it had been up to Janie Thorne, she wouldn't have been invited.

A friend of Janie's, Rex Lerner was all muscle and had been a star football and basketball player in high school.

Twenty-two-year-old Zach was the undisputed leader of the group. His dark brown hair was kept neatly trimmed and short, his hazel eyes always seemed to be smiling, and it was obvious from the way his shirt fit that he put in many hours of hard labor on the ranch. Bria thought he was about the cutest guy she'd ever met. She felt sorry for him now; she could tell that all the contention was upsetting him.

"I shouldn't have invited Caden," he had whispered to her when Caden had again begun taunting her that morning and making smart remarks to the others.

Caden Pendleton was new to the community, and he was not particularly well liked by even the few people who knew him. He claimed to be twenty-one, although he looked older. From the first time Bria had seen him, he'd given her the willies. He was cocky and vulgar, and Bria tried to never be alone with him, and now with his radical and violent stance against those he perceived to be endangering the earth, she was convinced he was mentally unstable.

Brought out of her thoughts, Bria could hear someone approaching, and she figured it was someone on their way back to camp with another deer. The two deer the group had already shot were hanging from a high branch at the edge of camp. Their horses roamed and grazed in their hobbles in the nearby meadow. Since she'd decided not to hunt for the day, she had left her rifle in the tent she shared with the other girls. Even if the others didn't get a deer, she was thinking she would take her rifle, bedroll, and a little food, and hike out of here the next day—she wanted to get away from Caden. She would call her mother and have her come to Moon Lake to pick her up. She hated to hurt Zach's feelings, but she really didn't think he'd care if she left. It would probably make Sage happy.

In two or three minutes, Janie, Caden, and Rex appeared at the edge of the camp. They didn't have a deer, but Janie shouted to Bria to grab one of the packhorses for them. "We have to go get Rex's deer," she said. "It's too big to carry, and none of us wanted to drag it."

"Actually, it's *my* deer," Caden said haughtily. "And you guys both know it."

"You missed it by a mile," Janie said, throwing her arms wide. "I saw it all. Rex killed it. Your bullet kicked up dust way behind it."

"Well, you better make up your minds, because somebody's got to tag it before you move it," Bria said, irritated at the squabbling. She got up to get a horse for them. She didn't mind. It got her away from the contention for a few minutes.

"Think you're the fish and game?" Caden called after her. "Who are you to be telling us what to do? From what I hear, your old man didn't even have the sense to wear a life jacket."

Bria stopped, shocked by his comment, but she didn't say a word or even look back. She just strode angrily into the meadow.

Rex's face reddened. "You didn't know Rich Phillips. He was a great guy. So you just keep your mouth shut."

Caden ignored Rex. "You oughtta just go home, Bria," he called as she continued to walk away. "You are such a wuss. You're scared by a little wind in the trees. I'll tag my buck when I feel like it."

"It's not your buck, Caden," Rex said, his deep voice full of anger. "And you better lay off Bria. She's not the only one who got spooked by the sound last night."

Caden said something else, but Bria couldn't tell what, and frankly she didn't care. She also didn't care who had shot the buck. What hurt her was how callously Caden had talked about her father. She made up her mind then that she would leave first thing in the morning. She couldn't stand another day around Caden.

She caught Zach's tall bay packhorse and took the hobbles off its front feet. As she led it back to camp, she could still hear the argument. But she didn't say anything more except, "Here's your horse," as she threw the lead rope to Rex.

"Thanks, Bria," Rex said with a smile. "You didn't have to do that. I could have gotten it myself."

"It's okay," she said with a halfhearted smile.

Rex put a packsaddle on the horse, and the three hunters left. Bria was glad to be alone again. She stood near her tent and watched them as they started out of camp. Rex led the way, with Caden following behind him, still sulking. She watched Janie as she followed the other two. Janie was attractive. Her skin was clear, and she had expressive blue eyes and pretty blonde hair that came to her shoulders. She was fairly popular with guys. But unlike her pretty face, her personality, as far as Bria was concerned, was the pits.

But who was she to judge? Bria just needed to go home and back to school. Her mother hadn't been particularly pleased that she was skipping classes. It's not that she wasn't a good student, because she was. She had earned good grades in high school and was doing just fine in college.

Rex, Caden, and Janie hadn't been gone more than ten minutes when Zach, Jay, Sage, and Walt appeared.

Walt said, "Hey, you need to come with us, Bria. We're going out again after we grab a sandwich, but we'll take some horses this time, so you can ride."

"Thanks, but I'll stay here," Bria said.

Jay moved close to her and, with a lopsided grin, said, "I have a better idea. You and I will go one way, and those three can go another. I'll help you find a deer."

Sage's round blue eyes narrowed. "Not even," she said. "Walt and Bria can go together. He's got his deer, and now he can help Bria get hers. You and I are going to stick with Zach, Jay. Since he already got his deer, maybe he can find us a couple of them."

Zach smiled easily, but Bria could see the frustration behind the smile. He winked at Bria, making her heart flutter.

"Bria, you come with me," he said decisively. I'll help you find a deer, but I know you won't need any help shooting it. I've heard that your dad claimed you were a crack shot with that .30-30 of yours. We'll let those two and Sage hunt together."

Despite herself, Bria was tempted. She looked at Zach and smiled shyly. She gave him an almost imperceptible nod. He was not only good-looking, he had a big heart. A compliment from him went a long way with her.

"Maybe I will," she said.

Both Jay and Walt looked slightly stunned, but neither of them said anything. Sage grinned and looked longingly at Zach. Zach shrugged, looking a bit guilty, and then asked, "Have you seen the others, Bria? I heard some shooting a while ago. I was hoping maybe one of them got something."

When Bria finished explaining what had happened with Rex, Janie, and Caden, Zach's smile faded. "Caden is turning out to be a real pain in the neck. I wish I hadn't given in and let him join us. I still don't know why he wanted to come in the first place."

"Yeah, he tried to claim that little buck of mine, too," Walt said as his eyes drifted to the tree where he and Zach had hung their deer the day before. "He's a real jerk. Where did he come from, anyway?"

"He says he came from California, but who knows if that's true," Zach said with a frown. "He doesn't have a job that I know of, and yet he seems to have money when he needs it. I can't figure out what he does with his time. And what's with the environmental crap anyway?"

"I don't know, but I hope he moves on soon," Sage said. "I can't stand the way he looks at me. It gives me the creeps."

Bria didn't comment, but she was glad to learn that she wasn't the only girl he watched. That made it seem less personal and actually made her feel safer. She'd felt, even before this trip, that he had singled her out. She'd never mentioned it to anyone, not even her mother, but it had frightened her. It was a relief to know that he made Sage uncomfortable as well.

After they ate some sandwiches, Zach looked at Bria, his smile firmly in place again and full of good humor. "So you're coming with me?" he asked Bria.

She couldn't refuse. An afternoon alone with Zach was a dream come true. "Sure, I'll go," she said, ignoring the looks of jealousy on the faces of Jay, Walt, and Sage.

Chapter Three

As Bria, Jay, and Sage waited while Zach and Walt went to get the horses ready, Rex, Caden, and Janie returned to camp. The only thing different from when they'd left was the fine-looking three-point buck strapped to the back of the bay. Rex was still in the lead with the horse, with Caden trudging along right behind him, his face grim and his shirt wet with sweat. Janie brought up the rear, looking like she could barely place one foot in front of the other.

Bria sensed that the tension among the three had gotten much worse. Caden was still angrily claiming the deer, and as they entered camp, Rex said to him, "You know what, Caden, you can have this buck. I'll get a bigger one. But you can string it up by yourself. I've done all the work so far. If you want it, you take care of it from here on out."

Bria should have bitten her tongue, but she couldn't help it. Her father had always been a stickler for following hunting laws, and when she noticed that the buck still didn't have a tag, she said, pointing a finger at the buck, "If it's yours, Caden, why haven't you tagged it? I ought to report you to the game warden when we get back."

Caden didn't say a word, but he marched over and stopped right in front of Bria, his eyes glaring. "You mind your business, you nasty orphan," he said. "I oughtta slap you."

"Hey, that's enough!" Jay said as he approached Caden with his fists bunched up. The other guys were also coming toward Caden.

But before he got there, Bria said, "If you tag it right now, I won't say a word. But I do mean right now." She was provoking him, and she knew it, but she'd had it with him.

Caden slapped her so hard and fast that she stumbled back and fell to the ground. Her head hit a rock, and for a moment she thought she would pass out. Rex let go of the lead rope of the packhorse and ran toward her. With an angry shout, Jay laid into Caden with both fists, but Caden fought back. Sage screamed at both of them to stop.

Rex helped Bria to her feet. She swayed slightly, and he held her while she regained her balance. She touched her lip and found that it was bleeding. She wiped it with her hand and then wiped her hand on her pants. Her face was stinging, and it made her angry to think that she'd have a bruise and a fat lip.

As Caden and Jay continued to fight, rolling on the ground now, Sage shouted for Zach and Walt to stop the fight, since Jay was definitely getting the worst of it. It was Janie who saw the bay horse bolt and run back the way they had come only moments before.

"Hey, there goes your deer, Caden," Janie said, but she didn't seem to care enough to go after the horse.

Jay was too busy getting beat up to worry about it, and Rex was examining Bria's bruised face. Zach and Walt came running back to camp, leading two trotting horses. They quickly tied them to a tree, and in a moment, they pulled the angry combatants apart.

"What's going on here?" Walt asked.

Janie looked down her nose at Bria and said in a biting tone, "Bria thinks she's a game warden. And Caden thinks she isn't. He's a creep, but it looks to me like Caden won."

"Nobody won," Rex growled, and then his eyes darted about as he noticed that the horse with the buck he had shot was missing. "The packhorse is gone!"

"Walt, grab a saddle," Zach said urgently. "I'll get one too. We better get moving. Up here in these mountains we could easily lose that horse if we don't get right after him." Then he turned to Bria. "Are you okay?"

"I'm fine," she said unevenly.

"What happened? Your lip's bleeding," Zach said with a frown as he swung a saddle onto his tall black mare.

"Caden hit her," Jay said with a growl as he rubbed some of the blood from his face. "Somebody needs to do the same to him. I hate a guy who hits girls."

"I'll deal with you when I get the horse back," Zach said with an angry look at Caden as he pulled his cinch tight. "And you better knock off your nonsense in the meantime."

Caden glared at Zach and shook his head, his eyes narrow, lips pursed, but Zach kept working at his horse.

Caden turned toward Rex and said, "If you don't find that horse and get my deer back, I'll break your neck."

"Caden, that's not necessary," Zach said.

"It's not your deer that's been lost," Caden retorted.

"It's not yours either," Janie said. "You missed it by a mile. You're the worst shot I've ever seen."

"You can shut your mouth or I'll make it look just like Bria's," Caden said angrily. "It's your fault that horse and my deer are gone. You should have told me when it ran off."

"I did, but you didn't listen," she protested.

"You're a liar," Caden told Janie. "And you . . ." He pointed to Jay. "You'll wish you'd never laid a hand on me."

Zach swung into the saddle, his expression dark. Pointing a finger at Caden, he said, "You better hope we can find that horse. You'll wish you'd never been born if we don't."

"Rex let him go, not me," Caden said, seeming to be blaming everyone in turn. "He's an idiot. And Janie didn't move a hand to catch him when Rex let go of him."

Zach shook his head as he moved his horse toward Caden, one fist clenched. Bria was afraid that he was going to jump off of his horse and hit Caden himself. He did get off the horse and took a threatening step toward Caden, but then he stopped, his teeth grinding. He gave Caden a long, hard stare and then turned to Rex as his hand relaxed. "You and Jay get horses and come help us," he said with a tight voice. "And get one for Caden, too. He's going to help since it was his fault. And make it fast. That's our best packhorse."

Caden cursed. "It isn't my fault he ran off."

"Like heck it's not!" Zach thundered. "And you *are* going to hunt for him until we find him."

Janie grabbed her horse and made ready to follow the guys.

"I'll come too," Sage said, then looking hopefully at Zach, she added, "I'll ride with you."

But Zach didn't hear her. He was already swinging onto his horse again. The others, with the exception of Caden, sprang into action. Bria didn't go with them, but she did catch and saddle the big roan gelding for Caden.

Just before she rode out of camp with Rex, Janie said to Caden, "We'll find that horse, but there's no way you are going to get the deer. We all know you didn't shoot it. You're such a jerk."

Caden spun toward her, shook his fist angrily, and said, "I have friends, girl, powerful friends. You need to watch what you say to me if you don't want to meet some of them, and believe me, you don't."

"Oh, yeah, I'm sure you have lots of friends. You are such a *friendly* guy," she said with a laugh as she kicked her heels into her horse's side and rode out of camp.

Bria heard Caden say something that Janie missed as she rode off. "You think I'm kidding. You'll see. You don't want to meet my friends."

Bria led the horse she'd saddled over to Caden. "Here you go," she said.

He didn't bother to thank her. He just got on and, cursing, rode off through the trees and out of sight. However, in only four or five minutes he was back.

He got off the horse and said, "There. I hunted for him. Guess he's gone. I'm not going back out there again. Maybe you should go, game warden."

His eyes landed on Bria as he spoke, then the look on his face turned to a leer as he took her in. "On the other hand, maybe you should stay. You and I can get to know each other a little better." The look and the words he spoke caused her stomach to knot up.

"I don't think so," she said as she backed away and slipped into the shelter of the woods. She hadn't really known Caden until this trip, but he frightened her. She wasn't about to stay alone with him in camp. She sensed that he was a dangerous man.

Her heart pounding, Bria hurried away, praying that Caden wouldn't follow her.

"I'll be here when you get back. Don't go too far," he called after her.

She sped up, almost running through the forest. But when she didn't hear any sounds of pursuit, she gradually relaxed and slowed down. A few minutes later, Bria came to a small stream. She stopped and cupped water with her hands, washing the blood from her mouth and chin. Her head ached from where she had hit the stone when Caden knocked her down, and her cheek still stung where he'd slapped her.

An hour passed, and then two, as she wandered aimlessly through the trees, periodically tearing up as she thought about her father. How she missed him. She also thought a lot about her mother. Patty had become withdrawn and had acted strangely since her father had died. And she refused to ever talk about his death. It was like she was keeping it all in.

Bria's thoughts shifted to Zach. She hoped he had caught his packhorse. She thought wistfully about missing the chance to be alone for a few hours with Zach. That would have made the trip worth gold to her. But it wouldn't happen now. Nothing was going her way.

She heard a shot in the distance. She guessed that was a good thing. It probably meant that the horse had been found and that the hunting had resumed. She supposed it was time to start moving in the direction of the camp, but she was in no hurry. She didn't want to get back before some of the others had returned, since there was no way she would allow herself to be alone with Caden again—not even for a minute.

When a squirrel chirped and scampered up a tree, she stopped to watch it. Later, when she saw a large buck pass a few feet east of her, its huge rack gleaming in the late afternoon sun, she felt glad that she didn't have her rifle. The magnificent animal had a right to live. She stood and watched as it meandered slowly through a small meadow. She was upwind of it and kept quiet, so it never looked her way, apparently unaware of her presence. She watched it for fifteen or twenty minutes. When it finally moved gallantly into the forest on the far side of the meadow, she made the decision not to mention this deer to the others. She didn't want them to come looking for it, not even Zach. It was hers, and she wanted it to live.

She moved on, but after a few minutes she found herself near an outcropping of rock that she had already passed more than an hour before. Puzzled, she stopped and stared at the rock. She had to be walking in a circle. She stopped and sat down on the rock, and for several minutes she concentrated, trying to decide which way she should go to find the camp.

Finally, she admitted to herself that she was lost. In her wandering, she had failed to watch for landmarks in the distance—something she could position herself with. She'd always, thanks to her father, been at home in the mountains. And she usually carried a GPS unit, but it was back in the tent in her pack. She had let herself get upset, and in doing so she had allowed herself to get lost. Instead of panicking, she sat and pondered, trying to decide what to do. She prayed for guidance. And even though she didn't come up with an answer, she felt calm and relatively unafraid.

Her mind drifted to her father again. He had been a good man and her best friend. His fishing boat had been towed to their house, where it still sat in the backyard as if waiting for his return. On days like today, she felt like she was doing the same thing—waiting for someone who wasn't coming back. And sometimes her loss was so bitter as to eclipse all other worries.

Bria eventually stood up and studied the surrounding terrain. She decided to make one more attempt to find the camp before dark. If she didn't, she knew she had a long, cold night ahead of her. *Just me and some guy with a harmonica.* Where in the world had that thought come from? She shivered and began hiking.

* * *

Zach regretted ever planning this hunting trip. He should have just brought Walt and Sage as he'd first planned. He and his sister lived on the farm just east of Walt's. Their families had always been good friends. Walt even worked part-time for Zach's father, and he'd noticed since returning from his mission that Sage had really grown up. It also hadn't escaped him that she had developed an interest in him. He thought it might be nice to get to know her beyond her being *just* his neighbor and Walt's sister.

An avid hunter, Zach had thought that maybe others who might not get to hunt this year would enjoy going with him into the Uintas—one of the most breathtaking areas of northeastern Utah. This was his second hunt since returning from his mission eighteen months ago. His older brother was across the country with a new job. His younger brother was on a mission now. And his father was not in the best of health.

Zach had decided to stay home and help his father on the ranch this year instead of going back to Utah State University. But when his father insisted he not miss out on the hunt this year, he'd decided the break would be nice. So he'd reached out to a few others to accompany him. Obviously that had been a mistake.

He barely knew Caden, but somehow he'd heard about the trip Zach had planned and approached him, asking to go along. Zach had refused at first, but after Caden had begged several times, and despite his misgivings, Zach had given in. Jay, Rex, and Janie had jumped at the chance to go. And then there was Bria. Eighteen like Walt, she was a cute a girl, but a lonely one. If it wasn't for treading on Walt's shoes, he would have asked her out before now. Since her father had disappeared from his boat on Strawberry Reservoir, she seemed to be sad all the time. He had hoped that this trip might cheer her up.

Zach spurred his horse. His packhorse was still missing, but it was time to get back to camp. Darkness wasn't far off. The others, at his direction, had split up and ridden in different directions while he had continued to search alone. All of them had GPS units, and he'd made sure they knew how to use them, so he hadn't worried about any of them getting lost. He hadn't seen Caden, but he guessed he too was searching. The missing horse was old but one of his family's favorites. Zach wasn't looking forward to telling his father that he had lost the tall bay.

Zach rode through the lush meadow where they had been keeping the horses. There were three there now—the second packhorse, the little sorrel gelding Bria rode, and the large roan he'd let Caden ride. When he saw the roan, he was angry. Caden had apparently turned it loose with the saddle and bridle still on, and it wasn't even hobbled. The last thing he needed was to lose another horse. He rode next to it, leaned down, grabbed the roan's rein, and led it into camp. He was ready to tell Caden to hit the trail first thing in the morning. He'd had it with the lazy troublemaker.

However, he found that the camp was deserted, which worried him. He now wondered if Caden had been thrown from the horse somewhere. That would explain the roan still having the saddle and bridle on. He swung down from his mare and tied her to a tree at the edge of camp. Then he tied the roan to another tree.

With the horses secure for the moment, he looked around and called out, "Anybody here?"

No one answered. He stepped over to the girls' tent and said loudly, "Bria, are you in there?" She didn't answer.

He couldn't imagine where Bria and Caden were. He worried even more. The others should have been getting back soon. The sun was no longer in sight, and it was growing dusky. Everyone needed to be here before darkness fell, and in these mountains that would come quickly now. His eyes fell on a rifle that lay on the ground near a tree stump just beyond the girls' tent.

He walked over and recognized the old .30-30 rifle Bria had brought on the hunt. He hadn't seen her with it earlier that day. His brow furrowed as he bent to pick it up, but before he touched it, his eyes caught a glimpse of what looked like a boot just a few feet beyond the rifle. He straightened and stepped cautiously toward the bushes where the boot stuck out. To his horror, the boot was attached to a body that had fallen faceup into some thick bushes.

Caden Pendleton's lifeless eyes were staring straight up at him, his chest covered in blood. Zach stumbled back and turned to one side, grabbing a small tree for support as his legs buckled beneath him.

Chapter Four

Over the next half hour, everyone but Bria Phillips returned to camp. Zach didn't mention the dead man lying in the bushes until they had all gathered around the fire. He wondered how to tell them without creating mass pandemonium. Then he said, "Does anyone know where Bria is?"

They all shook their heads.

"I'm worried about her," he said.

"I'm sure she's fine," Walt said, but he looked worried. It was quiet for a moment. Zach noted that everyone's eyes were on Walt. "She was hating this trip," he added. "Maybe she just decided to hike back to the trailhead."

"By herself?" Sage asked. "I don't think she'd do that."

"She was afraid of Caden," Walt said. "That creep isn't here. Surely he hasn't hurt her. I wouldn't put it past him, though."

Zach spoke quickly then. "Caden didn't take her."

"How do you know that?" Walt demanded. "He was really mad at her."

"Caden is dead," Zach revealed, his voice suddenly weak. "Over there." He pointed and everyone looked toward the edge of the camp. Zach moved toward the bushes and pointed. "Someone shot him."

Sage screamed when she saw Caden's boots sticking out of the bushes. She grabbed her brother as she said, "Oh, my gosh! This is the most terrible thing I've ever seen."

Rex's first reaction was to say, "Couldn't have happened to a nicer guy." But after a moment, he said to no one in particular, "Who would do something like this?" He looked around at the rest of the group. "He's been murdered," he said. He stepped back, his hands in his pockets, but said nothing further. He simply stood and stared.

Jay and Janie looked at the body, their faces white, their eyes wide. Janie said, "I feel like I'm going to be sick." Jay put his arm around her and guided her to sit on a nearby camp chair. "Don't look at him anymore." Then they withdrew and huddled, whispering to each other and looking terribly worried.

"Could it have been Bria?" Jay finally asked. "Maybe he attacked her again."

"If he did," Sage began, still clinging to her brother, "I don't blame her." Everyone looked at her, and she added, "But I don't believe she would or even could kill anyone, no matter what he did."

An uneasy silence hung over the group. Zach finally said, "We don't have any idea what happened here while we were gone. All we know is that Caden's dead and Bria is missing. Exactly what took place will be for Sheriff Rutger and his deputies to figure out."

Even though his head was aching from the tension of the past little while, Zach gradually calmed the group down and got them organized. "We have to protect the crime scene," he said. "And we have to get the sheriff up here as soon as possible."

"We can't go out until morning," Janie protested. She looked terribly frightened and was shaking badly. "It's too dark to go tonight."

"So you think we should leave Caden lying there in the bushes all night long without the cops even being notified until morning?" Zach asked.

"Yes. No. Oh, I don't know." She said, rubbing her eyes as tears welled up in them.

"I'll go," Rex volunteered. "I can find my way in the dark. And I have a cell phone back at my truck. As soon as I can reach a place where there's a signal, I'll call in."

"Walt, will you go with him?" Zach asked. "I don't want anyone going alone. And you guys should maybe take two extra horses so at least a couple of officers can ride in and save some time."

"You can take mine," Jay said. "He's got lots of endurance."

Zach couldn't quit thinking about the shocking possibility that someone in the little group of hunters he had assembled had shot and killed a man in cold blood. And what really disconcerted him was that the one most likely to commit murder was the victim. If anyone could have acted out in violence, it would have been Caden. Emphasis on the "would have been."

Until the sheriff and his deputies gave them permission, Zach told the others that no one was going anywhere except for Rex and Walt. He told the two of them to stick close together. "Don't get separated," he warned.

He also gave instructions that no one was to touch Caden's body or Bria's rifle and that no one should go close to the crime scene.

Within a few minutes, Walt and Rex were in their saddles and ready to go. "Wait at the trucks for the sheriff and his deputies," Zach said.

"We might have to go quite a ways before we can get a signal on my cell phone," Rex said.

"I understand that, but as soon as the sheriff's department is on the way, you guys go back to the trailhead and wait there." He paused, then he added, "Watch for Bria along the way. And if you don't see her, check at the trailhead. I think she must have decided to leave us."

The two young men nodded and headed for the trail, each with a saddled horse on a lead rope behind him. Zach told the others that he was going to grab a tarp and cover Caden's body. Then, thinking that some normalcy would help them make it until the police showed up, he suggested they get a meal ready, for those who could actually eat. After that, all they could do was sit around the campfire and wait. "If any of you gets too tired, you can go in your tents and go to sleep, but not me. I'm going to sit right here and make sure nothing disturbs the evidence, especially Caden's body."

* * *

Sheriff Lee Rutger was sound asleep when the phone rang. That was one of the downsides of this job; he was on call twenty-four hours a day, every day of the year. When the phone disturbed his sleep in the middle of the night, he always got up and did what the voters had elected him to do. Tonight it was a fatal shooting that had been reported as a possible murder—something he rarely saw in his rural jurisdiction.

He asked the dispatcher to call Chief Deputy Marlon Sessions and Detective Andrew Wakefield and have them meet him at the office. He explained that there were two horses waiting for them at the trailhead. But they would need more, and he asked the dispatcher to tell Andrew, who had several horses on his dad's farm, to saddle one of them and bring it if he could.

His next instruction was for her to call out search and rescue and more deputies. They were to come to the scene as soon as possible. There was a lot of work to do. That done, he hurriedly dressed, buckled on his gun belt, and headed for the office.

Lee knew all but one of the young people involved in the hunting party. Caden Pendleton was new in town, and although Lee had seen him around, he'd never actually met him. There were rumors that he sold drugs—he had no other apparent source of income. Lee had been told that Caden was the victim. Sheriff Rutger couldn't understand what he was doing up there with Zach and the other young people in the first place; he didn't seem their type. Rex Lerner had reported the crime on his cell phone from near the trailhead at Moon Lake and had given the dispatcher the names of the people in the hunting group and had told her that Caden Pendleton had been shot and killed. That was all that Lee knew.

* * *

Unable to find her way back to camp, Bria had built a small shelter, with branches that she'd gathered, beneath the low-hanging limbs of a large pine tree. She had left camp in fear of Caden and hadn't even brought a match or a jacket. It had been an unseasonably warm day, and she'd shed her coat before noon. She regretted that now, knowing she had a long, bitter cold night ahead, but she also knew that trying to find her way out of the mountains at night could be suicidal. So she hunkered down in a makeshift bed of pine needles and tried to sleep. Despite the cold and her troubled thoughts, she finally drifted off.

She awoke sometime later to the sound of a soft whinny. For a few moments, she was disoriented, but she finally remembered where she was and sat up, shaking the pine needles off her clothing and brushing them from her hair. Then she stepped out of her shelter and listened. She was pretty sure she'd heard a horse, but she couldn't be positive.

"Here, horse," she called out tentatively.

For a moment, all she could hear was the breeze whistling through the branches above her. Then she heard twigs breaking. She was nervous and a little bit afraid. Even though she'd spent a lot of time in the mountains with her dad, she knew to be cautious. So she didn't step any farther from her shelter. But she again called out, "Here, horse."

When she heard it again, the whinny startled her, coming from just a few feet into the darkness. She called again, and a moment later a shadowy form stepped close to her. She shuffled forward and touched the head of the horse. She discovered that it had a halter on but that the lead rope was broken. It had a packsaddle, and so she figured Zach's missing packhorse had found her. The packsaddle, however, was empty, meaning that somewhere in its hours of wandering, the big bay had lost the buck Rex had strapped to its back. That rekindled her anger toward Caden. It had been a nice buck, and now, because of Caden, it was wasted—its death in vain.

Since there was only a minute amount of light shining through the tree limbs above her from the bright stars, she mostly worked by feel as she pulled the packsaddle and double layer of saddle blankets off the bay's back. Then, using one of the straps from the packsaddle, she tied the horse to a small tree a few feet from her shelter. Then she crawled back in, shivering uncontrollably. At least she had the two saddle blankets now. Her shivering stopped a short while after she'd worked her way deep into her pine needle bed with the saddle blankets over the top. Feeling reasonably warm and less alone now with the gentle horse tied nearby, she soon fell back asleep.

When she woke up a short time later, she wasn't sure what had disturbed her sleep. Without moving, she strained to listen. The horse snorted and stamped his feet. Thinking that the horse's noises were what had woken her up, she closed her eyes again. Then she heard it: the sound of a harmonica playing an unfamiliar, mournful song.

It wasn't the wind! And it wasn't her imagination. Someone was out there somewhere. The sound suddenly stopped—right in the middle of the song. The silence that followed was almost as frightening as the song. She shivered and cried, never having been more frightened. There was no way she could go to sleep now; she wasn't even going to try. She reached around the edge of her blankets and found a stick, holding it next to her.

An hour must have passed. She sat shivering with the two saddle blankets held close. The horse whinnied again, and she could hear it stamping its feet and moving back and forth on its short lead rope. Her eyes were wide open, and she gripped the stick tightly, allowing one of the saddle blankets to fall away. Before she could pull it back, however, a gloved hand came from nowhere and covered her mouth. She couldn't even scream. She kicked and writhed, but it didn't last long. Whoever had grabbed her was strong and restrained her from running. Bria was trapped. *Caden followed me,* she thought in panic.

* * *

Sheriff Rutger was shocked and worried sick when he learned that Bria Phillips was missing and that her rifle was the one found on the ground near the body of Caden Pendleton.

"Why didn't you tell us she was missing when you called in?" he angrily asked Rex.

"When we didn't find her on the trail or back here at the trailhead, I just thought she was hiding from Caden and us—that maybe she had killed Caden in self-defense but wasn't sure if he was dead or if he'd continue pursuing her even after he'd been wounded—and that she'd show up after a little while," Rex said. "I'm sure she's back with the rest of them now. There's no way she's lost. We all have GPS units."

"Did she have hers with her?" Sheriff Rutger asked. The boys looked at him blankly. "You don't know if she did or not, I take it?"

"Yeah, I guess that's right," Rex said lamely. "But I can't imagine . . ." He didn't finish his sentence but hung his head slightly.

As they were getting the horses ready to ride to the hunting camp, Sheriff Rutger asked Rex and Walt more questions. From their answers, one clear picture emerged—Caden Pendleton had provoked the others to anger. It also became apparent that the hunters had all been separated at one time or another between the time they'd left camp to hunt for the missing packhorse and when they'd returned. That meant, theoretically, that any of the seven could have pulled the trigger. And it would be nearly impossible for any of them to come up with an alibi. He inquired about other hunters in the area. Rex responded that they had seen some on the main trail when going in but that they hadn't seen anyone since then. He and Jay both said that they'd heard some shooting, but it was not close to where they were hunting.

Before the team of officers and two hunters left the trailhead, they wrote down the description and license number of every vehicle parked there. With that done, they headed up the trail. It was early morning, with bright streaks of light breaking over the eastern horizon by the time the three officers and two hunters rode into camp. Zach sat by a low fire, his head in his hands. The rest were in the tents, trying to sleep.

Zach jumped up and approached the sheriff. "I'm sorry to get you guys up here like this, Bishop," he said. Sheriff Rutger had been Zach's bishop and had helped prepare him for his mission, conducting the necessary interviews and completing the paperwork. Lee Rutger knew Zach was incapable of murder, and yet he had to keep an open mind—a cardinal rule in all criminal investigations.

The first thing Lee did was check to see if Bria had taken her GPS with her. He was disappointed to find that it was in the girls' tent, along with her coat. He worried that she was lost and very cold.

After that, he set up an area adjacent to the campsite as a command post, and he had all the kids move there, with strict orders not to enter their camp again until given permission. He and his deputies worked carefully and thoroughly, anxious for the two additional officers who were on their way. The search-and-rescue men were also headed for the camp. Besides the need for collecting evidence, there was a missing girl who had to be found. Bria's whereabouts and safety were the sheriff's greatest concern.

As his men began the preliminary work at the crime scene, Sheriff Rutger used his radio to order an aircraft search for the missing girl and to start the process of getting permission from the U.S. Forest Service to land a helicopter in the meadow next to the camp to pick up the body of the victim. He also dispatched officers to contact Patty Phillips and advise her that her daughter was missing. Others were instructed to find out where Caden Pendleton had come from and attempt to locate his next of kin.

* * *

Patty Phillips was putting breakfast in front of her seven-year-old son, Cody, so he could be off to school, when the doorbell rang. "Say the blessing, Cody," she said. "Then I'll see who's at the door."

"Heavenly Father," he began, "please bless this food to make us healthy. And help Bria be safe. I miss her when she's gone." He closed his little prayer, and Patty hurried to the door in the other room. Her heart nearly failed her when she saw two uniformed officers standing there.

"May we come in?" one of the offcers asked as she stood there, staring at them, her heart in her throat.

"Uh, yes, please," she said weakly. The officers entered and asked her to sit down. "What has happened?" she asked, not wanting to hear but knowing that something was terribly wrong.

"I'm sorry, Mrs. Phillips," one of them said. "Your daughter is missing. Apparently she wandered away from camp."

Patty looked up at them. "That can't be," she said, knowing full well that they wouldn't be here telling her so if it wasn't true. Then she had a positive thought. "She has a GPS," she said. "She knows how to use it. Her father . . ." She trailed off at the look she got from the officers.

"It was in her tent. I'm sorry," the officer said. "A search is underway. They'll find her for you."

After they left a few minutes later, their devastating message delivered, she dropped on her sofa and sobbed uncontrollably.

Every word of the mysterious call she'd received the evening her husband had fallen from his boat into the lake came back to her. She had not uttered a word of it. She hadn't dared. She still didn't dare. And yet, if she had, would her daughter not have gotten lost? She dropped to her knees and pled with her Heavenly Father for direction. She stayed on her knees until little Cody came in and stood quietly, waiting for her to drive him to school.

She took him in her arms and hugged him. She wasn't sure she wanted him to go to school that day. She needed him here with her. But he said impatiently, "Mom, I need to go. It's the spelling bee this morning. I don't want to be late."

She had forgotten about the bee. He had worked hard preparing for it.

She exhaled slowly and then said, "Okay, son. Get your backpack."

She didn't say a word about the sister he adored, even though she was breaking up inside. She didn't want to distract him from the goal he had today. As soon as she'd left him at the school, she drove to the sheriff's office.

* * *

Sheriff Rutger was notified by radio that Patty Phillips was at his office wanting more information. He took a deep breath. She had the right to know more, but he didn't want it sent by radio. He pushed the button on his radio and told his dispatcher, "I'll be coming off the mountain shortly, and when I do, I'll call her so I can tell her what's happening in person."

He hoped that would satisfy her for now. In the meantime, he was anxious to get the rifle that belonged to Bria Phillips back to his office and have it fingerprinted. It was critical, as far as he was concerned. He prayed that it would have fingerprints other than Bria's on it. Whose might he find? He couldn't imagine any of these young people committing such a heinous crime. But someone had. There was no indication that Caden had accidentally shot himself, especially with his body being deliberately dragged into the bushes. As for Bria, the search-and-rescue folks were actively looking for her now.

Chief Deputy Marlon Sessions entered the camp. He'd been with the search commander for the past hour. He approached the sheriff. "There will be two dogs here in the next hour or two that I hope can follow Bria's scent from the camp and hopefully aid in finding her sooner."

"Excellent," Sheriff Rutger said. He looked up as he heard the drone of a plane. "And it sounds like the planes are in the air. That will help a lot. I'm afraid there's not much else we can do."

Marlon looked at him and asked, "What about a helicopter to take the body out of here?"

"I have permission from the Forest Service. It should be here before too much longer. I'll fly down in the chopper. I need to get to the office as soon as possible."

"What's Andrew doing?" the chief deputy asked.

"He's interviewing our young hunters, one by one. I instructed him to tell them that they will be interviewed further at the sheriff's office when they are back in town."

Marlon nodded as two deputies arrived at the scene. Sheriff Rutger continued. "Marlon, I'd like you and these guys to search every square inch of the camp and surrounding area. Mark the spot of every boot or shoe print so that Andrew can photograph them for comparison purposes later."

"We'll do that," Chief Deputy Sessions said. "And we'll pick up and bag anything we find."

"Specifically watch for candy wrappers, bullet casings, matchbook covers—anything and everything that might have even the most remote possibility of being of evidentiary use later," the sheriff instructed him. "And let me know of any important developments."

As Detective Wakefield interviewed the young people he also took photographs of the soles and heels of each of their shoes and boots. He collected all the spare footgear they had and photographed it as well. Bria had a spare pair of sneakers that she had left behind. He included those. He inventoried all of their possessions, in case anything—or the lack of any items—would give them some clue.

The planes were flying an organized pattern over a large area of the mountains. The pilots and spotters were asked to report anyone they observed moving anywhere within a several-mile radius of the hunting camp. As a result, several calls were made as various sightings occurred. They reported teams and groups of hunters in bright orange at various locations. Of course, he already knew that Bria did not have her hunter orange on. It was in the tent with her coat, her GPS, her blaze-orange hunting cap, and the rest of her belongings. She had last been seen by the others wearing a pale-blue, long-sleeved shirt and blue jeans.

One plane reported seeing a horse tied to a tree on a main trail about four or five miles from the camp. It was dark in color, they reported, either bay or black, but there was nothing on its back as near as the men could tell from the air. There was no one near it that they could see. They also reported that there was a pair of hikers, one with a large backpack, heading down the trail toward one of the trailheads.

Neither of those hikers was carrying a rifle as far as they could tell, but both were dressed in hunter orange. A second plane reported that there were three people in hunter orange hiking away from the horse, close to a mile north of its location. Other pilots reported that there were three different groups of hunters on horseback in different locations, none of them closer than two or three miles from the sheriff's command post.

The sheriff sent two of his search-and-rescue men to get Zach's packhorse, if it was indeed the one that was tied to the tree several miles away. They had to cross a major mountain pass to reach it, and he encouraged them to hurry. An hour later, he lifted off in a helicopter, accompanying the dead body back to town. He was also taking Bria's rifle back to be sent to the crime lab in Salt Lake City for fingerprinting, and if a bullet was recovered from the victim, for ballistics work as well. As they flew, he had the pilot take the long way out, since he wanted to check on the horse. It was still tied where it had been reported earlier. They hovered low enough to see that it was bay, the color of the missing packhorse. They didn't see either the three hunters that had been hiking north or the two hikers who'd headed south.

* * *

Every time the phone rang, Patty Phillips's stomach twisted. Friends, neighbors, members of the ward, relatives, and others called to offer assistance, to bring in meals for her and Cody, or simply to extend a hand of friendship. Those calls helped, and she appreciated the concern that so many folks showed her. She anticipated more bad news and honestly didn't know how much more she could stand.

She was in the living room vacuuming carpet that didn't need to be vacuumed when the shrill tone of the phone again battered her nerves and caused her to tremble. She shut off the vacuum and went into the kitchen. After she picked up the phone, she held her breath for a moment then exhaled and said, "Hello?"

She recognized the voice now. The message was short and to the point, after which, the man said, "Do not, under any circumstances, repeat so much as one word of what I just told you."

"Okay," she said, her voice full of emotion.

"Don't even mention that you received this call. Is that clear?" the voice asked.

She told him that she understood, and the call was terminated.

With a shaking hand, she put the receiver back and moved to the sofa, where she sat down, dropped her head in her hands, and sobbed.

Chapter Five

By the time the helicopter carrying Sheriff Rutger landed in an open spot next to his office, a hearse was waiting to pick up the body of Caden Pendleton and head to Salt Lake to have an autopsy performed. In his office, the parents of seven of the eight hunters waited to meet with him. There was no one there for Caden as he had no known relatives in the area, and so far none had been located anywhere. Lee had instructed an officer to take the dead man's fingerprints before the hearse left with his body. He wasn't at all sure that Caden was who he said he was. But whoever he was, they needed to find his next of kin.

He braced himself when he entered the building. The families were waiting for him in the squad room, and he knew they would be full of questions. All he planned to do was tell them the basics—that Caden was dead of a bullet wound, that no one in the group admitted to knowing anything about how it happened, and that Bria was missing. The location of her rifle was something he'd release later, after the autopsy and ballistics testing were completed.

He was not about to speculate regarding who was responsible for the young man's death. He feared that they would draw their own conclusions from the details he was about to give them, and he didn't want to give them any more fuel for their speculation than was necessary. He worried about community backlash once further facts were released. The Phillips family was well liked in the area, and there was a lot of sympathy for them since the loss of their husband and father. However, they were relative newcomers with no family anywhere close to Duchesne. Sheriff Rutger was afraid that who to blame would be the big question on everyone's minds, regardless of the outcome of the search for Bria—which he prayed would end soon and with positive results.

Sheriff Rutger met with Patty Phillips alone in his office before meeting with the others. He told her what was being done in the effort to find her daughter. She thanked him, apparently satisfied that everything that could be done was being done. She had questions she didn't want to ask in front of the other families.

"Bishop, what exactly happened up there?" she asked.

Lee sensed that she doubted her daughter had just run off. "There was some contention in the camp," he said. "Caden, the young man who was killed, stirred up some trouble. For some reason, he was particularly rude to Bria. Apparently she stood up to him, and he slapped her hard enough to knock her down and cut her lip. She was upset and went off on her own."

Mrs. Phillips looked at him, but she didn't seem to be seeing him. Her mind was somewhere else. Suddenly, she shook her head and said, "Bria spent a lot of time in the mountains with her father. She knew how to take care of herself. I'm not saying she couldn't get lost, but if she did, she would take care of herself and find her way to safety. If she doesn't show up soon . . . maybe she had an accident . . . or . . ." She seemed to consider a few other things. "Whoever killed this young man might have hurt Bria."

"That is on the mind of every person searching for her," Lee said. "More people, including volunteers, are heading into the mountains to help."

Patty looked worried, and she kept wiping at her eyes.

"I need to meet with the other parents," the sheriff finally said with a sigh.

"Yes, I know that. I'm sorry I've kept you."

"Why don't you join us," Lee insisted. "We'll meet in the squad room."

"Sure," she said as she rose to her feet. She looked at Lee, her eyes questioning. "Who is Caden? I mean, he's new to Duchesne. Who is he really?"

"I have the same question," he said. "We are going to find out."

"Sheriff . . . ?" She was wringing her hands.

"What is it, Patty?"

"There's something . . ." she began. "Never mind. Let's go meet with the others."

The sheriff looked at her searchingly, wondering what was going through her mind. She seemed seriously worried about something beyond her missing daughter—almost as though she knew something about her daughter that the police didn't.

The meeting lasted about thirty minutes. The families had lots of questions, but Lee didn't have many answers. Several expressed sympathy to Patty Phillips. Things got tense right at the end when the sheriff was asked if any of their kids were suspects. He had feared this question would arise and had carefully considered what he'd say if it did. He answered, "At this point in the investigation, we have not focused on anyone. Now, I need to get back to work. Thank you for your patience."

* * *

Zach Barlow was no fool. He knew that he was innocent, but he also realized that the sheriff and his deputies would evaluate every one of them. He wasn't afraid of the investigation for himself, but he was for the others, especially for Bria. His heart told him that she had not shot Caden, either in self-defense or in anger. He prayed he was right. He was also afraid for her—alone out in the mountains. It was the last week of October, and even though it was unseasonably warm and dry, the nights were still below freezing. He had invited her on this ill-fated trip and felt keenly responsible for her terrible situation. He was determined to do everything within his power to help her—if there was anything he could do.

Accompanied by a couple of deputies, Zach and the rest of the hunters had finally been cleared to gather up their belongings and ride out of the mountains. All of the other hunters were worried, but they didn't talk much about what had happened. However, Walt, at one point, stated emphatically that Bria was innocent. "Just because Bria's gun was used doesn't mean she did anything," he argued. Even though Zach quietly agreed with Walt, he kept his thoughts to himself.

Rex Lerner had been mistreated by Caden. He had shot and cleaned the buck Caden declared his. To Zach, he said, "They are probably thinking it was me. Caden was a dirtbag, but he wasn't worth the trouble of killing. I shot that buck." He clenched his fists. "He claimed it, even though he clearly missed it." Rex closed his eyes and rubbed his forehead, shaking his head as he did so. "It made me mad, but I guess it wasn't that big of a deal. I could easily have gotten another one. I think everyone is going to suspect me."

"None of us is being blamed," Zach told him as they finished tying down the load on the one remaining packhorse. The second had been recovered but was still miles away, the searchers on their way back with it. It would be delivered to the Barlow ranch the next day, Zach was informed. The rest of the hunters' gear would be loaded on the saddled horses that Bria and Caden had ridden. When the remaining hunters left, there was still a lot of activity going on. The sheriff's command post was buzzing as searchers came and went, as sandwiches were consumed, and as information was received and dispensed.

* * *

In the early evening, Sheriff Rutger, who was still in his office, was notified that the tracking dogs had led searchers to a makeshift bed of pine needles beneath a large tree. He learned that the missing packsaddle and saddle blankets had been found there, and the horse's tracks, along with two sets of footprints in addition to Bria's, led away from that location. The search dogs followed those tracks, indicating that Bria had been at the shelter and had left it with someone else.

Lee rubbed his short gray hair as he absorbed this latest information. An unknown person had entered the picture. Bria was now much worse than lost. Had she been kidnapped? They now knew that Bria and whoever had taken her had left the horse on the trail on the far side of the pass and had then continued on in the direction of a distant trailhead.

He concluded that Bria and her kidnapper must have been the two individuals who were seen heading out of the wilderness, both wearing hunter orange, the larger of the two carrying a backpack. He ordered that the dogs be taken to the trail where the hikers had been spotted by the aircraft personnel. He had little hope of finding her in the mountains now, though, because a missing person had become a kidnapped person, as far as he was concerned. Her description was immediately sent out over the airways.

Chief Deputy Sessions entered the sheriff's office a few minutes later. The two men were both exhausted, but there was no rest in their immediate future. That immediate future had barely begun when a call came in from the state lab. The sheriff put his phone on speaker, and he and Marlon received the report together. There were a number of fingerprints on the rifle. Some of them matched the prints that the medical examiner had taken from the dead man's fingers. There were others that were smaller, but they had nothing to compare with since Bria had never been printed. Some of the prints were smudged and illegible.

"So Caden touched the gun at some point," Sheriff Rutger mused. "Why?"

Chief Deputy Sessions said, "I wonder if he has a record anywhere."

"With any luck at all, we'll soon know," the sheriff responded. "Now that we have his prints, they are going to be run through every computer database available. I don't have a good feeling about the guy. But back to the gun; we need to find out who else handled it."

"We can't assume that all the prints are Bria's," Marlon reasoned. "We'd better do a couple of things."

"And what would that be?" Lee asked, expecting his chief deputy to confirm his own thoughts.

"First, let's get fingerprints from the rest of the group, all six of them. And then we need to see if Mrs. Phillips will allow us to get Bria's prints from something in her home—some personal item, perhaps."

Marlon had in fact had the same thought as Lee. But Lee asked, "Like what? A dresser drawer or something like that?" he asked.

"Yes, or a can of hair spray or a stick of deodorant or tube of toothpaste. We can be almost positive that some of the prints on the rifle are hers. After all, it is her rifle."

The sheriff sat back with a sigh. "And who do you propose talks to Mrs. Phillips about this?"

His chief deputy gave Lee an exhausted smile. "The buck stops with you," he said.

Lee nodded. "Guess you're right. Let's get the others in first. They'll be brought here as soon as they get off the mountain. We can print each of them then. Once that's done and the comparisons are made, we can deal with Bria's fingerprints."

Neither officer spoke for a minute.

Finally Marlon said, "At least we know that the .30-30 was the weapon used to shoot the victim."

The second half of the report they had received from the crime lab was on ballistics. The bullet removed from where it had lodged against the victim's spine perfectly matched the riflings of Bria's .30-30.

Marlon got wearily to his feet. "I better get busy comparing the pictures we took of the hunting party's footwear with the pictures we took of prints on the ground up there."

"And I'll let Detective Wakefield know that he's going to have to go back up and start getting pictures first thing in the morning at the place where Bria apparently tried to sleep. And we'll also need to take more over where the horse was found tied up beside the trail," the sheriff said. "After that, I'll give Bria's mother an update. And I suppose that while I'm there, I might as well talk to her about the fingerprints."

* * *

It was the same voice on the phone. This was the third call. Patty Phillips would never forget that voice. She had to sit down as the man delivered his message. As was the case each time before, it was short and to the point. And just like when he had called the night Rich had been thrown overboard on Strawberry, she was told to say nothing about his call to anyone. Once again, he disconnected before she could respond.

She was beside herself and paced back and forth through the room. She had almost told the sheriff about the calls when she had spoken with him in his office, but at the last second she'd obeyed the order the mysterious man on the phone had given her. When the doorbell rang, she was so deep in thought that it startled her.

Her former bishop was standing there. "Sister Phillips," the sheriff said. "May I come in? We need to visit for a while."

"Yes, please," she said. After the door was closed, Patty said, trembling and with tears in her eyes, "You didn't find her." It wasn't a question.

He shook his head. "I'm afraid she's been taken out of the mountains." He explained what they knew. She listened quietly, not saying a word as he spoke. Her eyes were red, and she shifted nervously in her chair. "I'm sorry," he said as he finished his hard tale. "We are doing all we can."

"I know you are," she said after a moment. "Is there . . . is there anything else you can tell me?"

"Yes, we know now that Caden left his fingerprints on Bria's rifle. And we know that whoever killed him did it with that gun. There are other prints as well, but we don't have anything to compare them with." He went on to explain that they had fingerprinted the other six young people. And he told her what they were doing about footprints. Then he asked her about getting fingerprints from something that belonged to Bria.

Patty didn't hesitate. "Anything I can do to help," she said. "Let's go to her room and see what we can find."

When Sheriff Rutger left a few minutes later, he had several items taken from Bria's room in large plastic bags. He promised to bring them back first thing in the morning. "And I will let you know the moment we learn anything important. I'm so sorry about all this."

She looked at him tearfully, patted his hand, and said, "Bishop, I'm sorry that you have to go through this. Thank you for all you do."

He hesitated, looking deeply into her eyes. She dropped her gaze. "Patty, is there something you need to tell me?" he asked gently.

Again, she was tempted to confide in him, but she didn't dare. The man on the phone had been very specific. Without meeting his penetrating gaze, she mumbled, "No. I'll be okay."

* * *

By ten o'clock that night, there were several new developments. First, there were a couple sets of boot prints at the campsite that didn't belong to any of the hunters in Zach's group. That and learning that someone had taken Bria from her makeshift camp in the night confirmed that there had indeed been others in the area who might have taken Bria. The extra tracks also pointed to the fact that it could have been someone other than the young hunters who had killed the victim.

The second development was that Bria's fingerprints were all over the gun. They were the only prints they could identify besides Caden's. Third, the other young hunters had haltingly expressed the idea that if Bria had shot Caden, she'd done so in self-defense.

Fourth—and this was the most important development of the four—Caden Pendleton was a very bad person. His name, according to the results of a fingerprint search, was Calvin Portman. Same initials; different name. And he was actually twenty-five—not twenty-one, as he had claimed. He even had an extensive criminal record in various states.

Once again, the sheriff and his chief deputy were in the sheriff's private office discussing the developments. "Considering what we just learned, I suppose that Bria might have acted in self-defense," Sheriff Rutger said as he drummed his fingers on the desk. "The man has several assaults on his record and an attempted kidnapping. Who knows what's *not* on his record."

Chief Deputy Sessions sighed heavily and said, "I wish we had known this about him days ago. The whole thing would have been prevented had we known that there was an outstanding warrant on him."

"I wonder what other aliases he might have used," the sheriff mused. "His fingerprints can't be changed, but I would guess that his name and birth date were things that he adjusted whenever he felt like it."

"We may never know," Marlon said. "But I can certainly understand now why there is such animosity toward him among the other hunters."

"Why did he work so hard on Zach to get him to let him go on the hunt?" Lee asked, as much to himself as to Marlon. "Why did he want to be there with this bunch of young people who he clearly didn't like and was not averse to antagonizing? There has to be a reason. If we knew that reason, it might help us to understand why he was killed."

"Attempted kidnapping might be a clue leading to why he was killed," Marlon reminded Lee. "Remember what the other girls, Sage and Janie, said about him. They both felt very uncomfortable around him, and they thought that Bria had felt that way too."

"And assault. He did hit Bria. Maybe he hit someone else, one of the guys—not counting the fight that he and Jay had. Maybe there's a motive that someone isn't telling us about." Lee was thoughtful for a moment. "Tomorrow, I suppose we'll need to question the other guys again, in light of what we now know about this man, this Calvin character."

CHAPTER SIX

THE HUMAN BODY CAN ONLY go so long without sleep. Lee Rutger had reached that point early Thursday morning, and both he and his chief deputy had gone to their homes to get some rest. But the sheriff tossed and turned in his bed, unable to fall asleep.

"Honey, are you okay?" his wife, Myra, asked.

"I just have a lot on my mind," he said. "I've got some real problems to deal with and a lot of people to worry about." He didn't mention Patty Phillips, but he couldn't get rid of the feeling that something other than worry over her missing daughter was eating at her. Twice, he'd felt sure that she wanted to tell him something but was afraid to.

Just before he drifted off to sleep sometime around two in the morning, he made a commitment to go see her when he got up. Maybe he could persuade her to tell him what it was that had her so distracted.

* * *

Sheriff Rutger was out of the house by eight, showered and shaved but only partially rested. After checking on duty with the dispatcher, he drove directly to Patty Phillips's house. He rang the doorbell and waited. When Patty didn't come to the door, he rang it again. There was still no response, so he knocked. Finally he pulled out his cell phone, looked up her number, and called it.

The phone rang and eventually went to voice mail. He walked around back and knocked at that door. When she still didn't answer, he began peering in the windows. At the garage, even though the window was dusty, he could see her pickup—the one her husband had driven—parked there, but her van was gone. He stepped back from the window and thoughtfully rubbed his jaw. Perhaps she was at the store or had just taken her son to school. As he walked back to his truck, he made a mental note to come back later.

When a major crime occured, it didn't mean that all the other work of law enforcement took a sabbatical. It continued, and such was the case when Lee entered his office that morning. He dealt as quickly as he could with a variety of complaints, papers that needed his signature, a personnel problem, and some jail issues.

When that was done, he turned to the pressing matters of the day. He had a killing to solve and a missing, possibly kidnapped girl to be found. Reports were coming in from the mountains. The dogs had tracked Bria's scent to a trailhead, where the dogs lost interest. She had left the mountains—a huge concern for the sheriff. He issued a directive for the search teams to return home. Bria wasn't in the forest anymore.

Detective Wakefield had left at daylight for the area where Bria had spent part of the previous night. He found and photographed the tracks of whoever had escorted Bria out of the wilderness. The men manning the command post reported that they didn't know what else they could do, so the sheriff told them to come off the mountain.

Marlon joined Lee a few minutes later. "We need to make some plans," Lee told him. "We need to decide how to proceed on the investigation."

Marlon took a deep breath. "I've been thinking about it. Perhaps—"

The sheriff's secretary stuck her head in his door just then and said, "I've been screening your calls the best I can, but I have one that I think you might want to take."

Lee picked up his phone. "Sheriff. This is Sister Smith. I'm worried and thought I should call you." Sister Smith was the Relief Society president in his ward, someone he had a great deal of confidence in.

"What's troubling you?" he asked. Then, covering the phone, he whispered to Marlon to let him know who was calling.

Sister Smith quickly went on. "My counselors and I have been over to Patty Phillips's house this morning. I was hoping we could help her in some way. But she didn't answer the door. I tried to phone her a few minutes later. She isn't answering her phone. We went back to the house again a little later. She's not home."

"Yes, I've been there as well. She's gone somewhere in her van," Sheriff Rutger said.

"I assumed that, but I also called the school. Cody has not been at school today."

The sheriff tried to shake off the uneasiness that began to play at the edges of his mind. "I suppose that she and Cody have gone to be with their family somewhere. I think her parents live down in St. George. They may have gone there. I sure wouldn't blame her."

"Or maybe they just decided to get away for a few hours," Sister Smith suggested.

"I'll keep checking," he promised. "I don't know what her parents' names are or I'd consider giving them a call."

"Will you let me know if you learn anything?" she asked.

"Of course. Why don't you give me your cell phone number."

After he'd completed his conversation with her, he sat back in his chair for a moment, thinking. Then, shaking his head, he said to Marlon, "Patty Phillips has gone somewhere. I can't imagine why she would leave without at least letting us know where she's going, just in case we have any news about her daughter."

"Maybe she'll call in a while," Marlon suggested. "Now, back to making some plans."

"Yes," the sheriff said, his brow still furrowed in thought. He hesitated for a moment. Then he said, "Would you see about getting the other six young hunters to come back in? I'd like you to talk to them again about Caden or Calvin, or whoever the guy is."

* * *

Following still another interview with Chief Deputy Sessions, Zach left the sheriff's office and drove home. He was deeply troubled. He had allowed Caden Pendleton, who he now knew to be Calvin Portman—a dangerous, wanted criminal—to join his group of hand-picked hunters. Tragedy had resulted because of his bad judgment, and he felt totally responsible.

He had no idea who had killed Caden, but he was certain now that it wasn't Bria. She was on his mind almost constantly. He would do anything to find her if he could, but what could he do that the sheriff and other law enforcement professionals were not already trying to do?

Back home, he went inside and booted up his computer. It was probably futile, but he decided to try something that the cops might not have thought of. He had a picture of Bria that he had obtained from one of her friends last night. He scanned it into his computer and then put it on the Internet with social networks and other public sites, along with a notice that she was missing. Maybe somebody out there would see her.

He finally went out and spent some time on the ranch. He had to stay busy, or he'd go crazy.

* * *

At noon the sheriff again went by Patty Phillips's house. There was still no one there. At one o'clock, as he returned to the office, he heard a highway patrol officer call in a plate number to dispatch, explaining that it was from a Dodge van that had been parked for several hours at the rest area near the Tabiona Junction, about seventeen miles west of Duchesne.

When the plate registry came up for Richard and Patricia Phillips of Duchesne, he grabbed his mic and called the officer that was with the car. "Don't touch a thing," he said urgently. "I'm on my way out there."

The car was locked, but it didn't take the officers long to get into it. The engine was cold, indicating that it had been there for hours. The registration and other papers were in place, but there was no purse, luggage, or anything of Patty's in it. He had the car towed and sent a couple of deputies to process it for fingerprints. Then, along with Marlon, he went to the Phillipses' home.

"I think we better go in," Lee said with a grim expression when there was no response to his repeated knocking and bell ringing. "If someone stole her car and then abandoned it at the rest area, it scares me to think of what we might find inside."

He tried the door. When it didn't open, he turned to Marlon again. "Let's go around back. If that one's locked too, we'll check the windows."

They finally managed to remove a screen and get in through an unlocked window. They quickly walked through the entire house, checking every room. No one was home; there was no damage anywhere, and nothing seemed to be disturbed. They then conducted a closer inspection.

"Sheriff, this isn't good," Marlon called from the master bedroom as Lee was checking in the living room.

"What have you got?" he asked as he hurried to join his deputy.

Marlon was holding a purse. "Women don't leave home for long if they don't have their purses," he said, shaking his head.

"No, they don't," Lee agreed as he felt a chill pass through him. "I suppose it's full."

"Her driver's license, credit cards, temple recommend, cell phone, house keys, and some personal items are in it," Marlon said. "It was on the dresser."

"Let's see if we can figure out if they took suitcases," Lee suggested.

Both Patty's and Cody's closets and drawers were full. There were suitcases in the basement. The sheriff knew that they still might have taken luggage, but he doubted it, since there had been none in the car. *But her purse?* It seemed unusual that she would have left her purse if she was going . . . just about anywhere.

The officers collected several important items, locked the house behind them, and returned to the office. They now had a murder and not one but three missing persons to worry about. The sheriff felt like he'd been run over by a truck. His chief deputy didn't seem to feel any better.

Back in the office, they discussed the missing family. "It must have been hard for her," Marlon said. "You know, with her husband gone so much with his work. What did he do, anyway?"

"I'm not sure," Lee said. "I only know what you just mentioned—he worked for a company that sent him all over the world. I think it might have been in some sort of sales. I do know that his wife worried a lot when he was gone for long periods of time. Maybe his work took him into parts of the world that aren't considered safe."

"My wife would worry if I traveled a lot. She's always worried about plane crashes. You were his bishop. I don't suppose you could give him much in the way of callings when he was gone so often," Marlon suggested.

"That was hard, but I will say this for him: when he was here, he'd do anything he could to help out. For example, he volunteered to substitute in Sunday School or priesthood meetings for people who couldn't be there. And he did an outstanding job. He also helped out with the Scouts a lot. The boys loved him. They are a good family. I feel terrible about what has happened to them," the sheriff said. "I just wish there was more we could do to find his wife and children."

Later that day, a search warrant was executed at the apartment where Caden Pendleton had lived for the few weeks he was in Duchesne. Nothing of value to the investigation was found until a scrap of paper was discovered in a ragged old briefcase. Two words appeared on it.

"Look at this," Detective Wakefield said as he held the paper with gloved fingers.

The sheriff looked at the two words written there. "Earth Militia." He gaped as he read, then he said in a slow voice, "Eco terrorists. It was all over the news, remember? That's the group who claimed responsibility for blowing up a coal mine and other places, and who also claimed to have caused that train wreck in Nevada, the one hauling coal to the coast from here in Utah."

"Yeah, we were warned to keep an eye on some of the oil rigs in the county," Andrew recalled. "But nothing further has happened for a long time."

The sheriff looked at the paper as Andrew examined it once again. "Who is this guy?" he asked.

About ten minutes later, Lee was talking to an official from the Department of Homeland Security. When he finished the call, he said to Marlon and Andrew, "Looks like we'll have federal agents here by morning."

The sheriff was so exhausted that he fell asleep quicker that night, even though he had more than ever on his mind. The phone rang at about one in the morning.

"Sheriff, I'm sorry to bother you," Detective Wakefield began as Lee rubbed the sleep from his eyes. "The dispatcher called me first, but I'm afraid you'll need to get over to the Phillipses' place too."

"What's happened now?" the sheriff asked as he reached for his pants with his free hand.

"There's been some kind of explosion, and the house is now fully engulfed in fire."

"I'll be right there," Lee said wearily, as though a great weight seemed to press down on him.

The night air was filled with sirens, and neighbors were pouring from their houses when Lee parked across the street from the Phillipses' home. He looked in total dismay at the flames that leaped high into the night sky. Duchesne's volunteer fire department arrived with the first of their fire trucks, and they began to set up their equipment.

As Lee walked across the street, Andrew met him, shaking his head. He took a deep breath and pointed toward what was left of the garage. "The explosion originated from there."

"There's not much left of the garage. I can't even see their truck," Lee said. He glanced toward the closest house. "It looks like the Jorgensens' home is also damaged."

"Yeah, Mr. Jorgensen said the explosion was so powerful that it shook their house. When he ran outside, his siding was burning. He put it out with a garden hose while his wife called 911."

As firefighters sprayed water at the main part of the Phillipses' house, the roof collapsed, showering the neighborhood with sparks.

"I feel so helpless, Andrew," Lee said as they backed away, brushing at the cinders on their heads and shoulders. "But I'm grateful that no one was home."

"I wonder what caused the explosion?" his chief deputy asked behind him.

He turned. "Oh, hi, Marlon. They called you out, too, I see."

"I guess we don't need to sleep," Marlon said with a tired shrug. He looked at the blazing home for a moment, and then he reworded his first question. "Do you think it was a gas leak?"

"If it weren't for all the things that have happened the past few days, I'd think it might be something like that." He paused, checking out the remains of the garage. "It was a bomb of some kind. I'd bet on it. But you and I don't have the expertise to determine that, and neither do these guys." He waved in the general direction of where the first truck was already pumping water and a second truck was just pulling in.

"I guess we'll need some backup from the state fire marshal's office," Marlon said.

"That's exactly what we'll need. Those guys can figure out what caused the explosion."

Chapter Seven

The next couple of days brought little encouraging news to Zach. Like the rest of the community, he had been stunned when he learned about the explosion at the Phillipses' house. The more he thought about Bria, the more concerned he was. The fire investigators had ruled out any kind of gas-related explosion. They had determined that the cause of the explosion and fire at the Phillipses' home was a crude bomb that had been detonated from a remote location, probably from a car on a nearby street.

Somebody hated Bria and her family. He prayed that she was somewhere safe, even though he had to admit that she might not be. Zach was discouraged when the sheriff informed him that they hadn't received a single lead about where Bria, her mother, and her little brother were.

The sheriff kept Zach posted on developments in the murder investigation. For one thing, they had confirmed with footprint patterns that the same man who had stolen into Bria's makeshift campsite and had led her and the packhorse over the mountain had also been in and around their main hunting campsite. Similar footprints were also found to the south of the campsite—the same direction that Bria's prints indicated she had gone when she left. However, there was another set of unidentified prints that differed from the first ones.

Suspicion was leaning more toward an unknown man, or men, and less toward the young hunters. He had also learned more about Caden's criminal past. He felt terrible about having included him in the hunting party.

He not only thought about Bria and prayed for her, but he also woke up at night, over and over again, in a cold sweat. At other times, he woke up feeling very close to her, like he'd just spoken with her in person. Bria was becoming such a large part of his life, even though she was gone, that he felt like he needed to do something for her if he could.

When he was planning the hunting trip, he had corresponded with Bria and the others via e-mail to give them specific directions for planning what supplies, clothing, and equipment they needed. He suddenly had the impulse to send an e-mail. As he thought about it, it seemed silly to think that she would be in a position, wherever she was, to receive an e-mail from him.

However, he went straight to his computer, accessed his e-mail account, and began to compose a message to her.

Bria, I am worried about you. I pray for you constantly. If you get this, please let me know how you are. If there is anything I can do to help you, please let me know. Your friend, Zach.

He read it over and then sent it out into cyberspace with a prayer that it would find Bria, wherever she was.

* * *

Deadly bombs had been detonated in West Virginia and Pennsylvania seventeen months before by a previously unheard-of terrorist group. The scrap of paper found in the briefcase of Calvin Portman, aka Caden Pendleton, containing the name of that group, Earth Militia, had brought several FBI agents into Duchesne. That Monday afternoon, as those agents met with the sheriff in his office along with Sessions and Wakefield, they dropped a stunning revelation on the local law enforcement officers.

Lab work over the weekend confirmed that there were several similarities between the explosive and detonation devices used in the bombing of the Phillipses' house and those used in the earlier bombings.

However, the agents were vague about what the significance of all of it was. They made passing comments about the coal-mining counties of Carbon and Emery, the oil exploration in the Uinta Basin, and the coal-powered plants in Utah, including one in the Uinta Basin. But they did not attempt to disclose any possible ties to the Phillips-house bombing.

After they had left, the sheriff turned to Marlon and Andrew and said, "I think we're missing something here. What may be quite clear to those feds is a total mystery to me."

Marlon said, "I guess what we need to figure out is if there is a connection between the explosion at the Phillipses' home, the disappearance of the family, the explosions carried out by the Earth Militia, and the death of Caden. His death may be nothing but a coincidence. A case of his being in the wrong place at the wrong time."

Andrew looked Marlon in the eye and asked, "Do you really believe there's no connection?"

Marlon shifted in his chair. "I don't know. I just think we need to consider it."

The sheriff spoke up as he slid a legal pad over and picked up a pen. "Let's consider the facts as we know them.

"First, our victim, Caden Pendleton, is convicted felon Calvin Portman." He began to write. "Second, Portman may have had a connection to a deadly environmental terrorist organization, hence the scrap of paper."

Marlon leaned forward and said, "Third, he was killed in the hunting camp after alienating every member of the hunting party."

"Fourth, he committed at least one act of violence in the camp—the assault on Bria Phillips," Andrew added. "He also made threats to several of them."

"And we must include the fact that the weapon used to kill Portman belongs to Bria Phillips. And, of course, her prints were on it, as were the victim's," Marlon added.

The sheriff chewed on his pen for a moment before saying, "Also, Bria disappeared into the mountains, leaving on her own, while the others were out hunting for the missing packhorse."

Andrew looked at the sheriff and interrupted. "We don't actually know that she left on her own," he said. "Could someone have taken her right from the campsite, someone who left some of the other tracks not made by Zach's group?"

The sheriff grunted and said, "That is possible. We do know that she later left the mountains with some unidentified person whose boot prints are found both in her makeshift camp and in the hunters' main camp."

"Add to that the fact that there is still another set of tracks that appear at the campsite but not at the makeshift camp," Marlon said.

"Which is why I think she left the camp alone," the sheriff said. "If someone took her from the camp, why did she need to make herself a shelter that night?"

They all agreed and then were thoughtful for a moment. Finally Marlon said, "Also, Bria's mother and little brother disappeared shortly after she did."

"Then comes the most unbelievable part," Andrew added. "The Phillipses' house is blown up in a manner resembling terrorist acts committed last year by the Earth Militia."

"Anything else?" the sheriff asked.

Marlon thought for a moment then said, "Back to the killing . . . Not one of the other six young people in the hunting party can establish alibis for themselves or for each other. That means we can't rule out any of them."

"That's right," Andrew said. "And the general attitude of the hunters was that Caden may have been killed by Bria, but if so, in self-defense."

"Have we missed anything?" the sheriff asked as he glanced first at Andrew and then at Marlon.

"Yes," Andrew said. "This may be a stretch, but I think we must consider the drowning of Rich Phillips. I know it was closed, but can we be sure there isn't a connection to the troubles with his family?"

The sheriff nodded as he wrote. "I've had that same thought. What else?"

"I don't know if we can include this as a fact . . . yet . . . but I'm not convinced that the members of the hunting party are being truthful with us," Andrew said.

"So you think someone in the group may be lying?" the sheriff asked, his pen poised.

Andrew nodded. As the sheriff wrote again, Marlon asked, "Can you be specific about who you think is lying?"

"I felt more resistance from Rex Lerner and Jay Kilpatrick than from the other guys. In fact, I believe Zach Barlow has been totally open and honest with us," Andrew stated. "And Walt Hinshaw seemed nervous, but I don't think he was lying. However, I gathered that he was very reluctant to point fingers at Bria. He seems real keen on her and would protect her, perhaps. He may be hiding something."

"Jay seems real nervous, and he doesn't want to point fingers either," Marlon added. "Those two have both dated Bria. And yet he does admit that it could have been her, but that if it was, it had to have been in self-defense."

Lee looked at Andrew for a moment and then at Marlon, shaking his head slowly before saying, "I'd bet my life that Zach didn't kill Caden, but I do think he is hiding something."

"What are you talking about, Sheriff?" Andrew asked.

"Yeah, what do you see that we don't?" Marlon asked.

"I think that he's attracted to Bria, and I think it's more than a passing thing. She's four years younger than he is, but when he mentions her, I get the feeling that he cares about her more than just as an unfortunate girl who's been caught up in a terrible tragedy," he disclosed.

Both Andrew and Marlon sighed at the same time.

"Am I wrong?" the sheriff asked them as he noted their reactions.

Both shook their heads. Marlon said, "Now that you mention it, I think you're right."

"I have to agree," Andrew said. "And I can't say I blame him. She's a mighty cute girl. And a good one, from what I know of her."

"I was her bishop," Sheriff Rutger said. "I can tell you that she is a good girl. That's why I can't believe she would gun Caden down, no matter what the motivation, unless she was defending herself."

"The poor kid," Marlon said. "I sure hope she's okay."

The sheriff nodded and then looked down at his pad for a moment. He looked up and began tapping thoughtfully on it with his pen. After a short pause, he asked, "What about the girls, Sage Hinshaw and Janie Thorne?"

He was looking directly at his detective as he spoke. Andrew answered slowly, "Sage is okay. If she's hiding something, it's to protect someone, possibly Bria. But Janie—I can't quite put a handle on it. She seems squirrely to me. She could be lying about something, but she could also be nervous. She makes no bones about disliking Caden."

The sheriff wrote for a minute before looking up. "Is there anything else I need to write down here?"

"I think so," Andrew said with a nod. "Just because we only found fingerprints from two people on the rifle, it doesn't mean that none of the others in the group didn't handle or fire the gun." The older officers looked at him questioningly. "Every one of the hunters had gloves with them, and it was chilly up there. Wearing gloves makes a lot of sense. And some of the prints we found were smudged. What I'm suggesting is that whoever shot Caden may have been wearing gloves," Andrew said.

"Good point," the sheriff said, twisting uncomfortably in his seat. "That means that any of them could have fired the fatal shot."

"Any of them," Andrew agreed.

"Or someone else who left footprints there," the sheriff said, shaking his head gloomily. His list was growing. He added the possible use of gloves to it. Then he said, "Keep talking, men. This list is getting awfully large, but I suppose we haven't listed everything."

"There is something else that I suppose we should note," Andrew said. "We found Caden's hunting knife on the ground beside his body, in the bushes."

Lee nodded and made a note, and then he said, "I suppose it could have just fallen out of the scabbard when the killer dragged his body there."

"Or he might have used it to threaten someone," Marlon mused.

Lee nodded as he wrote. "Okay, what else?" he asked.

Marlon smiled narrowly. "The feds are hiding something. That's not conjecture; that's fact. And I think it's important, whatever it is."

The sheriff noted that as he said, "They are probably hiding a number of things, either about the bomb or about Caden."

"I hope whatever they're hiding isn't something that would help us solve the murder," Marlon said with a frown. "But there is one more thing—Mrs. Phillips left her purse before she disappeared. That's significant, I think."

That was added. But none of them could think of anything else. So the sheriff put down his pen, sighed as he glanced over the list, and then read it to the others. When he had finished, he said, "If we think of anything else, we'll add it. But for now, what is there here that we should work on first?"

"So far none of the kids has lawyered up," Marlon said. "But I suppose that if we asked for them to talk in front of a polygraph operator that might happen."

"Probably, but we might have to do just that," the sheriff said. "They were all read their rights, correct?" he asked Andrew.

"I have it in writing, and on a digital recording," Andrew answered with a nod.

"Good," the sheriff said. "Then let's concentrate on the hunters again. And let's use the threat of a lie-detector test as leverage. If bluff doesn't work, I'll arrange to get someone to come and administer the tests. I'm afraid there's not much we can do that hasn't already been done about the missing family, but we can work on these young people. I want to know if any of them is lying, and if so, why."

* * *

Working on the ranch was helping to alleviate some of the stress Zach was feeling. As he worked feverishly at his task, he felt someone watching him and looked up to see Sage standing near the bull pen. Her blonde hair shone like spun gold as it caught the sun. He leaned on his shovel waiting to see what she wanted.

"Hey, Zach."

"Hey, Sage, what's up?"

"I just wanted to say thanks for being so calm at the camp. That was one of the scariest things I've ever been through. I felt like I was going to lose it, but your calmness helped me to keep it together. So . . . just . . . thanks." She shrugged as she said it then turned and walked away.

"You're welcome," he called after her. Sage had always been the girl next door, but now he realized even more how beautiful she was—not just physically but as a person as well. She had always been kind to those around her, especially those less fortunate, wherever she was. She even volunteered at the school regularly, helping the handicapped and resource kids. He knew she couldn't have killed Caden.

Zach drummed his fingers on the pitchfork he was leaning on as his thoughts shifted to the interview that afternoon with Detective Wakefield and Chief Deputy Sessions. He felt good about their recommendation that the hunters each take a polygraph test and welcomed the chance to take one. He had nothing to hide. Most of the questions he'd been asked were ones he'd already answered at least twice, and he'd certainly not worry about answering them again while hooked to a polygraph. He thought about the questions he'd been asked by the officers. He smiled to himself when he remembered how Andrew Wakefield had caught him off guard when he'd asked, "Are you romantically interested in Bria Phillips?"

He remembered how his face had flushed. And finally, he'd said honestly, "I hadn't thought of it in that way, but now that you ask, I suppose that's possible. At least, I think about her a lot, and she is amazing. When she comes back, which I hope with all my heart she will soon, then I'll probably see if she wants to date."

He'd been glad when they didn't follow up on that. A yes or no was all they seemed to want. Thinking about it now as he pitched hay to a pen filled with bulls, he couldn't help but wonder if they suspected him of trying to cover for her in Caden's murder. But that wasn't the case at all. He didn't believe she'd shot Caden, in self-defense or otherwise. *He had nothing to hide.*

He suddenly remembered the e-mail he'd sent to her, and a twinge of guilt ran through him. The sheriff and his men didn't know about that. But, then, he didn't expect to get any results from that.

The chores that he was working on were soon finished, and he returned to the house. His mother was busy in the kitchen, and his father was reading the paper in his recliner. He said hi to both of them as he headed for the stairs and to his room. As he closed the door a moment later, he looked at the computer on his desk and moved toward it.

Telling himself that he was being foolish for even trying to communicate with Bria, he booted up his computer and accessed his e-mail account. He gasped when he looked at the newly received messages. Third from the top was one from Bria's e-mail address! With trembling hands, he opened the message and hoped for some luck.

Chapter Eight

After finishing his call, Sheriff Rutger sat in thought. He'd finished arranging for a polygraph operator to come help him with Zach and his friends. The operator couldn't be here until Thursday, because he would be coming from Los Angeles. There were others that Lee might have been able to get here sooner, but he was told that this man was the best in the western states.

The sheriff had met with the county attorney while Andrew and Marlon were again interviewing the young hunters. He had agreed that they would do whatever they had to in order to arrive at the truth. There was always the danger that they might be forced to bring charges lighter than might be warranted if the use of the polygraph led them to solving the case.

Later, after Marlon and Andrew had completed the interviews, the three of them had met. The kids' parents had been allowed to be in the interviews, and Andrew reported that they hadn't gotten far with Rex or with Jay before the two of them, advised by their parents, had decided to say nothing more without having an attorney present. Once they'd mentioned a polygraph test, Janie Thorne's father had stood angrily and told them that since they seemed to be calling his daughter a liar, he would seek the advice of an attorney before allowing Janie to say another word to them.

Zach, Sage, and Walt had all answered their questions, and the three of them had indicated that they had nothing against being tested. Their parents agreed with them, and they had each left, their parents thanking the officers for what they were doing to bring the case to a head.

Lee had met again with the prosecutor, and the two of them had agreed on a strategy. They would get the polygraphs completed, if at all possible, no matter which attorneys were retained. The worst that could happen was a delay in the administration of some of the tests.

In his mind, the sheriff had narrowed his focus to Rex Lerner, Jay Kilpatrick, Janie Thorne, Bria Phillips (albeit reluctantly), and some unknown person or persons—possibly whoever had taken Bria from the mountains.

* * *

The trembling of Zach's hands had subsided a little by the time he'd finished reading the e-mail message for the second time. There was no doubt in his mind that it was from Bria. He read it once more, even as he wondered what he could or should do about what he'd just learned. Bria had written,

Zach, I'm okay. Please don't worry about me. For now at least, I am safe. So are my mother and little brother. I'm afraid I can't tell you any more than that. I wish I could. But if I say too much and certain people find out, we would all be in a lot of danger. So please forgive me.

Thank you for letting me go on the hunt with you. I'm sorry if I spoiled the fun for you and some of the others, but that Caden guy really got to me. It wasn't your fault.

Thank you for caring. It means more to me than you can possibly know.

Zach, I must ask one thing of you. Please, please, please don't tell anyone about me contacting you. You've got to promise me you won't. If you tell anyone, it will make things much worse. But I trust you to honor my request. I hope I can see you again someday. Please forgive me for this. I was overjoyed when I heard from you. For a long time, I didn't know what to do, but I decided to send this. I'm rambling now. I wish I could just see your face. You give me strength. Thanks for including me in your life. I'm sorry I've complicated it for you. Gotta go now. Bria.

One more thing. When you finish reading this, delete it. You can't let anyone else see it or even know about it.

Oh, I'm still not through. Don't let anyone hurt you. Watch your back, Zach! Please be careful.

He shivered each time he read it. After going through it five times, he finally deleted it. By now it was burned into his memory as clearly as if he had it on paper in front of him. He'd heard that nothing sent over the Internet could be permanently erased, but it would be harder for anyone to find it if he deleted it and then emptied his trash bin. At least he hoped so.

He took another precaution, deleting his original message to Bria in the sent box. Then he sat and thought for a long time about what she'd said to him. She had rambled a lot, and at times she seemed to just be typing thoughts as they occurred to her. But he was pretty sure he'd gotten the message she had intended—she was safe for now but very much in danger. Her mother and brother were either with her or she knew where they were. And they, too, were apparently safe enough. He was convinced that there was much, much more than the murder going on in her life. In fact, it seemed like she didn't even know Caden had been murdered.

She had asked him not to tell anyone about this. That meant the sheriff, for sure. It also meant that if he took a polygraph test, he could run into trouble with it. And if he did, it could lead the sheriff and his deputies to think he was lying about the murder. He realized that having received this communication from Bria had put him in an extremely awkward position. If he could possibly manage it, he would never betray her trust.

He dropped to his knees and prayed for guidance. He begged the Lord to help him know what to do. As he pondered following his prayer, he decided he needed to act on his promptings before he talked himself out of it.

He started a new message to Bria:

Dear Bria, your message is safe with me. I respect your right to ask me not to share this with anyone else. I feel that I've got to do something. I know I don't know what's going on, but whatever it is, it must be dangerous. If I can help you and your family, I will accept whatever danger comes my way. Please, let me come to you. I know this probably sounds like some weird desire to be a hero or something. That's not the case at all. I feel that if I can come to you, there will be something I can do.

Please, think about it and let me know. I'll delete this message as soon as I've sent it to you, and I'll be waiting for your reply. Let me know how I can help. Zach.

He read it over, and then, before he could talk himself out of it, he hit send, and it was off at the speed of light. Before he got up from his computer, he entered his sent messages folder and deleted the message. Now all he could do was keep checking his e-mail and pray she'd respond again and that when she did, she would tell him how he could find her.

* * *

One of the search-and-rescue men came into the sheriff's office and asked for the sheriff. When the secretary told him that he'd just left, the man pulled a harmonica from the pocket of his coat with a gloved hand and explained that he'd found it in the mountains as they were searching for Bria. He'd forgotten about it until he put a candy bar in his pocket after leaving the store a few minutes ago. He was sure it meant nothing, but he thought he should give it to the sheriff anyway. He assured her that he had only touched it once without gloves on—when he discovered it in his pocket just a little while ago.

The secretary put the harmonica in a small evidence bag in a drawer, promising to give it to Sheriff Rutger when he came in again.

* * *

Sheriff Rutger was already at his desk Tuesday morning when his secretary came in and handed him a small plastic evidence bag containing a harmonica. She explained where it came from and left.

He was still examining it when Rex Lerner's attorney called. The attorney said that after meeting with Rex and his parents, he had decided that a polygraph would be in his client's best interest but that he would allow it only if he had advance approval of every question to be asked. And he also told Sheriff Rutger that it would be at least the following week before they would be ready, because he was going to employ an investigator to do a little work for him.

"I'll check with the prosecutor," Lee promised, "and then I'll get back with you. I'm sure we can work something out."

It was that afternoon before he heard from an attorney for Jay Kilpatrick. He also indicated a willingness to take a polygraph. But he too placed restrictions on what they could ask. He even told the sheriff that he would like to meet with him and the prosecutor first, because he wanted some ground rules established beforehand. And as in Rex's case, he made it clear that he would need at least a week while he reviewed things.

The last of the hunters who hired an attorney was Janie Thorne. Her attorney didn't call the sheriff at all. He called the county attorney directly. When the sheriff met with the prosecutor shortly after six that evening, they went over everything the three attorneys had demanded. Janie's was the most stubborn of the three, and it looked like she wouldn't be allowed to take a polygraph. That was suspicious to both the sheriff and the prosecutor. It made both of them wonder if she had something to hide that the others didn't.

The other three were set for Thursday afternoon. Zach was going to be first, Walt second, and Sage last. The sheriff hoped to learn something from the three of them that would help him decide how to proceed with the others next week.

* * *

There was finally another e-mail from Bria. It appeared Tuesday night, just a few minutes after eight. Zach had been checking his account when it popped up. He opened it instantly, holding his breath as he did.

Dear Zach, I've been worrying about what to tell you. I want you to come. I'd feel safer and less lonely if you were here. But I don't want to put you in more danger than you are already in. If you do come here, you cannot tell anyone where you are going, not even your parents. It will put them in danger if you do. But if you are serious, and you honestly feel that you should come, write me back and tell me so as soon as you can. But please don't do it unless you are absolutely sure. I'll be waiting for your response. Bria.

There's something else I wanted to tell you. Remember the harmonica sound we heard that night? I heard it again the next night. It wasn't the wind. I know it wasn't. Take care.

He didn't miss a beat. He deleted her message and wrote, *Dear Bria, I'm ready. Just tell me where to go and when. I'm serious about this. And I wonder what's up with the harmonica. Weird. Zach.* He hit send and deleted his message as soon as his computer screen told him it had been sent.

Then he sat at the computer and waited. Five minutes passed. Then ten. He got up and paced nervously around his room. After fifteen minutes he went downstairs and got a drink of water. Moments after he returned to his computer, it appeared. He opened Bria's message.

Are you absolutely sure? If you are, go west from your ranch. Don't drive, just walk. Someone will stop and ask you if you're looking for your lost dog. Say yes, and he'll invite you to get in with him. A man calling himself Frank will pick you up. If you trust me, you can trust him. He will bring you to me. Don't bring any ID with you or any credit cards or anything with your name on it. Also don't bring spare clothes. You'll be given what you need. I know this sounds surreal. Be careful. If anyone but Frank tries to pick you up, run. I don't think anyone will, but you need to be sure it's him. If you change your mind, let me know in the next hour. Otherwise, leave your place at midnight. I hope to see you soon, Bria.

Zach, are you sure? You don't have to do this.

Zach stared at the message. He rubbed his temples, stood up, and paced his room for a moment. Then he sat back down. He didn't know what he was getting into, but he was going to find out. He deleted the message and spent half an hour making sure that none of his messages was available in any way. Finally satisfied that he'd done his best, he shut down his computer.

He looked at his watch. It was almost nine thirty. He had just short of two and a half hours before he needed to leave. He took everything from his wallet that had his name on it. Then he put all the cash he had on hand in the wallet, a total of $320. He put his keys and ID in his sock drawer. He dressed in dark clothing—a black western shirt, blue jeans, black socks, and his black sneakers. He was thoughtful for a moment before he pulled his wallet from his pocket, took $250 from his wad, and stuffed it in his shoes.

That done, he went down to the basement and found the little .22 pistol he'd bought when he was sixteen and had only used for hunting rabbits and plunking at cans and bottles. He hadn't had it out of the gun cabinet since before his mission. He loaded all ten rounds, engaged the safety, and placed it in his pocket in addition to an extra dozen rounds of ammunition. He also retrieved his hunting knife from the gun cabinet and strapped it on. After that, he went back upstairs and pulled on a dark gray sweater. It was quite cold at night this time of year, and it was a good way to cover the knife.

"Going somewhere?" his mother asked when he came down around ten. She and his father were in the family room watching TV. He had to let them know that he was leaving, but he couldn't tell them more than that.

He didn't know of an easy way to say this. "Mom, Dad, something's come up. I've got to go away for a few days. Walt will pick up the slack on the ranch until I get back." He hadn't talked to Walt, but he knew Walt wanted more hours.

His dad muted the TV and looked at him over the top of his glasses. "Where are you going?" he asked.

"I'd rather not say," he replied. "But I know what I'm doing. Please, don't worry about me."

Worry showed on their faces, and his mother even began to brush at her hair. He'd never given them reason to doubt his word, but that didn't mean they wouldn't worry.

"When are you leaving?" his mother asked.

"I'll be leaving soon, and I hope to be gone only a few days," he said. He sat down as his parents looked at him.

"Is there something you need to tell us?" his father asked gently.

"Not really, but I was just thinking about something interesting. The second night in our hunting camp, a strange thing happened—something I forgot about until just a few minutes ago," he said.

"What was that?" his father asked.

"We thought we heard harmonica music outside our camp somewhere. We decided it was just the wind, but now I'm not so sure," he said. "Has anything like that ever happened to you?"

"That's strange," his father said, shaking his head. "No, I've never heard anything in the wind that might have made a sound like that, and I've spent a lot of time in those mountains."

* * *

At ten minutes to midnight, Zach slipped quietly from the house and headed up the road. He had been walking for close to fifteen minutes and was a mile from the house when a dark-colored pickup approached behind him. He'd seen a dozen or so vehicles so far, but none of them had stopped. This one, as he looked back, was slowly pulling up alongside him.

Zach slipped his right hand into his pocket and took hold of his pistol—just in case. The pickup slowed to the pace he was walking, and the passenger window went down.

"Are you looking for your lost dog?" the driver asked.

"Yes," Zach said.

"Hop in."

Zach opened the door. No interior light came on, but he could see a smile on the driver's face from what little light shined from the instrument panel.

"I'm Frank," the man said. "Glad to have you aboard."

* * *

The next morning around eight, Sheriff Rutger got a call from Zach Barlow's father. He reported that Zach had disappeared during the night. He told the sheriff that Zach had told them he was going to be leaving for a few days and not to worry about him—that there was something he needed to do.

"I assume his truck is gone?" Lee asked. When he heard the reply, he said, "I'll be right out."

On the way, he called his chief deputy. "It's happening again. Zach Barlow is gone. He left during the night even though his truck is still home and he didn't pack. According to his dad, he told them last night that he had to leave for a few days. When his parents asked him when he was leaving, all he'd told them was that it would be soon. They assumed he meant in the next few days. But this morning, when he wasn't up doing the chores at his usual time, they checked his room. They looked all over their property but didn't find him."

The sheriff heard Marlon groan. "Would you like me to meet you out there?" he asked.

"Yes, if you can," Lee said.

With the permission of Mr. and Mrs. Barlow, they searched Zach's room. They found his personal ID in his sock drawer. But the wallet was gone. As near as either parent could tell, all of his clothes were still in his room except for the ones he'd been wearing the night before.

They checked the basement, and Zach's father noticed that the old gun cabinet had been opened where dust had been wiped around the latch. After opening the cabinet, it took only a moment for the man to discover that the .22 pistol and Zach's hunting knife were missing.

As the officers were about to leave, Mr. Barlow stopped them. "Sheriff, there's one more thing I might mention. I'm sure it's nothing, but Zach told us the strangest thing last night."

Lee stopped and turned toward him. "What's that?" he asked.

"I suppose some of the others may have mentioned this, but the night before that boy was killed, the kids heard something that sounded like a harmonica coming from deeper in the forest." Mr. Barlow shook his head as Lee stepped back inside the room, glancing at Marlon, who looked as surprised as Lee was feeling. "They figured it was the wind, but Zach didn't seem so sure. If he was, he wouldn't have mentioned it to us."

"When did he tell you this?" Lee asked.

"Last night. We thought he had already gone to bed, but he came back downstairs to tell us that."

"A harmonica?" Marlon asked. "Are you sure that's what he said?"

"He said it sounded like one," Zach's father answered.

"Thanks for letting us know," Lee said, saying nothing to Zach's father about the harmonica that had been turned in to him. Back in the office a few minutes later, Lee and Marlon discussed whether or not to put an APB out on Zach.

Marlon said, "Maybe we didn't know Zach as well as we thought we did."

The sheriff shook his head. "Zach said that he feels like this whole thing is sort of his fault. He blames himself for allowing Caden to go with them. And he feels responsible that Bria is missing."

"Yes, and he even admits that he has some feelings for the girl," Marlon added.

"Is there any way he has some idea where she is and has gone looking for her?" the sheriff asked. "Or has he just decided to take a shot in the dark and go searching who knows where?"

"Why did he go without any ID or credit cards or even a change of clothes?" Marlon asked as he tapped his pen on the desk.

Just then, Andrew came in, and they filled him in on what was happening. When they reached the point they'd been discussing just before he arrived, Andrew said, "He must have met someone and left with them."

"But why?" Sheriff Rutger asked.

"To look for the Phillips girl, and maybe her mother and brother, too."

The three officers were all silent for a moment. It was the young detective who finally said, "Maybe Mrs. Phillips and the boy also left willingly. No ID, no luggage, no vehicle after a few miles. This is too similar to ignore." The others agreed with him, but then he added, "Maybe Zach knows something about them that we don't."

Andrew cleared his throat. "Who's to say Zach didn't leave because he was guilty of the murder?" he asked.

"Then why would he tell his parents he was going? And why leave now and not earlier in the investigation?" Marlon argued.

"On the other hand," Sheriff Rutger said, "it's possible that Zach left because he was in some way coerced."

"But he left on his own," Marlon said.

"He could have been responding to some kind of threat to him or to his family, or even to the other hunters," Lee reasoned.

"Some kind of blackmail," Marlon said with a nod of his head.

"Yeah, something like that. And the same could be true of Patty Phillips and her boy."

"I hope that's not the case," Marlon said.

They finally decided that they wouldn't report Zach missing just yet. A call to his parents confirmed their feelings. Even though they were worried, the fact that he'd told them he was going somewhere and not to worry gave them some comfort. But despite that, a nagging worry ate at Lee's mind.

"I guess he won't be here for the polygraph," Andrew noted. He chuckled and said facetiously, "Maybe he thought he wouldn't pass."

The sheriff allowed himself a short chuckle and then turned serious. "Andrew, you may be on to something there. When your men spoke to him about it earlier, he was probably okay with it. But what if he learned something that he didn't want us to know? He may have realized that he couldn't be candid with the polygraph operator the way he had planned to be. The more I think about it, the more I believe he's doing something he believes will help protect someone else. I think we'll need to wait and see if he contacts us. I have a good hunch about this."

"You are probably right," Andrew said thoughtfully.

"Oh, there's something else," Sheriff Rutger said. "Did any of the youth mention hearing what sounded like a harmonica being played in the forest outside their camp the night before the murder?"

"What?" Andrew said. "No, what are you talking about?"

The sheriff pulled the harmonica from his desk, explained where it had come from, and told him what Zach had told his parents the night before. When he had finished, Andrew said with a laugh, "Maybe we have a musical killer out there somewhere."

The sheriff smiled. "I've heard of stranger things," he said. "We ought to see if any of the other hunters have any thoughts on this."

Chapter Nine

When Zach had walked into the small cabin up Huntington Canyon well before daylight, it had been silent and dark. Frank had pointed at a sofa in the main room and said, "Get some sleep," then left.

After having slept very little for several hours, Zach heard a door open, and Bria entered the room. Her smile was radiant. For a moment, she just stood and beamed at him as he stood up from the sofa. Then she gave him a big hug.

"Thanks for coming," she said, her voice cracking.

He held her for a moment, amazed at how good it felt. Then he gently pushed her back and looked down at her beautiful green eyes and perfectly round face. It was like he was seeing her for the first time, and he couldn't get enough of her.

"You look amazing for a kidnapped girl."

She grinned. "I wasn't kidnapped. I'll admit that Frank scared me at first, but as soon as he told me what was going on and what bad men Caden and his friends were, I was glad to go with him."

"Your mother and brother—you said they are safe too?"

"They are. Frank's taxi service brought them near here. You and I will be joining them tonight," she said. "Frank is in charge. He says he has an assistant who is keeping an eye on the place where Mom and Cody are staying."

"Why aren't you together?" Zach asked.

"We were, but then Frank took us to another place, left them there, and came back here with me. He said that he didn't want to take you there until he'd had a chance to talk to the two of us alone. Then we'll go meet Mom and Cody."

"And I suppose that Frank will tell me what's going on then," he said. "He didn't tell me anything when he brought me here during the night."

"Probably, but I'm not sure. I still don't know everything. He gives me a little bit at a time. There's only one thing I know for sure. We are in a lot of danger," she said, her face clouding. "And that includes you now."

"That's what you told me in your e-mail," Zach reminded her. "And after what I've seen happen in Duchesne, it's easy to believe. But here I am. I just hope there's something I can do to help."

"Some cutthroats want to hurt my family. If my mother and brother had stayed home, they'd be dead now. Frank says that our enemies assume that they succeeded in killing them in the house bomb," she said, trembling as she thought about it.

"So you know about your house?"

"Yes, it's horrible. We see the news, and Frank knows a lot about what's going on."

"Who *is* Frank?" Zach asked.

Bria fidgeted and turned away. "He's a friend," she said vaguely.

"Where is he now?" Zach asked, stepping in front of Bria and taking hold of her arm so she couldn't easily turn away again.

She looked up at him, meeting his eyes for a moment and then looking toward the door. "He's outside keeping watch."

"Who is he protecting us from?" Zach asked. "Who would want to kill your family, and why?"

"I don't know," Bria said, ducking as she spoke. "Well, I mean, I don't know *exactly.*"

"I'm here now, Bria. I'm part of whatever's going on. I need to know. Please, tell me," he implored.

"I can't tell you, Zach. I promised Frank I wouldn't. Please be patient. We'll be leaving here tonight," she told him. She smiled. "Let's have some breakfast."

* * *

A dozen people filled a room in an old warehouse in San Francisco—all of them unflinchingly disgruntled; all of them extreme sociopaths.

All but one, that is. GR Roper, though embraced by the other eleven, was not who they thought he was. If they knew who he represented, he would never be allowed to leave the room alive, or at least they would attempt to stop him—GR was not a man easily brought down, even when outnumbered. He was not here today to say a lot but rather to observe and learn. He'd respond in the way he thought they wanted when spoken to, but otherwise he would keep silent.

The Earth Militia were angry. They numbered more than a hundred across the country. This small gathering, however, contained some of the most extreme of the group. They were accepted by the others as the authorities. The leader of the group, of the entire movement, was thirty-five-year-old Kerry Sunger, physically strong, demanding, and cruel. His dark brown eyes were slightly sunken beneath thick, black eyebrows. He kept his head shaven, but his face usually sported a three- to four-day growth of black whiskers.

"The agenda today is short," Kerry said as his eyes roamed over his faithful followers. "First, we need to decide what targets will create the most destruction and death. We have been ignored, and the time is fast approaching when we will make those who create the most pollution pay dearly. Once we have chosen our targets, we can begin to make specific plans."

"What else are we talking about today?" Harrison Bagshaw asked. At fifty-eight, he was the oldest of the group, albeit the newest member—a small, bearded man with sparse, graying hair.

Kerry waved one hand in front of his face. "I was coming to that. Damage control," he said, his dark, sunken eyes narrowing. "Calvin Portman failed us. He didn't learn a thing from the Phillips girl, and the fool lost his life in the attempt. Even though we got lucky when Agent Phillips drowned this past year, we can't take any chances if he divulged some of what he knew about us before his accident. We need to renew our efforts to learn what his family and any associates know. They could blow it for us."

"His family has vanished. They weren't in his house when we blew it up," Harrison reminded the group. "We need to find and eliminate them. I'm sure they know something. If they didn't, they wouldn't have disappeared."

"Probably true," Kerry agreed, even though he gave Bagshaw a dirty look. "The girl, Bria Phillips, was close to her father. If he said anything to anyone, it would have been to her, as well as his wife."

"Calvin probably learned something from her before he was murdered," Sylvia Morris, a thirty-year-old woman of slight build and wild, blonde hair, said.

"What makes you think that?" Harrison asked, his voice filled with doubt.

Sylvia glared at him, her round, blue eyes narrowing slightly. "He called me just before he left for the mountains. The Phillips girl fancied him. He told me he was going to spend time alone with her while they were on the hunt. I'm sure he did. And he probably got her to tell him some things."

"Not that it's any help to us now," Harrison reminded them. "Somebody blew him away. Our loss."

Kerry smiled confidently. "She's somewhere, and if we work at it, we'll find her. Somebody helped her get out of those mountains."

"Unless she was kidnapped," Sylvia said. "They say she's really pretty. So who knows? Maybe she's been taken care of for us."

"We can't depend on that," Harrison said. "We've gotta try to find her."

"And her mother and brother," Kerry added. "And we will."

GR Roper was taking it all in. He kept his true emotion from his face. He was a capable agent and had specialized in blending in when he was undercover. Though only five-foot-eight, he was strong and wiry. He'd grown his hair and beard long to fit in with the others.

He was glad when the conversation in the room turned back to the choice of sabotage sites. He was here to discover their next targets, so that the Earth Militia would be prevented from succeeding in their extremist goals.

As the meeting progressed, there was a lot of disagreement over where the strikes should be made and when. By the time Kerry dismissed them, the only decision that had been reached was concerning the states in which the attacks would be made—Utah and Nevada. Firm plans on how to find the Phillips family were never made, but several people were assigned to look for them.

GR left disappointed. He'd hoped to have a better idea of where and when the attacks would occur—to learn specific locations, not just states.

It took a few minutes to free himself from the company of two men from the meeting. They wanted to talk about what a big splash they were going to make when they unleashed their fury on those bent on destroying the beauty of their planet. Although GR joined in with their threatening talk, he shuddered when he finally walked away in another direction. These people were nuts.

Although anxious to make a phone call, he would wait until he was at a safer location. He couldn't risk jeopardizing his current success in infiltrating the organization. The cell phone he carried whenever he was around the Earth Militia was never used for private or government purposes.

He caught a cab several blocks from the meeting place. Not until he was in the hotel where he had stayed for the past couple of nights did he finally dial Frank's number. Even on his own phone, he was careful about what he said. The only time he ever spoke of specifics was when he met other federal agents face-to-face.

"I'm concerned about the Winsbergs' housing arrangements. Find them a cleaner home," he said.

Neither agent called the other by name. Nor did they talk unnecessarily. So when Frank replied, he simply said, "I'll take care of it. I'll see that all four of them are comfortable."

GR heaved a sigh of relief. That meant that the young man from Duchesne was safe. "Thanks, I'll be going, then." He looked at the phone in his hand for a moment then slipped it into his pocket. Then he headed for the shower. Whenever he was with the sociopaths, he felt dirty and contaminated.

* * *

Frank spent an hour with Bria and Zach that afternoon at the cabin. Mostly he questioned them about the hunting party and the conflicts they'd had with Caden. Frank still wouldn't answer Zach's questions about the danger they were in. He simply said, "Be patient, Zach. You'll be told what you need to know as you need to know it."

"Where are we going?" Bria asked when Frank appeared in the cabin that evening and told them it was time to go.

"It's starting to snow," he said, avoiding her question. "I don't know where this storm came from, but we need to get off this mountain before the roads are too bad. We'll pick up your mother and brother and then drive all night. You are in more danger than we thought." He turned to Zach and handed him a driver's license and social-security card. "You are now Joe Sowers. And from this point on, you should call each other by your assumed names—at least until this crisis has passed."

"Your real name isn't Frank?" Zach asked as he pulled out his wallet and put the two documents in it.

"That's right. To you, I'm Frank Harmon," he said as he opened the door and ushered the two of them outside and into the swirling snow. He opened the tailgate of the pickup and put Bria's small suitcase in the back beneath its vinyl cover. "We'll get you some clothes and personal effects in the morning. Until then, you're going to have to make do," he told Zach.

The two of them got in the front seat of the truck next to Frank. "Joe, this pretty little gal who got roped into this mess is Justine Winsberg. Practice that name, because that's what you'll be calling her."

"Hi, Justine," Zach said. "They can just call the two of us JJ—for Justine and Joe."

"That'll work," she said, chuckling. "By the way, my mother's name is Wendy and my brother's is Dillon. I guess we're the Winsbergs now."

"That's a lot for me to remember," he said. "But I'll work on it."

After reaching Huntington, they turned south on State Road 10. They drove steadily in the ever-increasing snow until they reached Ferron. Frank turned onto a side street and drove for a couple of blocks. He pulled into the driveway beside a white frame house with a For Sale sign on the front lawn. He went into the house for a few minutes. When he came back out, he was accompanied by Bria's mother and brother. They climbed into the backseat as Frank put what appeared to be brand-new, compact suitcases into the trunk. Bria turned and smiled at them. Her mother said hello to Zach and thanked him for coming. Frank brushed the snow off his jacket and climbed in, and they were on their way again, southbound once more.

Other than a review of everyone's assumed names and Frank's stern warning for them to use them, there was little conversation for the first few minutes. Patty Phillips finally asked Zach about what was happening in Duchesne. "I'm worried about Sheriff Rutger. He must be weighed down with worry," she said after Zach brought them up to date on what he knew of the murder investigation.

"He's stressed, that's for sure," Zach told her. "But he's a strong man."

"He is that," she agreed.

They talked about the destruction of the Phillipses' house and the damage to neighboring homes.

"Everybody is worried about you three," Zach said over his shoulder.

"And now they're worried about you," Patty said soberly.

"I doubt that," he said with a shrug. "After all the trouble I've caused, they're probably glad to see me gone."

Bria laid a hand on his arm. "That's not true," she said.

The conversation slowed as the snow picked up. Frank had to keep his speed down when the snow began to stick to the surface of the highway.

Bria's little brother had been quiet the entire trip. Zach looked back and saw him leaning against the door. He whispered to Bria, "I think Co—I mean, Dillon—is asleep."

Bria looked back. "Poor kid. He can't possibly understand what's going on," she said as she faced forward again.

"Just like me," Zach said.

Bria sighed. "Once you're told, you'll understand," she said seriously.

Again, they watched the snow as it fell outside the truck. The windshield wipers went back and forth hypnotically. Zach was deep in thought for a long time. Finally, he spoke up, his curiosity getting the best of him. "I didn't see a computer anywhere, *Justine.* How did you get my message?"

Frank answered before she could say anything. "She used my laptop," he said. "I told her to check her e-mails. We'll continue to do that. We'll check yours, too. We need to see who is trying to get in touch with either of you."

"Why?" Zach asked.

"Listen and you'll understand," Frank said brusquely.

"Sorry," Zach said. "It just seems strange. But then this whole thing is strange."

"I understand," Frank said. "Anyway, I had Justine open her e-mail so both of us could look at it. When she saw the one from you, she begged me to let her answer it. I said no until she opened one from an unknown source."

"It scared me," Bria said, taking hold of Zach's arm and gripping it tightly.

"What did it say?" Zach asked, patting her knee gently.

Frank answered again after glancing in the back and making sure that Bria's little brother was still sleeping. Patty leaned forward and listened. "It said that Caden, or Calvin, as we know him now, said some things to her that he shouldn't have. She was told to keep her mouth shut. We already knew she was in danger; that's why I escorted her from the mountains. But it also said that she was too close to you, and that she should tell you to keep your mouth shut as well."

"Who are these people?" Zach asked as he felt Bria's grip on his arm tighten.

"We'll fill you in later. For now, just know that they are dangerous," Frank said, glancing over at Zach in the murky darkness of the truck. "I felt like you were a potential target too, *Joe,* so I told Justine that we needed to do something to protect you. I watched her type the messages, edited a little, and told her she was fine to encourage you to come. I hope you don't regret it, but now I can keep an eye on all of you."

Zach shook his head. "Wow," he said. And then he sat thoughtfully for a moment. Bria released her grip on his arm. He finally expressed the concerns that were running through his mind to Frank. "If I'm in danger, aren't the others?"

"Are you referring to the others from your hunting party?"

"Yes," he said. "I feel responsible for them."

"Joe, get one thing straight," Frank said. "What's happening is not your fault in any way. Calvin Portman was targeting you guys in a way that we'll explain later. Believe me, nothing is your fault."

Zach grunted. "Now I feel better."

Bria looked up at him. "You sound like you don't mean it," she said.

He smiled grimly in the dim light. "You're right. If Caden was targeting us, then I'm not exactly feeling like Rex, Walt, Jay, Janie, and Sage are safe."

"You may be right," Frank said. "I've been thinking the same thing. We'll stop in a few minutes, when we get to a rest area, and I'll make a phone call or two."

He wasn't any more specific than that, but Zach thought he sounded like he was sincere, and he did feel better. But he had another thought. "So I'm not here so I can help . . . I'm only here to be protected. Is that it?"

"That's my main concern," Frank conceded. "But Justine thinks there might be some way you can help. We'll see about that."

"I'm willing," Zach said. "I just need to know what to do."

"It's only the first week of November. What's with all the snow?" Frank grumbled as he slowed down a little more. "I'm not sure we'll get to where we're headed by morning at this rate."

No one bothered to ask him where that was. They were fast learning that Frank Harmon shared information when he was ready and that no amount of coaxing would change his mind.

Chapter Ten

The sheriff was trying to relax in front of the TV for a change. He was watching a ball game and was finally getting into it. He hadn't had a break for days, and it felt good to relax for a little while. The phone rang, and he groaned as he got out of his recliner and walked across the room to answer it.

The number was blocked by the caller ID. He let it ring once more before answering.

"Hello," he said, trying to keep the irritation he felt out of his voice.

"Sheriff Lee Rutger?" the voice asked.

"Speaking," he said.

"Don't look any further into the death of Calvin Portman. And forget about the fire at the Phillipses' house. It's not your business. Forget about everything that's happened the past week, and you may live to be an old man."

"Who is this?" Lee demanded angrily.

"Either do as you're told or watch your back every second. No funny business."

"Who are you?" he demanded again.

There was a chuckle on the line, followed by a click.

Sheriff Rutger stared at the phone. *What in the world was that about?* he wondered.

His wife walked in. "Who was that, honey?" she asked.

Lee slowly shook his head. "I don't know, Myra." He noted the worry that suddenly clouded her face, and he added, "Some prank caller. I sometimes wonder if I should do like a lot of the other sheriffs and have our number unlisted."

She nodded, but the worry didn't leave her face. "It wasn't exactly a prank, was it?" she pressed, stepping close and tenderly touching his arm.

Before he had to answer her, the phone rang again. "Hello, this is Sheriff Rutger."

He breathed a sigh of relief after listening to the other person on the phone for a moment and then handed it to his wife. "It's for you," he said, forcing a grin. "It's not a prank this time. It's Kathy."

Lee wasn't able to get interested in the ball game again. All he could think of was the threatening call. He considered himself a brave man, but he would be a liar if he said the call hadn't been cause for concern. Backing off on an investigation—especially one this important—was not an option. That meant he would have to be careful for the next few days.

After a few minutes, Myra came back into the room and put the receiver back. She smiled at Lee and left. The phone rang again. Lee slapped the arm of his recliner in frustration and headed for the phone.

"Hello," he said, hoping it was for his wife again.

He wasn't that lucky. "Sheriff, this is Rex Lerner. I've been trying to call for several minutes."

"Sorry, my wife's been on the phone," he said as he thought about the panic he was certain he heard in the young man's voice. "What's the problem, Rex?"

"I just got a call. I was threatened," Rex said, his voice rising.

The sheriff felt a chill pass over him. "I don't suppose you know who was calling you?" Lee asked.

"He wouldn't say, but he said that I better forget anything and everything Caden—uh—Calvin said to me. I told him I didn't know what he was talking about." Rex paused, breathing hard into the phone.

"Rex, did Calvin say something to you or any of the others that might indicate that he wasn't who he claimed to be?" Lee asked.

"Well, he did go off about the environment and how it was being destroyed by pollution, and he did say that he had friends that could cause us a lot of trouble, or something like that. But I never thought anything about it at the time. I just thought he was up in the night," Rex replied.

"What else did the caller say to you a few minutes ago?" Lee asked. "You said you were threatened."

"Yeah, he said that if I tell anybody about what Calvin might have said to me, I'd be as dead as Calvin. Sheriff . . . I don't know what to do. I tried to tell the guy that Calvin didn't tell me anything, but he wouldn't listen. He just told me to shut up. Honestly, all Calvin did was talk about the environment and mention some friends. Anyway, the guy said that I better convince you to do what you'd been told, and he hung up." Rex's voice had broken by then, and Lee could tell he was fighting his emotions.

Lee tried to calm him down and offered to meet him at his office in a few minutes if he'd like to. Rex agreed to that. "My dad wants to come too," he said.

"Great, I'll see you shortly. I've got a couple of things I need to do first."

What he didn't say was what he had to do. *He had to wait for more phone calls.* He was almost certain they were coming. So he wasn't even vaguely surprised when the phone rang again. It was Walt Hinshaw, Sr., Sage and Walt Hinshaw's father. It was an almost identical story to the one Rex had just told. That call was followed by one from Jay Kilpatrick, and then finally Janie Thorne called. Lee told all of them the same thing—they were to meet him at his office in just a few minutes.

His wife came in again. "Lee, what's going on?" she asked, her face creased with lines of worry. "You've had a flurry of phone calls."

"I'll say. I've got to run to the office," he said. "It's about the killing on the mountain. Getting more complicated, I'm afraid."

"Lee, this is too much for you," Myra said as she approached and put her arms around him.

"I ran for the office," he said. "It's fine. Now quit worrying. I'll try not to be too long."

She laid her head against his chest. He stroked her hair for a moment, and then he said, "I love you, Myra. I'm lucky to have such an understanding wife."

She smiled up at him and then gently kissed his cheek.

"I better call Marlon. I'll need him there," Lee said.

But before he could dial his chief deputy's number, his phone rang again. "Now what?" he said as he looked at the phone in his hand. His wife stood near him, looking faint. "Sit down, Myra, and try not to worry. This is probably for you again, anyway. It's your turn, that's for sure."

It wasn't for Myra. "Sheriff Rutger, you don't know me, but I'm calling to warn you that there are people who could be a threat to you."

"You think?" Lee said as he left the room with the phone in his hand. He didn't want Myra to overhear something that would cause her more worry.

"Yes," the caller answered, rather tentatively now. "I'm with the CIA and am in receipt of information that I think you need to hear."

The sheriff suddenly felt anger begin to surge within him. "First FBI and now CIA. If you feds know something that I need to know, it's about time you came clean. I've got my hands full here, and I don't need anyone, even you, keeping information from me."

"You're right, Sheriff. That's why I'm calling. And if you haven't already guessed, this case you're working is more than a simple murder. Until I can get someone to speak with you in person, you'll just have to take my word for it that you might be threatened."

"I already have been, and so—" Lee began.

"I was afraid of that. The young people involved with the matter are also in danger."

The sheriff's anger dissipated. "Listen, we've all been threatened in the past few minutes. I'm going up to my office to meet with the kids in just a minute. What do you suggest I do?"

"I'm not sure. I guess that's your call. But I suggest that you take the threats seriously. Do something to keep those people safe."

"I'll try to do that, but I need to know what you aren't telling me," Lee reminded him curtly.

"You have my word, Sheriff. My boss will be in Duchesne tomorrow. He'll contact you as soon as he gets in town."

The sheriff called Marlon then grabbed his coat and headed for the door. Myra called after him from the doorway, "Be careful, Lee. It's snowing out there."

* * *

The snow had let up a little. They were parked at a small rest area in the tiny town of Emery in the southern end of the county by the same name. Zach had watched as Frank talked on his cell phone outside the car. When he was finished, everyone took a restroom break, then they piled back into the truck and left. When they reached I-70, Frank entered the freeway, heading west.

Frank told them that he'd called Sheriff Rutger, but he offered no details on the conversation. He was driving with complete attention to the task at hand. Plows were busy on the freeway as they drove over the pass and headed toward Richfield. As they drove into the Sevier valley, the snow became lighter but did not entirely clear up.

Bria was tense, and as vehicles passed them, she'd grab Zach's arm tightly. At one point, she turned toward him and said, "I hate snowy roads. They scare me."

"Frank's a good driver," Zach assured her. "And he's not rushing. Relax if you can. We'll be fine."

"I'm thinking of stopping in a few hours and finding a hotel," Frank said. "I'd planned to drive all night, but this is tiring. Are you guys okay with that?"

"I am," Bria said quickly.

"Whatever you think," Zach told him. He looked in the backseat. Patty and Cody were both asleep. "Looks like they're okay with whatever," he added with a grin.

A couple of hours later, they were on I-15 driving south. The storm let up more as they continued on. Bria relaxed, and after a while her head settled against Zach's shoulder, and she fell asleep. Zach shifted a little so she would be more comfortable and closed his eyes but did not fall asleep. He was nervous, wishing he knew exactly what was going on.

Frank stopped at a gas station in Cedar City and filled up. Everyone got out and walked around. Frank bought some snacks, and when they got back in the truck, they busied themselves with the food. Less than an hour later they stopped in St. George, where Frank arranged rooms for them.

"We'll leave again around ten or eleven," he said. "You guys get some sleep. I'm sure that no one has any idea where we are, but as a precaution, don't let anyone into your rooms. If anyone knocks, call my cell number."

"Where is the other agent—the one who was keeping an eye on us in Ferron?" Patty asked.

Frank looked at her for a moment. "I've got to keep you all close together now. He's been sent on another assignment. He left when we moved you from the house in Ferron. I'll keep a close eye on the four of you." She nodded and said nothing more.

At nine in the morning, Zach had almost finished shaving when there was a tap on his door. He peered through the peephole and then swung the door open to Frank, who stepped in carrying a laptop computer case.

"The gals need a little more time," Frank said. "Maybe while you and I are waiting, we could check your e-mail. Do you mind?"

"Of course not," Zach answered.

There were several messages there. Only one looked suspicious. Frank had him open it at once. Zach found his hands shaking as he read,

Zach, if you think you can hide, you are sadly mistaken. You'd better forget whatever Calvin Portman told you and just go home and mind your own business. If you don't, we will hunt you down. Watch your back wherever you are. We are coming for you.

"Wow," Zach said as he looked up. "How do they know I left Duchesne?"

"That's a good question. It's clear that they know too much," Frank said. "Let's type a response. There is no way they can tell where we are from their computer."

Without a word, Zach hit reply, embarrassed at the way he was shaking. But Frank didn't mention it. He just studied the screen and said, "You type, I'll dictate."

"Good. Because I don't know what I'd write," Zach said as he poised his fingers over the keyboard.

"Let's see. How shall we do this?" Frank asked, more to himself than to Zach. "I'll talk slowly. Okay, how about this?

Are you nuts? I'm not running from anybody. I'm on a trip. I don't know what you're talking about. Caden invited himself on the hunt. I barely knew him and frankly didn't like him. He didn't say anything important to me, and I wouldn't have taken the time to listen had he tried. I went to hunt, not to listen to a whiner like Caden. Don't write again. Zach.

Frank straightened as there was a knock on the door. "Hi, are you three ready to go?" he asked as he opened the door for Bria, Cody, and Patty.

Bria's eyes caught Zach's as he looked up from the computer. She smiled, and when he grinned in return, she blushed. "Good morning," he said. "Sleep well?"

She nodded and walked to the table where Zach was sitting at Frank's laptop. "Anything interesting?" she asked as she looked over his shoulder. Then she gasped. "Oh, Zach!"

"Joe," Frank said mildly. "You've got to remember."

"Sorry, but what is this?" she asked. She rested her hand on Zach's shoulder as she read on.

She gasped a couple of times and then finally straightened up, keeping her grip on Zach's shoulder. "I'm sorry . . . I told you this would be dangerous."

"It's okay," he said. "I'm just glad to be here with you and your family." He smiled at her and reached up and placed his hand over hers, where it still rested on his shoulder. "So, any suggestions?" he asked. Frank was also looking over Zach's shoulder. Patty, standing next to him, was studying the message Zach had typed.

"I do have a suggestion," Bria said.

"What is it?" Frank asked.

"Tell him that I'd like to scratch his eyes out," she said angrily.

Frank chuckled. "I don't expect that any of you will ever meet the author of this e-mail, but if you do, you have my permission to scratch his eyes out and even break his arms if it will make you feel better."

It only took a couple of minutes for Zach to check his other messages and delete them. There was nothing he wanted to respond to. He got up and stepped away from the computer. "It's your turn, Justine," Frank said, waving his hand toward the chair.

She sat down, and Zach stood behind her, both hands on her shoulders, looking past her short brown hair as she accessed her account. There was one from the same e-mail address as the one Zach had received. Bria stiffened when she saw it.

It was shorter than Zach's but just as threatening. As Bria was checking her other messages, a new one popped up at the top of the screen. She took in a sharp breath. "It's from Walt Hinshaw," she said, looking up at Zach.

"Open it," Frank said.

Bria did, and the color drained from her face as she began to read Walt's message.

Bria, I know this is crazy, because you'll probably never see this. I guess this is kind of like talking to myself. Things are getting really scary. Somebody called Sage and me and threatened us if we said anything to anybody about what Caden told us. But he didn't tell us anything. I wish we'd never gone hunting. And I wish I knew where you and Zach are. I don't know what to do. The sheriff said he'll protect us, but what can he do? A deputy is sitting outside right now, but what can one guy do? I miss you, and I miss Zach. I hope you're okay. I hope you're even alive. Sage is as scared as me. She says to say hi. We don't know anything. Why would anyone do this to us?

Frank said, "We won't get anywhere by responding to this message. The sheriff is working something out for Walt and the others. Delete it and let's get on our way."

Frank packed up the computer, and they all grabbed their bags. After breakfast, they did the necessary shopping for Zach and then headed toward Las Vegas. Frank still hadn't said what their final destination was, and nobody bothered to ask.

Chapter Eleven

The sheriff had been up much of the night again. He'd arranged for several of his deputies to provide security for Zach's friends. It was cutting him real thin on resources. He and Marlon had spent a long time after that trying to come up with a way to keep the young people safe over the long term while this thing came to a head. Even after he finally got to bed, he didn't sleep well.

It was late when he finally managed to drag himself out of bed to face the day. He looked out the window at six inches of snow blanketing everything. The snow glistened under the bright morning sun. It was the kind of beauty that usually brought him a feeling of joy. The first snow of the year, following such an unusually mild October, had caught him by surprise. A snowplow passed, piling the wet, heavy snow against the curb.

He tried not to think about the angry and unsettling meeting with the kids and their folks about the threats they'd received. It had consumed over an hour of his night, not to mention the work he'd done after that. There was plenty of time to worry and think and try to come up with a firm plan to keep people safe while still moving forward in his murder investigation. After showering, shaving, reading scriptures, and eating some breakfast, he pulled the snow blower from the garage and cleaned his sidewalks and driveway.

An hour later, he was in his office. Marlon and Andrew met him there, and they sat down together to analyze where they were and decide where to go from there. "We clearly can't just close the case on Portman's death," Andrew said. He had missed the previous night's meeting, and it had taken a few minutes to fill him in.

"You're right," Lee said. "And yet we've somehow got to protect our kids from whoever is out there messing with people of our town."

"Sheriff, is it possible that something has already happened to Zach and the Phillipses?" Marlon asked.

"We can only hope they're okay. I wish we would hear from them, but I'm afraid that's not likely. There will be a ranking CIA agent here today who can hopefully tell us something. I'm expecting to get a call at anytime."

They almost felt like they were killing time as they went over the list they had made earlier. They added another item—the threats that had been made. Somehow, in some mysterious way, the death of Calvin Portman had stirred up a hornet's nest. They discussed things but came to no more conclusions.

The CIA agent from the night before called at noon. "My boss will be there this afternoon. Hopefully he'll help you make some sense of all of this."

* * *

The last place that Zach would have expected to go was the Las Vegas strip. Frank explained briefly that, in his judgment, it would be safer there than most places. "Sometimes it's easy to get lost in a crowd. This place is crowded," he said.

Frank grinned as they walked to the front of the Mirage and said, "I don't want anyone gambling." His face grew sober. "We are going to check in separately. I'll stand where I can see you at all times, but you go first, Joe." He handed him a wad of cash. "Pay for four nights in advance. There is a reservation in your assumed name. After you're done, go into the casino, because we have to go through it to reach our elevators. Wait there and watch for us. I'll send the Winsbergs first, and then I'll follow a ways behind them. Make sure Wendy sees you, and then move out ahead of them. Don't get too close to each other. Go right to the elevators and to your rooms."

"Why are we doing this?" Patty asked.

"Because these places have cameras everywhere. I don't want us to be seen together by the cameras. It's just a precaution."

It made sense to Zach, so he did as he was instructed. He waited for a long time in the casino for Bria and her family to appear. He was starting to get worried, and he even thought about moving back toward the check-in area when he finally saw them. They were looking around, and Bria's face broke into a smile when she spotted him. He smiled back then moved toward the elevators.

The rooms were clean, large, and attractive. Zach had a room to himself, connected to the one that Bria and her family were assigned. They were on the nineteenth floor, with a view of the large pool area far below. Frank had booked a room for himself directly across the hallway from the Phillipses' room. He again warned them to let no one in but him and room service people when they needed meals and snacks delivered. And they were told not to answer the room phones. If anyone tried to get in, they were to call Frank's cell phone.

The first thing Zach did was shower, shave, and put on clean clothes. Then he pulled out a copy of the Bible from a bedside stand and began to read in the New Testament.

* * *

After his office door had closed behind Agent Jim Crooney, Sheriff Rutger sat back in his chair with his hands behind his head, fingers locked, and stretched. A ranking officer from the Central Intelligence Agency, Agent Crooney had met with the sheriff for the past two hours, and the meeting left Lee's head spinning. A moment later, he pushed his chair back from his desk and approached the window. He stood staring at the snow as his mind wrapped itself slowly around the disturbing information he'd just received.

He'd been sworn to secrecy and wasn't even allowed to tell his chief deputy. And yet he had to involve Marlon and others of his department if he was to keep the members of Zach's hunting party alive. He didn't have the manpower to have deputies protect them one on one for any extended amount of time. At the same time, he had to watch his own back.

He reviewed his conversation with Jim Crooney as he stared out the window. There were still some things that the agent hadn't told him. Not that he'd admitted as much, but Lee could tell. There were gaps that hadn't been satisfactorily filled. Lee supposed that there were reasons for the omissions, but what Crooney *had* told him generated more headaches than anyone could reasonably handle. For just a moment, he considered resigning. But it was no more than a fleeting thought. He had a job to do, and he would find a way to do it.

His secretary interrupted his thoughts as she rang him on the intercom, letting him know there was a call for him. Taking a deep breath and turning back to his desk, he sat down and picked up the receiver. "This is Sheriff Rutger," he said.

"Lee, this is Rudy Alfonso. I'm sure you've got a lot to worry about with the killing and all that you've got going on over there . . ."

"More than enough," Lee agreed, wondering what his friend, the sheriff of Emery County, wanted. "So I hope you don't have something more to keep me occupied." The two lawmen chuckled.

"This may be nothing," Sheriff Alfonso said, "but I thought you should know."

"I sincerely hope it's nothing," Lee said. "But let's have it."

"I got a call around noon from a concerned citizen," Rudy said. "He told me that the house next door to his is for sale, but he's pretty sure someone has been there the past day or two. Sometime last evening, after the snow started to fall, a pickup pulled up to the side of the house. A man went to the door and knocked. A moment later, a woman and child came out. They each had small suitcases, which the fellow took from them and put in the back of his truck."

"In the snow?" Lee asked.

"No, the bed had a vinyl cover on it," Rudy explained. "Anyway, as he was doing that, the woman and child got in the backseat of the truck. Then the guy got in and drove off. My informant was behind his house. He'd gone out to feed his dog, and he hadn't turned any lights on. He had just finished when the truck pulled up next door. He says he was curious, especially since he thought the house was vacant."

"So he watched," Lee said. "Did he say if he could see anyone else in the front of the truck?"

"That's what's strange," Sheriff Alfonso said. "When he opened the door, no interior light came on. But when the driver started the engine, the dashboard lights were just bright enough that he could distinguish two people in the front seat. The one in the middle was short; the one on the passenger side was taller."

Lee quickly counted in his head. He was missing three from the Phillips family and Zach. The math added up. But he was jumping to conclusions. He asked, "Was that all? And if so, why did the guy wait until noon to call?"

"About ten this morning, two guys drove up in a small white car. My informant was at work, but his wife called and told him about them. She told him they had driven into the driveway, just like the pickup, but that they had had a hard time with the snow. They slipped and spun but finally made it. Then the men got out and went to the back door where she couldn't see them. She was cleaning the house, and every few minutes she'd look out and see that the car was still there. Then it was gone."

"How long did that go on?" Lee asked, wondering where this was going.

"Probably thirty minutes," Rudy answered. "Maybe a little more. She called her husband, and he apparently didn't think it was any of his business. But for some reason, it kept coming to mind as he tried to work. Finally, he called the realty company that has the place listed. They dodged his questions and told him they had no idea about people living there. But when he said that two men had been there this morning, the real-estate agent asked him if he was sure. He told them that he was, and they seemed concerned at that point."

"So tell me again how you got involved," Lee said.

"The neighbor came home for lunch, and when he did, he says he walked around behind the empty house. The door was hanging open and the glass in it was broken. He didn't go in the house, but he did approach the back door and could see that things were a mess inside. So he called me," Sheriff Alfonso told him.

"Did you go over yourself, or did a deputy go?" Lee asked as he nervously turned his pen over and over in his fingers.

"I went, and two of my men went with me, but not before I tried to call the realty company. They didn't answer their phone, so we just went," Rudy said.

"And what did you find?" Lee asked.

"The place had been torn apart. There wasn't a lot of furniture in the house, but there were a couple of beds. They'd had bedding on them, and the bedding was torn off the beds and the mattresses thrown off and ripped open. There was some garbage in a couple of garbage cans, but it had been scattered. It looked to me like more than someone searching for something. It was like someone was in a rage and did the most damage they could."

When Sheriff Alfonso quit talking, Lee asked, "So what are your thoughts?"

"Well, you have a woman and her little boy missing. I was thinking about them," Rudy said. So was Lee.

"Thanks. If you learn more, let me know," Lee said.

Lee urgently dialed the number Jim Crooney had given him. But he got no answer. The agent was probably in one of the numerous dead cell phone areas west of town or else he'd turned off his phone. Either way, it wasn't helpful to him. He got up and anxiously paced his office. He'd known that the Phillips family had been in Emery County until last night. That was one of the things the agent had made him promise not to divulge. It didn't take a rocket scientist to figure out that whoever had been in the little white car in Ferron was closing in on them.

He sat down at his desk again and called Sheriff Alfonso back. "Did your witness get a license number to the car?" he asked, afraid of what the answer would be.

"No."

Not good, Lee thought. "Did she at least get the make?"

"Nope, sorry. Why?" Rudy asked.

"I've been threatened, and so have some of our residents," Lee said. "I just thought it would be helpful in case the men in the white car come here next."

* * *

Time was dragging. Zach wasn't used to sitting around doing nothing, even though he enjoyed visiting with Bria and her family. He still didn't know what was going on, and Frank hadn't given him any clue as to what he could do to help out. It was frustrating to feel so useless.

He hadn't seen Frank for several hours. As afternoon wore into evening, Zach wasn't the only one getting edgy. Patty Phillips, try as she might, looked worried. But she said nothing about what was on her mind. Cody was content because he had food and the TV. Bria reflected her mother's concern.

The three adults were in Zach's room, Cody in the other one, when the room phone rang. That surprised Zach. He looked at the phone and moved toward it.

"I don't think you should answer it," Patty said.

Zach looked at Bria. "I think she's right," Bria said. "We have no way of knowing who it is. If it were Frank, he'd be calling on the cell phone."

It must have rung fifteen or twenty times before it finally quit. "I'm going to call Frank," Zach said a minute later. "He needs to know that someone's trying to reach us. It might only be the front desk, but we shouldn't take any chances."

He picked up the receiver and punched in Frank's room number but got no response. He tried a second time. Again, there was no response, so he tried the agent's cell phone. He'd barely hung the room phone up when it began ringing again.

"Maybe that's Frank now," he said. "I better take this."

After picking up the phone, he said hello.

It was the front desk. The woman's voice sounded panicked. "Sir, I have a message from someone who says his name is Frank. He's been shot, and he wanted this room notified."

Zach's heart began to pound unmercifully. "Where is Frank?" he asked.

"He's on the main level near the elevators. He's badly injured. We've called for an ambulance and the police. Come down here at once. Frank is in terrible shape."

"It's a trap!" Bria wailed after Zach explained the call. "You can't go down there."

"You aren't even armed," Patty said. "And how do we know it's the truth?"

"We don't, but I've tried to reach Frank," Zach said as a rush of adrenaline made him feel ill. "What if it *is* true? We've got to know for sure either way."

Zach felt in his pocket for his little pistol. "I'm going. You guys keep the doors locked."

Bria grabbed his arm, but he shrugged free and left the room. She was crying as the door shut behind him. He sprinted to the elevators and punched the down arrow. He scanned the area, having no idea who the enemy was but remaining determined, despite his fear, to reach Frank.

An elevator door finally opened, and he leaped in and punched the close button. When the elevator stopped, an elderly couple got on. Zach pushed the close button again, willing the elevator to reach the bottom quickly. It felt like it was descending at a snail's pace. His heart pounded fiercely, and his palms were drenched in sweat. His gut was churning. Finally the elevator came to a stop, and the door opened. Zach stepped out and looked around.

Chapter Twelve

Security officers were trying to shove people back, but the crowd, many of them under the influence of alcohol, pushed forward, trying to see what was happening in the hallway just outside the elevator lobby. Zach joined the fray. A security officer grabbed him by the arm and pulled him back. "Let me through. It's my friend in there. He sent for me," Zach pleaded urgently.

"The paramedics will be here in a moment. Nobody gets near," the officer said gruffly.

"Please, Frank needs me," Zach pleaded.

Just then another officer stepped over, pushing a drunken woman away, and asked, "Are you Joe?"

"Yes," Zach said.

"Let him past," the officer ordered. "The victim is asking for him."

As the crowd parted to let Zach and the officer into the circle, Zach saw Frank on the floor in a pool of blood. Two men were working frantically to stop the bleeding, but they were clearly losing the battle. Zach rushed over and knelt beside him.

"Frank, it's me."

Frank's eyes opened and he said, "Joe?"

"Yeah, it's me," Zach said as he leaned close. "Who did this?" he asked.

"It was one of them," Frank said slowly, even as bloody froth oozed from his mouth. "I'm dying. Take care of the others."

"What do I do?" Zach asked desperately.

"Stay put," Frank said, and he gasped as more blood spewed from his mouth. For a moment, his mouth worked silently. Then he managed to speak again, although it was very faintly. "Help will come."

He began to cough, blood showering Zach's clean shirt. "Take this," he said as his hand moved, his fist clenched.

Zach touched Frank's hand, and he passed his hotel key card to Zach. He shoved it into a pocket while he continued to watch Frank's eyes. They were growing dim, like the life was slipping from them.

"Harmonica player . . ." Frank said. "An agent . . . disappeared . . . couldn't find him . . . might be dead."

Wondering if he had heard right, he leaned closer and asked, "What about a harmonica, and who might be dead?"

The paramedics crowded past the security men who had been giving first aid, ordering everyone to give them room. But Frank spoke again. "Joe stays . . . must . . . speak to him . . . Joe, you . . . still here?"

Frank's eyes closed, and Zach got the terrible feeling that the end was near.

"I'm here, Frank," he said.

Frank's lips moved, and his head turned slightly toward Zach, but his eyes remained closed. Every breath he took was ragged, full of blood. One of the paramedics began working on the gaping stomach wound while the other put a blood-pressure cuff on one arm. "They don't know . . . where you are . . . Stay hidden," he finally managed to say in short, staccato bursts.

"You'll make it, Frank," Zach said. "Hang in there."

Frank shook his head weakly and gagged, coughing up more bloody froth, and said, "I . . . didn't . . . kill . . . Caden. B . . . Pro . . ." Blood filled his mouth. He tried to spit but couldn't. He began choking. "B . . . pro . . . tect," he tried again, but he couldn't say more. The paramedics shoved Zach aside, and he didn't resist as the importance of what Frank had tried to say hit him. He didn't say a name, but twice he said the letter B and the word *protect. Bria. Protect.* And yet it couldn't have been her, even in self-defense. He knew it, *didn't he*?

He stood up, watching as Frank's eyes finally opened. For just the briefest moment, they focused on Zach's face. Again his mouth began to work.

"Go. Get out of here. Now!" he said forcefully. Then his eyes rolled back into his head before closing one last time.

Zach backed away, tears streaming down his face. The curious crowd parted, letting him pass. They were still trying to move forward, defying the orders of the security officers, as he caught one last glimpse of Frank.

A paramedic with the blood-pressure cuff attached to his arm said, "We've lost him." Zach broke free of the remaining crowd, rushed back to the elevators, and pushed the up arrow. A moment later, an elevator opened, and he got on. He rode to the nineteenth floor alone. Then he ran as hard as he could down the long hallway to his room and pounded on the door.

"Zach!" Bria screamed as she opened it and he rushed inside. Her pretty, round face went pasty white. "You're hurt! We've got to get a doctor."

"I'm fine. This is Frank's blood," he said as he bent over and gasped for air, his hands resting on his knees.

Patty came rushing in from the adjoining room. "How bad is Frank?" she asked.

Zach took a few more deep breaths, and then he said, "Frank's dead. We're on our own now."

Patty collapsed onto the nearest bed. Bria grabbed hold of Zach as he stood upright again and clung to him like she was also going to topple over. He helped her to the sofa at the far end of the room as she began to cry, her sobs wracking her. Just then, little Cody Phillips stepped into the room. "What's the matter?" he asked.

"Go back and watch the TV," Bria ordered softly.

With a shrug, the boy did as he was told, blissfully ignorant of how critical things had become. Zach left Bria on the sofa and turned to her mother, who seemed to be feeling weak and was struggling to sit up. Her eyes were red, and she said, "When is it going to end? Poor Frank. He was such a good man. Why did they have to kill him?" She began to sob quietly.

"It's terrible," Zach agreed. "I barely knew him, and yet he gave his life for us." He couldn't help but choke up a bit as he spoke.

Patty was still struggling to sit up. Zach helped her and offered to get her a glass of water.

He rushed to the sink, filled a glass, and returned it to her. She drank it, and then she said, "Thanks. I'll be okay now."

Zach did the same thing for Bria. She was getting some color back in her face, and she had finally managed to quit crying. "He was such a nice man," she said.

Zach tenderly touched her arm. "Wait here while I make sure the doors are bolted," he said, thinking he should already have taken care of that. If they found Frank, they could find them, too. He shuddered, thinking how grateful he was that they had checked in separately. And he prayed no one had seen him with Frank just now.

Once he'd ensured that the doors in both rooms were secure, he checked on Bria and Patty again. "We'll be fine now," Patty said. "You might want to get cleaned up."

He looked down at his shirt and gasped. It was soaked with Frank's blood, as were his pants. Blood had gotten on his face and hands, too.

"I'm sorry. I didn't realize. I'll shower quickly," he said, "and get some clean clothes on."

He reached into his pocket and brought out the small .22. After walking to Bria, he said, "Hold this while I'm getting cleaned up. Don't let anyone in. I'm sure we're safe for now. Frank said that they don't know where we are yet. I don't know how he knew that, so we need to be ready, just in case."

Patty and Bria went back into their own room, leaving the connecting door ajar as Zach fished some clean clothes from his small suitcase. He stuffed the ruined bloody shirt in a laundry bag he found in the closet.

As he showered, he thought about what Frank had told him in his dying moments. Frank had known who killed Caden and had even tried to tell him, but all he got out was the letter B and *protect*. What was he trying to say? And if what Zach had heard was correct, there was another agent who'd been in the mountains and a dead man there as well. Was the agent dead? He couldn't be sure, but he suspected that the dead man was the person who had killed Caden. He wondered if Frank had in turn killed the other guy, but he couldn't imagine why he would do that. It was all so confusing. Somehow, he needed to contact Sheriff Rutger. But he wasn't sure how to do that without compromising their location.

He told Patty and Bria what Frank had told him, excluding his use of the letter B. Bria was shocked. "You mean all this time he knew who killed Caden and didn't tell us?"

"He didn't say that, only that *he* didn't do it," Zach said.

"But do you think it could have been the harmonica player who shot Caden?" Patty asked.

"That could be it. Yes, it might have been him." He hadn't mentioned the harmonica until then and chuckled at Bria's startled look.

"I knew I heard a harmonica," Bria said, her shock at Frank's death temporarily replaced by a feeling of vindication, "even if the rest of you thought it was the wind."

"Frank said it," he told him. "There really was a harmonica; the other guy was playing it."

Patty's face was still white. She said, "Frank—he tried so hard to protect us, and now look what's happened to him. I feel sick. We've got to get in touch with Sheriff Rutger."

"I was thinking the same thing, but the question is how to do that without letting anyone know where we are."

"There's got to be a way," Bria said.

Zach had an idea—one that might work. He bounced it off the women.

"That's a good idea, but we need a computer," Bria said after he'd outlined his basic plan.

Zach turned to his dresser, where he had placed the spare bullets and his knife and other items from his pocket. Turning Frank's room key in his fingers, Zach said, "I need to go to Frank's room."

"It's too dangerous," Bria said, her eyes growing wide.

"I've got to. The sooner I go, the better."

With downcast eyes, she nodded. "Take this with you," Bria said as she shoved the little pistol into his hand.

"Be ready to open the door when I get back. I'll hurry," he said as he accepted the pistol.

Zach opened the door and glanced into the hallway. There was a man approaching from far down the hallway. He slipped back inside and shut the door. "Someone's coming. I'll wait until he's out of sight."

He looked through the peephole. The fellow didn't appear. Finally, Zach opened the door again and cautiously checked the hallway.

"Must have gone into a room," he whispered and then slipped across to Frank's room. For a moment he just stood there, an emptiness settling over him as he realized how quickly life could be taken away. He had to force himself to look around.

He spotted the computer on the second bed beside Frank's open suitcase. Frank's shaving kit was on the counter beside one of the sinks, and a couple shirts hung in the closet as if awaiting his return. Everything else was apparently in the suitcase. Zach was unsure of himself. He hated to just leave the agent's things for someone from the hotel or the police to clean up. Out of respect for Frank's sacrifice, he began to gather his things up. He carefully folded the shirts and placed them in the suitcase. He added Frank's shaving kit and started to zip the suitcase shut. But on an impulse, he checked through the contents, feeling vaguely guilty. On the bottom, beneath Frank's clothes and a couple books, Zach found a pistol and holster.

Zach pulled it out, checked the clip, discovered that it was fully loaded, and then put it back. A moment later, he was tapping on his own door. Bria opened it quickly, and he stepped in. She shut the door behind him and bolted it.

"Let's get started," Zach said after setting down Frank's suitcase and the computer. He took the computer out of the case. "Are we doing the right thing, or is there a better way to contact the sheriff?" he asked, as much to himself as to Bria and Patty.

Neither of them said anything in response as he set the computer on the desk by the window and plugged it in. He booted it up and looked at Bria, who stood next to him, watching him intently.

"I wonder if it's password protected," he said. "If it is, we might not be able to use it."

Bria looked at him and bit her lip. "I saw him type his password," she said. "I didn't mean to but I did. I've been feeling guilty about it, but now I'm glad. And I know he'd want us to use it," she said.

"Okay, I'll move and you can take over."

As soon as Bria was seated, she entered Frank's password, and then she opened her e-mail account and typed in Walt Hinshaw's address. Then she paused before continuing. Looking at Zach, she said, "I'm so glad you're here with us," and she tenderly touched his arm. Their eyes met, and for a moment their gaze held. "I'm especially glad after what happened to Frank. I don't know what we would have done without you."

"I don't know what we'll do now," he said. "But we'll do the best we can. Okay, let's see if we can contact Walt."

She looked up at Zach, her eyes teary again. "I'm ready."

"Go ahead," he said as he knelt beside her chair.

She nodded, wiped her eyes, and typed, *Walt, it was good to hear from you. I'm okay and so is my family.* She stopped and looked over at Zach.

"That's good," he said. "Now, just tell him that you need to get in touch with Sheriff Rutger but that you can't call him. Ask him to find out the sheriff's e-mail address and get it to us."

She typed for a moment then looked over at Zach again. He once more nodded his approval and she sent it. "Do you think he'll get it?" she asked when they were finished and she had shut the computer down.

"I don't know. I hope so," he said. "But if he's been threatened, it may be that the sheriff has them all someplace safe for a while. We'll check every so often, and if we hear nothing, we'll have to try something else."

"Like what?" she asked as the two of them moved away from the computer and sat together on the sofa.

"Like make a short call from a pay phone," he said.

Bria shivered. "I don't like that idea. Somebody out there killed Frank and is close to finding us."

"Yes, that was what I was just thinking," he said. "But we've got to talk to the sheriff. And, speaking of necessities, I've got to know what this is all about. Since Frank is gone, I guess it's up to you and your mother to tell me. And let's do it now." He was firm, and she nodded in agreement.

She went into her room and asked her mother to come in and talk to them. They told her what they wanted, and she slowly nodded.

"But first," she said, "Cody's hungry, and I think we could all use something to eat. Let's have something brought up."

Once the order was made, Bria and Patty sat on the sofa in Zach's room while Cody watched TV again in the other room. Zach brought the chair from the desk and then sat down and faced them.

"Okay, shoot," he said.

There was a knock on the door. "That can't be room service already," Patty said, her face suddenly creased with worry.

Zach got up and headed for the door, stopping long enough to open Frank's suitcase and get his 9mm pistol out.

"What's that?" Bria asked.

"It's Frank's," he said. "It must have been a spare. It's bigger than mine." With the pistol in hand, he looked through the peephole and into the hallway.

"I don't like this," he whispered. "I don't recognize this woman. She's standing there looking around . . . There's a man with her now."

Bria and Patty joined him. They took turns looking through the peephole. When Zach looked again, the man and woman were swaying and pushing each other.

"I think they're drunk," he said as the man reached up and pounded on the door. Zach kept watching, hoping they'd leave. Finally, they staggered across the hall and started knocking at Frank's door.

He told the women what was happening but kept his eye to the hole. After standing and swaying there for a while, they talked for a moment, and then they both laughed and moved to the door next to Frank's, where they knocked again. That door was opened in a matter of moments; the pair laughed some more and went in.

"Whew," Zach said. "They had the wrong door. I hope that doesn't happen again. I can't take the tension."

They returned to their seats, and Patty began to tell Zach things that gave him chills. "My husband worked for the CIA for many years. He was assigned to work on the case that Frank was involved in. He was trying to get information on this organization called Earth Militia. I didn't know that until after the accident at the reservoir. Then I got a call from Frank." She choked up for a minute. "They are terrible people. I wish we'd known that Caden was one of them."

She explained a little more—things she had learned from Frank over the past few days. When she finished, Zach said weakly, "This is unbelievable. Does the sheriff know any of this?"

"I don't think so," Patty said. "My husband was pretty good at keeping his true occupation secret. Sometimes I even forgot what he was really doing when he was gone. At home, he didn't seem like a CIA agent. He was just a great guy, a wonderful husband, and a doting father," she said.

Bria looked at her mother, a question in her eyes. Her mother nodded, her face serious.

"Zach, there's something else you need to know," she said, leaning forward and putting a hand on his knee. There was an anxious look in her eyes, and he felt his stomach begin to churn.

Chapter Thirteen

The attorneys for Janie Thorne, Jay Kilpatrick, and Rex Lerner convinced the parents in each case to move the three to a safe place, which they stubbornly did not disclose to the sheriff. Sage and Walt Hinshaw and their parents sought Lee's help, and so, on a temporary basis, he arranged for them to stay in a safe house in Salt Lake City. They were at the safe house when the sheriff received a call from Walt.

He was surprised at how excited Walt sounded on the phone. "Sheriff," he said, "Bria is safe. She's okay."

"How do you know that?" Lee asked in amazement.

"I got an e-mail from her. She says her mom and little brother are okay, too," Walt reported.

"That's great," he said, wondering why Bria would contact Walt and not the sheriff's department or even him personally. "Did she say where she's at?"

"No. She said she needs to get in touch with you but that she can't use a telephone."

"Did she tell you what she wanted to communicate with me about?" Sheriff Rutger asked.

"Nope, but she said that if I can give her your e-mail address, she'll e-mail you," Walt said. "Isn't that great?"

"As a matter of fact, it is," he said, even as he realized he had just learned one of the things the CIA agent had failed to tell him, namely that the Phillips family was alive. *If they even knew.*

Lee gave Walt the e-mail address he needed and said, "Get this to her right away. I'll have my computer on and be watching for a message from her. And thanks for calling me, Walt. Are you and Sage doing okay?"

"A lot better now," he said. "At least I am. Well, so is Sage. We were afraid that Bria was dead. And Sage is really worried about Zach. So am I. I was thinking maybe he was with Bria, but I don't know if he is or not."

"I'm glad you've learned what you have," Lee said. "Now get that address to Bria. And if you hear more from her, please let me know."

It was less than half an hour before a new message popped up for Lee in his inbox. He supposed it could be Bria's address. He opened it and started to read.

Sheriff, there may be another dead man somewhere near our hunting camp. He could be the one who shot Caden. He played a harmonica. That's all I can tell you for sure. My mom and brother and Zach and I are okay for the moment, but there are dangerous people after us. They already killed a man who was helping us, and they are close by. We are hiding. Please delete this message after you've read it. Let us know what you find out. Bria.

He stared at the message for several minutes. So Zach was with Bria. Why didn't that surprise him? He was relieved. What now concerned him was that he might have another murder on his hands. It was also a concern that the CIA had not told him everything they knew. He felt a rush of anger and picked up the phone. Before he did anything else, he was going to speak to the agent who'd visited him, Jim Crooney.

He was lucky and made contact right away. "Why didn't you tell me that my missing people are alive and safe?" he demanded as soon as he'd identified himself.

"What makes you think they are?" the agent asked.

"I just received an e-mail from Bria Phillips," he said. "She told me that she and her mother and brother, along with Zach Barlow, are hiding somewhere. Don't tell me you didn't know that. I'd just like to know why you didn't tell me. It makes me wonder what else you know that I don't." The longer he talked, the madder he got. He finally said, "Your turn to talk. Open up, Crooney, and tell me what is going on."

It was silent on the line for a long moment—a moment in which Lee continued to boil. Finally, the agent said. "We didn't see where it would make you or the others any safer if you knew. But since you do, I guess it's okay to tell you that they are under our protection. But don't mention that to anyone."

"So was the man who was killed protecting them an agent with the CIA too?" Lee asked.

"I don't know what you're talking about, Sheriff. We have a man protecting them right now. There were two earlier, but the second man has been reassigned."

"Are you certain of that?" Lee asked. "Bria tells me that someone who was supposed to be protecting them has been killed."

There was an ominous silence on the line. He could hear the agent breathing deeply. "Are you sure of this?" Crooney finally asked, his voice taking on a much more serious tone.

"Bria claims they are in hiding and that the man who was protecting them was killed, and that whoever did it is close by," Lee said, trembling with anger. "It sounds to me like your man is dead."

"If he is, I didn't know it," the agent said. "Are you sure the message is from Bria?"

Lee thought for a moment, then he asked, "Do you have any agents who play a harmonica?"

Crooney didn't answer for a moment, but when he did, chills ran down Lee's back. "How did you know that?"

"I have the harmonica," the sheriff said. "And I think your man is lying dead somewhere in the Uinta Mountains under the snow. Is that the man you say was reassigned?"

"No, there was another agent. This is complicated. Listen, can you meet me at the Duchesne airport? I'll have someone fly me out right away. It sounds like we have some serious problems," Crooney said.

"You don't say." The sheriff was having a difficult time calming down. "Zach Barlow and the Phillipses are in serious trouble."

"I'll come out right away," the agent said.

"Good, but also do something to protect my missing friends. Or else tell me where they are so I can protect them," Lee said.

"I don't actually know exactly where they are. But I will find out. I'll get on the phone while my secretary lines me up a plane."

"You do that, Mr. Crooney, and I'll meet you at the airport. And if you're planning to go with us to look for your harmonica player, you might want to bring snowshoes."

As soon as he hung up, he called for Chief Deputy Sessions and Detective Wakefield to join him in his office. While he was waiting for them, he typed a reply to Bria's message. He wrote,

Thanks for contacting me. I'm grateful to hear that you are okay at the moment, but I'm worried about you. I'll take immediate action on your information, but in the meantime, be very, very careful. If there's any way you can let me know your location, I'll arrange for someone to meet you, someone who can protect you. Get back with me right away. Sheriff Rutger.

He had barely sent the message off when his deputies came rushing into his office, shutting the door behind them.

"Come around here," he said before either of them seated themselves. "There's something I want you to read on my computer screen."

He opened Bria's message again and watched the men's faces as they read. They both had the same look that he suspected he must have had the first time he read it. Neither of them said a word as they moved back around his desk and seated themselves.

Leaning forward on his chair, Marlon finally asked, "Does that mean our missing people are safe?"

"It means they were when they sent this message," Lee clarified. "I just wrote them back. I told them to be careful and to let me know where they are so we can send someone to protect them."

"Protect them from who?" Marlon asked.

"I wish I could tell you that, but I can't—at least not yet. I just got off the phone with Special Agent Jim Crooney of the CIA. He'll be here as soon as he can get a plane to fly him to the airport. We need to meet him there."

Both deputies nodded. Marlon asked, "Did you say CIA? You didn't mean FBI, did you? I thought you met with an FBI agent yesterday. What does the CIA have to do with all this?"

"This agent was from the CIA. And I haven't sorted it all out myself."

The two deputies exchanged puzzled looks, and then Marlon asked, "Will he tell us what he told you?"

"I don't know, but I hope so. This thing is big, and it's complicated and dangerous," Lee said.

"Sheriff," Andrew began as he thoughtfully rubbed his chin, "do we have another body on the mountain?"

"I think so," Lee acknowledged.

"And you have his harmonica," Marlon stated.

"I think so," Lee repeated.

"So how do we find him?" Marlon asked. "There's snow up there."

Lee nodded. "I know, but we are going to try. We'll need to arrange for some cadaver dogs. That will probably be our only chance."

"And maybe they can't do it with all the snow on the ground," Andrew suggested.

"You are probably right. I don't know. All I know is that we have to try." He paused and added, "I told Agent Crooney to bring his snowshoes. There is one thing in our favor. This storm we got came in from the south. That usually means that there is more snow here than in the mountains north of us."

"That's true. Would you like me to see if I can find someone who can at least give us an estimate of how much snow is up there?" Andrew asked.

"I'd appreciate it," Lee said. "And Marlon, let's see if some of our search-and-rescue guys are willing to brave the elements. Check on the availability of cadaver dogs as well. The handlers can probably tell us if it will do any good to even take them up there."

* * *

Zach, Bria, and Patty read over the e-mail from the sheriff several times. "Maybe we should tell him where we are," Bria suggested. "He can probably send someone from the local police here in Las Vegas to protect us."

"As soon as they know we're here, they are going to want to question us about Frank's death. Who knows, they might even try to blame us," Patty said, shaking her head.

"I hope they won't blame us, but at the very least they'll want to question us," Zach said. "They're probably already trying to figure out who I am. Dozens of people saw me talking to Frank as he was dying. And who knows how many of them saw me take the elevator."

"So what should we do?" Bria asked tearfully.

Zach touched her arm. "I don't know. If we go out of the rooms, they might see me and have enough information to grab me." He paused for a minute. "Do you remember how careful Frank was when we registered? He didn't want us on the cameras at the same time. He said that they have cameras everywhere in the casino. That means I'm almost sure to be on their system. So they must know what I look like."

Patty chewed thoughtfully on her lower lip. Finally she said, "They would have pictures of all of us from when we came in, but only Bria and Cody and I were ever together. They would have no reason to connect us to you."

"That's right, and we all paid with cash. They've probably recorded all of us on their system, but they don't know who we are and that we are together," Zach agreed. "But they do know me, and they could be waiting at the elevators for me to come down," Zach said. "They might even have pictures of me checking in, and if they do, they'll know when I checked in and be able to tell what room I'm in. I don't like that."

"Zach, I'm scared," Bria said, trembling and taking hold of his arm for support. Her mother also put her arm around her. "Do you think the Earth Militia could also figure all this out?"

Zach hated to scare her worse, but she had a point. He said what had to be said. "Yes, I suppose in time they could. But if Frank was shot right there where I saw him, they also should have images of the killers on camera. And the police might be watching for them instead of me."

"Oh, I hope so," Bria said.

"And that would also make it harder for the killers to find us, because they are going to be watching out for the police," Patty reasoned.

"That's true," Zach said.

Bria, still holding Zach's arm, said, "If the police can see whoever it was that killed Frank in the act of shooting him, they wouldn't have a reason to come after you, would they?"

"Good thinking, Bria. Maybe we should tell Sheriff Rutger where we are."

"Can we wait a little while at least?" Patty asked. "If the police come to the door, we can let them in. Otherwise, I think I'd feel better just waiting things out for a while, until things calm down. By then, maybe they will have found whoever killed Frank."

Bria caught Zach's eye and said, "I think Mom's right."

"If they come to the door, it will be to mine," Zach responded, "not yours. From now on, we need to answer our own doors. We need to have room service deliver separately to each of our rooms and make sure that none of the staff, cleaning people, or room service see us in the same room."

"And there's one other thing," Bria reminded them. "He only had us pay for four nights. We've already used one of them."

"Very well. Then we'll wait, but not for more than three days. So let's send a message to the sheriff to tell him we can't disclose our location just yet," Zach said as he sat down at the computer.

Chapter Fourteen

The snow was light on the mountains according to the report that Marlon had received. "We can go in on horses, and even the dog handlers are willing to give it a try," he said to Agent Crooney, who had joined them only minutes before. "Do you ride?"

"Not a lot," Crooney responded. "But I can handle it."

"You don't have to go with us," the sheriff reminded him.

"Actually, I do. I have orders."

"Then we'll get you a horse. By the way, do your orders include letting these two men in on what's happening?" Lee asked, nodding toward his deputies.

"Yes, I think we can tell you two, but not anyone else. So we need to be careful not to say anything in front of other deputies or your search-and-rescue men," Crooney said.

"How do we explain you?" Lee asked.

"I am someone who is interested in what happened to Calvin Portman." He produced an ID that indicated he was a deputy sheriff from a county in Colorado. "If anyone asks," he said as he handed the ID around to the other three, "I'm *Deputy* Jim Crooney and I'm looking for a missing man."

"Got it," Lee said. "So fill these guys in."

As they were listening to the agent, a message came into Sheriff Rutger's e-mail from Bria. Without interrupting Crooney, he opened it, read it, and deleted it. It was short and its tone was one of caution mixed with fear.

After Crooney had finished briefing them, Lee told them what he'd just learned.

The agent said, "We'll figure out where they are soon, and we'll send help to them. We have one of our best men working on it. They're wise to wait where they are."

The trip into the mountain was cold and exhausting, but the snow depth wasn't a problem. At the hunters' campsite, it measured only four inches. More was forecast in two or three days, so those involved in the search began in earnest. Unfortunately, darkness came without having found a body.

The sheriff, Special Agent Crooney, and several of the others spent the night in the mountains. The search resumed at daybreak. Lee wondered if there was really any chance that they were doing any good. Then, shortly after noon, one of the dog handlers met with success. A body was found lying at the bottom of a ten-foot drop-off in a thick clump of brush. It would have been easily missed by searchers earlier who were working without dogs. It had been somewhat mutilated by scavengers, but Crooney was able to identify the body.

He didn't refer to him as an agent in the presence of the searchers; he simply identified him as the missing man from his county. They loaded the body on the back of a horse and headed toward the trailhead.

It was the next morning before the medical examiner called Sheriff Rutger with the results of the man's autopsy. He had died of a broken neck, presumably having fallen off the cliff. The man's identity was revealed as Boyd Swift of Baltimore, Maryland. Unfortunately, even though it was possible that the man was responsible for Calvin Portman's death, there was no evidence to that effect.

The first polygraph tests were conducted with Sage and Walt Hinshaw. The results indicated that neither of them was lying about anything. If the same kind of results came back when they finally got the others to submit to the testing, it would make it easier to conclude that the late Boyd Swift was responsible for the killing, even with a lack of evidence.

* * *

The waiting was getting on everyone's nerves. Bria and her mother snapped at each other several times, and Cody began acting agitated.

He couldn't understand why they had to stay in the rooms. His constant whining was even getting on Zach's nerves. He stayed in his own room most of the time while the Phillipses stayed in theirs.

An e-mail from the sheriff had informed them that a body had been recovered near their hunting camp and identified, but it didn't give any of the details. Zach had written back, asking what the man's name was. The sheriff refused to disclose that online. Finally, Zach typed a short request. He wrote, *Sheriff, can you at least answer one question? Does his name start with a B? Zach.*

A couple of hours later, he received a reply. The sheriff asked him why he wondered, and that, yes, his name did start with B. Zach had felt a huge relief come over him. Surely that was what Frank had been trying to tell him. The B didn't stand for Bria but for the name of the mysterious harmonica player. However, he didn't mention that to Bria. She didn't know about Frank's use of her first initial, and Zach didn't tell her about his short series of communications with Sheriff Rutger. He carefully deleted each e-mail as soon as he was finished with it.

At about nine that evening, someone knocked on his door in a peculiar pattern. There were three loud knocks followed by three soft ones, then a pause and one louder one. He grabbed Frank's pistol and went to the door. He peered through the peephole, his heart pounding. Standing outside was a bearded, long-haired man who looked to be just shorter than Zach. The man was looking up and down the hallway as he waited. Zach gripped the pistol tighter. After a moment, the man moved away, presumably to the Phillipses' door. Zach stepped in there, put his finger over his lips, and whispered, "Someone's about to knock."

As he'd predicted, there was a knock on the door. It was the same peculiar pattern. Patty Phillips came to her feet in a single bound and rushed toward Zach. She looked through the peephole and let out a gasp. Bria had already joined them. She looked out and then stepped back, her hand covering her mouth in a look of astonishment.

Patty reached for the security chain. "Don't!" Zach said in alarm, grabbing her hand and pulling it away from the chain.

But she shook him off and grabbed it again. Patty grabbed the door handle, turned it, and pulled the door open. The long-haired man bounded in, kicking the door shut with his foot, and reached for Patty.

Zach reacted, ready for a fight, but Bria grabbed him by the arm and said, "Don't, Zach. It's Dad!" Tears streamed down her face as the man fiercely hugged Patty.

Cody, who had been sitting on one of the beds watching the TV, leaped from the bed and scrambled toward the rest of his family. "Daddy, Daddy!" he called.

"My boy, my boy," the man said, his voice choked with emotion as he tenderly tousled the boy's hair.

Patty Phillips held her long-absent husband and Bria while Cody pushed between their legs and threw his arms around his father's waist. Time stood still for Zach as the reunion took place. He quietly stepped back and through the connecting doors into his own room. Bria and Patty had shocked him earlier with the news that Rich was alive, not lying dead at the bottom of Strawberry Reservoir. It had been hard for him to believe, but they seemed sure, even though the only way they'd known it was from what Frank had told each of them. Cody was not told for fear he might say something that could endanger them or his dad.

Zach would never have recognized Rich. The long hair and beard had him completely fooled. But it hadn't fooled his family. Five minutes passed before the connecting door opened and Bria entered, her face glowing. She reached for Zach and enveloped him in a big hug. Her tears ran freely as she rested her head against his chest.

"Even though Frank told me he was alive, I had my doubts. But it's him, Zach. It's really him."

A few more minutes passed before Rich and Patty, followed closely by Cody, came through the connecting doors. Bria slipped away from Zach, who stood awkwardly, his eyes darting from one to another of the Phillips family.

Rich smiled brightly at Zach. "They've been telling me about you, Zach," he said. "Thank you for being here for my family. You'll never know how much it means to me." His eyes were red, and his cheeks, above the long brown beard, were wet.

Rich held his hand out to Zach, and the two men shook. "It's nice to see you," Zach said. "Like everyone else, I thought you were dead."

"And except for you guys, my secret has to stay that way a little longer," he said. "This is one of the hardest things I've ever had to do, faking my own death and breaking the heart of my wonderful family."

"Why did you do it?" Zach couldn't keep himself from asking.

"That's a fair question, and considering the fact that you've been willing to risk your own life for them," he said, fondly taking in each member of his family with his eyes, "it's only fair that I tell you."

"You have a wonderful family," Zach said. "I really admire them." His eyes met Bria's as he spoke, and her face glowed.

"All of you need some answers. But I'm starving. Why don't we have some food brought up, and I can tell you what I'm allowed. Then we'll be leaving right away. I'm afraid that it won't be safe here much longer. They found Frank. It's only a matter of time before they find you, and I'm not taking that chance."

Bria shivered and stepped back beside Zach again.

After giving her a reassuring hug, Zach stepped into his room and called room service. Patty called from theirs. Then they sat together in Zach's room while they waited for the food to come. Cody had been planted in front of the TV again since they were about to discuss things his parents didn't think he should hear.

Rich said, "I guess you all wonder how I got out of the reservoir alive," he said.

Patty nodded, and she said, "When Frank told me you were alive, I asked him how that could be. He said he didn't know how you'd done it, only that the whole thing was staged."

"It was risky, but we set it up well," he said. "It was critically important that no one know I was alive, especially members of the Earth Militia. I had worked hard and made some huge inroads into their operation. We got word that they were after me, and my superiors decided that I needed to vanish so I could then infiltrate them with a new identity. So far it has worked. They know me as GR Roper."

"So you're with the CIA," Zach said.

"Yes," he said to Zach.

"That's dangerous work."

"It is dangerous work," he agreed. "I've been with the agency for eighteen years now. Patty knew, but until just a couple of years ago, Bria thought that I was an international businessman."

"Yeah. I was shocked when he finally told me. It was when I turned sixteen. I've been scared about his work ever since then, but I've also been proud of him," Bria said, blushing lightly.

Rich looked fondly at his daughter. "She has faithfully kept our secret," he said. "Let's go on. The mystery man in the old blue boat is another agent. He and I planned and carried it out. He had waited until we had an audience—witnesses who could say I went down and never came up."

"How did you do that, Dad? You came up, didn't you?" Bria asked.

"Not for quite a while, I didn't. We had placed some underwater gear on the bottom of the lake. After I went overboard, I swam to the bottom, put on the gear, which included a tank of oxygen, and then headed for another location around the point where I wasn't likely to be seen.

"My colleague picked me up there, and we rode in the boat, with me lying on the bottom in case anyone saw us, then we sank the boat and swam to shore. We drove off in the vehicle he'd left near the lake," Rich explained.

"Mom says she knew about it before Frank picked me up in the mountains," Bria said.

"That's right. Frank called her. The director didn't want to let her know, but I insisted. But she had to be sworn to secrecy. Frank told her that my drowning was a diversion. She was also told that your kidnapping was another tactic. That's all she knew," Rich said as he squeezed his wife's hand. "It was cruel but necessary because of the many lives at stake. I'm not finished yet. Things will be coming to a head soon."

"Knowing was still a great comfort to me," Patty said. "But it was a burden, too."

There was a knock on Zach's door. The Phillipses hurried into their room, and then Zach looked to make sure it was room service. He let them in. As soon as his meal was on the table, the same man knocked on the Phillipses' door. The five of them ate together. Zach couldn't help but notice how Bria, Patty, and Cody kept looking at Rich's bearded face, love shining in their eyes. He thought of his own family and the worry they must be experiencing by now. He hoped it didn't have to go on for too long.

As soon as the meal was finished, Rich said, "Okay, it's time to go. Get packed up."

Zach fidgeted with the snaps on the sleeves of his western shirt. Bria noticed first. "Zach, are you okay?"

"Just wondering about getting out of here," he said.

"We'll be fine," Rich said. "Or is there something I don't know about?"

"When you came in, were cops or security officers watching the elevators?" Zach asked.

Rich pulled on his beard for a moment. "You know, there were, now that I think about it. Why do you ask?"

Zach explained about the cameras and how he was afraid that people were looking for him in connection with Frank's death.

"That won't do," Rich said. "What size pants and shirt do you wear?"

Zach told him. Rich said, "You'll have to part with that western getup until we get you away from here. Have everything ready. I'll be right back." He went to the door, peered out, and then he was gone.

Bria grinned. "Looks like Dad's going to get you a disguise. I can't wait to see what he comes up with." Bria gently touched his arm. "Whatever he gets, you'll look great. I'm so glad you're here with me."

The time it took for Rich to return was close to an hour. When he finally came in, he was carrying a couple of large bags and one smaller one. He handed one of the large ones to Zach. "It took longer than I expected. Those guys are being pretty observant down there. Get the clothes on, and then I'll help you with the rest."

"What do you mean . . . 'the rest'?" Zach asked with apprehension.

"Trust me," Rich said. He turned to Bria. "This bag's for you."

"Dad, I'm fine. I don't need anything," she protested, pulling a face.

"Yes, you do. The two of you need to look like a couple. And in addition to that, you need to be a distraction. Go get dressed." Bria gave him a strange look, but her father didn't offer further explanation.

When Bria and Zach emerged from their respective bathrooms, they were wearing formal attire—a lime-green formal gown on Bria and a black tuxedo on Zach.

"Okay," Rich said as he dumped the contents of the smaller bag on the dresser, "let's get the rest of this done. Patty, all Bria needs is some makeup."

"Dad, is this really necessary?" Bria asked.

He put an arm around her shoulders and pulled her close for a moment. She blushed at the way Zach was watching them.

Rich said, "In my business, you do a little more than you think is needed. That's what keeps us alive."

Zach thought about Frank. *It hadn't kept him alive.* But he kept that thought to himself.

"Okay, Zach, let's see what we can do here. And don't worry, I've had a lot of experience with blending in. If Patty could see the way I've looked at times in my work, she'd cringe. Here, sit down," he said as he turned a hardbacked chair to Zach.

By the time Rich had finished, Zach was wearing a black toupee that covered the top of his ears and collar. Rich clipped a ring to one ear and made his eyebrows and eyelashes black. He wore a pair of fashionable glasses with darkened lenses. Rich glued a small goatee to his face. The final touch was darkening Zach's skin with some base.

Bria stared at him and then started to giggle. "Sorry, Zach," she said. "You're pretty good-looking, but I prefer the cowboy getup."

For his part, Zach was blown away by how Bria looked. Her mother had turned a pretty girl into a fashion model. She was a knockout.

He said, "Wow, Bria. Before we get out of here, somebody will probably hit on you."

"You won't let them," she said as she stepped close, took hold of the sleeves of his tuxedo, and gave him an impish look. "You'll intimidate them with that beard."

"Okay, enough with the compliments. Here's the plan," Rich said. He looked at his watch. "There will be a black limo waiting for us at the front doors. We'll go first. Patty, I'll walk a little bit behind you and Cody. I'm afraid that we don't look much like a couple right now."

"But I feel whole again," she said, her face serious. "You'll never know how much I've missed you."

"Me too," Rich agreed. "Anyway, you two follow, not too far back but enough that it doesn't look like we are together. But keep close enough that I can intervene if I have to. Not a lot of the terrorists have seen me, but enough that I need to try to avoid drawing attention to myself." He paused. "Do you have Frank's gun on under that suit?"

"I do," Zach answered.

"And I have his little gun in my purse," Bria said.

"Good. Now, there's one more thing we need to do before we walk through that door. I'd like to offer a prayer. No matter how well we plan, we always need the added help that only God can provide."

The plan worked perfectly. Bria and Zach walked close together, chatting about nothing, smiling at each other. She had her arm through his, and despite the seriousness of their situation, her nearness was wonderful. The only tense moment was when they passed a couple of officers who stood near the elevators on the bottom floor.

Both officers did a double take as the two of them strolled past. Zach felt his breath catch in his throat. Bria's arm tightened on his. But neither officer took a step toward them or even spoke. Zach kept his head down, and they kept moving. Zach's impulse was to run, but he made certain that they kept the same leisurely pace they'd adopted since leaving the elevators. Zach also had to fight the impulse to look back. Zach spotted Rich, his back to them, and he let out a deep breath. He also felt Bria relax, and, with his free hand, he gently patted her arm.

Rich, clearly trying to be as inconspicuous as possible, glanced only briefly at the two of them then began to move quickly toward the front doors, his head down.

Chapter Fifteen

Myra Rutger was a light sleeper. When she nudged Lee in the middle of the night, he stirred and rolled over to face her.

"I heard something," she said.

The sheriff was instantly awake. He lay still for a moment, listening. He could hear the refrigerator running. An electric baseboard heater was clicking softly, the way it did whenever the elements were cooling. A car passed by on the street out front. The floor creaked—*a sound that shouldn't be there.*

"Crawl to the bathroom," he urgently whispered to his wife. "Lock the door and then lie down in the tub."

"Lee, be careful," she whispered back.

"I will. Now go."

He slipped from one side of the bed as she slipped from the other. He had always kept his guns unloaded and locked up when not in use—until the threats had come. His pistol was loaded and lying on the little table next to the bed. He silently picked it up and listened until he heard the soft click of his wife locking the bathroom door. Rising to a crouching position, he moved slowly to the bedroom door.

The floor creaked again in the living room. Almost simultaneously there was a shuffling sound to the left of the creaking. *Two invaders,* he thought. He slipped into the hallway, the gun in front of him, his index finger on the trigger. He kept his back to the wall and slipped as silently as possible along it, knowing that the floor was less likely to creak there than if he walked in the center of the hallway.

He stopped after a few silent steps. He could hear the invaders inching their way through the house. One of them whispered to the other. The second whispered back. He couldn't tell exactly what was said, but he heard enough that he knew they were planning to plant a bomb but wanted to make sure Lee and Myra were in the house before they did.

Both men were close to him when he backed into the open doorway of a spare bedroom. His heart was pounding so hard that he hoped the men didn't hear it. His palms were sweating, and his knees felt like they were ready to smash into each other. He took a silent but deep breath and waited, his pistol ready. The shadow of a man appeared in front of him, just a foot or two away. He raised the pistol and brought in down with all the force he could muster on the intruder's head. There was a sharp crack and a soft grunt. With his left arm, the sheriff caught the falling man and pulled him into the bedroom, all the while on alert for the second man, wondering where he was.

There was a loud whisper, and although Lee couldn't tell what the man was saying, he could tell that he was anxious. He had to have heard the slight commotion when Lee knocked his partner out. Lee bent and swiftly checked the unconscious intruder for weapons. He removed a pistol and a knife and slipped them into the closet as he carefully listened for the second man.

Finally, he heard him moving toward the hallway again, whispering for his comrade as he passed the door where Lee waited. Lee struck hard again, but the man ducked the glancing blow. He came straight at Lee then, his fists pumping. Lee backed rapidly into the bedroom, avoiding the prone man on the floor while dodging the blows. The intruder, however, stumbled over his partner and fell. Lee struck again as the man tried to get to his feet. This time, the barrel met its mark, and the intruder went down again, falling on top of the first man.

Lee hurried past the men and turned on the light. As soon as he confirmed that they were both unconscious, he called out, "Myra, come help me."

His wife was there before he'd finished searching for weapons. She gasped, throwing her hand over her mouth. "Call for backup," he said as calmly as he could.

By the time an on-duty deputy arrived, both men were coming to, but the sheriff had them handcuffed. "Keep them in separate isolation cells," he instructed. "We'll interrogate both of them later."

Shortly after the culprits were hauled to jail, Marlon Sessions and Andrew Wakefield arrived. A bomb was discovered on the floor in the kitchen. Quickly determining that this homemade explosive was triggered by a timing device only and not by motion, Chief Deputy Sessions gently lifted the bomb and rushed it outside. He carefully set it down in the center of the sheriff's large backyard and then rushed back into the house.

Lee and Myra watched out the kitchen window while they waited for the volunteer fire department to arrive. "It's probably not set yet," Lee said hopefully.

His wife leaned against him. "Lee," she said with a trembling voice, "what are we going to do?"

"Hopefully, we've got the men who were an immediate threat, but there could be more coming. I think we should have you go stay with one of the kids for a few days," he suggested. "I don't want you to be in danger anymore."

Myra nodded. "Thank you. I'll go to Judith's in the morning. But what about you? I'm scared for you."

He forced a smile. He was admittedly scared, but he said, "Maybe I'll stay at the office. I can't leave town. I have work to do."

Myra nodded.

A siren sounded. "Sounds like the fire department is—"

Myra was cut off by a loud explosion in the backyard. A sheet of flame rose high into the air, and several windows in the sheriff's house shattered. Lee pulled his wife to the floor as glass sprayed around them. Myra trembled and clung tightly to Lee as they stood up together.

"Can we go right now?" she asked. "I know that Judith won't mind."

"I'll take you," he said. "Why don't you go pack while I see how much damage there is."

The fire department was spraying water on the area where the bomb had exploded. The lawn, flowerbeds, and shrubs were a mess. Lee and Marlon checked the house. Luckily, the only apparent damage was to the windows on the back side of the house, where four had been blown out. "Would you like me to get someone to come fix the windows while you take Myra to your daughter's home?" Marlon asked.

“Yes, if you don’t mind. I should be back before noon,” Lee said. “Also, get with the county attorney on the two guys who did this. And let’s get the feds back here. I’m guessing that this bomb was much the same as the one that destroyed the Phillipses’ house.”

* * *

When Sheriff Rutger got back to Duchesne at eleven thirty that morning, the first thing he did was drive to his house. Workers were already replacing his windows. He went inside and spent a few minutes cleaning up the broken glass. Then he grabbed some lunch and was off to his office.

He was still tired, despite the two-hour nap he’d taken at his daughter’s home before heading back. But there was a lot to do. First on his list was an interview with the two bombers. Both he and Marlon met them in a small, secure room at the jail. The two men were smug and uncooperative. They asked for an attorney and refused to answer any questions. Disappointed but not surprised, Lee and Marlon went to meet with the county attorney. He had already formally charged the two men with a host of serious charges, including two counts of attempted murder. The charges had been delivered to the district court, and the men were to be arraigned on those charges the next morning.

The county attorney had also called a judge and discussed holding the men without bond. The order was made. That afternoon, federal agents began their investigation at the sheriff’s house. They assured the sheriff that federal charges would also be brought against the two men.

Once again, Agent Crooney flew into Duchesne. With a grave face, he said to the sheriff when he met him at the airport, “I’m sorry about your house and yard, but I’m glad you and your wife are okay.”

“I just wish the men would talk, but they’ve refused without attorneys present,” the sheriff told him in frustration. “They’ve been given their phone calls, and we are just waiting to hear from their lawyers.”

“I’ve got news,” Agent Crooney said. “The Phillips family and Zach Barlow are safe, and there is an agent with them as we speak.”

The sheriff felt some relief as he opened the door of his car and got in. After he started driving away from the airport, he asked, “How long will this thing go on? Are your people making any headway on this so-called Earth Militia organization?”

"We hope to wrap things up fairly soon. Having these two in custody may prove to be a big help to us," he said.

"If we can get them to talk," the sheriff said wearily.

"We will," the agent said confidently. "When we bring enough charges against them, they'll want to make a bargain."

* * *

Rich Phillips arranged for another agent to come and provide some security. He was still with his family in a house in Los Angeles when he got a call on the cell phone he used in his undercover roll as GR Roper. It was from Kerry Sunger, leader of the terrorist organization. Rich hadn't seen or spoken to him since their last meeting.

"GR, I've made some decisions. I can't speak over the phone, but I'd like to meet you in Las Vegas tomorrow," he said with excitement in his voice.

"You name the place and time, and I'll be there," Rich said, hoping that he would finally be able to learn enough information to put an end to the insanity.

Zach was watching him as he spoke on the phone. He couldn't believe how calm Rich was. He was clearly cut out for this kind of work. His wife and daughter, on the other hand, both looked like the world might end.

When Rich completed his call, his wife asked, her voice trembling, "Do you have to go, Rich?"

"I'm afraid so, but you'll be safe here," he said, his face showing the tenderness he felt toward his wife. "I'm sorry, dear, but all of this should soon be over. That was the man behind all the trouble. I'll be meeting with him tomorrow."

"Where?" Zach asked.

Rich looked at him. "I better not say, but I'll be flying out of L.A. I need to get arrangements made, but before I go, there is one thing I need to do—I need to get you guys a cell phone."

An hour later, he delivered two phones, which he instructed them to use only when it was absolutely necessary. "For example," he said, "if you need groceries and only one of you goes, you'll need to be able to make calls if any problems arise."

"Is there any way we can call you, Dad?" Bria asked.

Rich tugged nervously at his beard. Finally he said, "I'll give you a number. Call only if it is a serious emergency. If you have to call, do not use any names, either real ones or the ones you are currently using. Just state the problem. If I answer but don't respond like you would expect me to, you can assume that I'm with our enemies, and we'll just have to wing it. That's the best I can do. But I will not be calling you on these phones unless it is life or death. Will that work?"

"That's better than what we've had, Dad," Bria said with a weak smile. "I just need to know that you are still out there for us."

Rich put his arm around his daughter and pulled her close. "I'll be there for you, Bria. I'll be there for all of you."

Rich left his family and Zach that afternoon, admonishing them to be very careful. After he was gone, Bria suggested she look at her e-mail messages. "Hoping to have another one from Walt?" he teased.

She pushed him playfully on the shoulder. "He's just a friend," she told him. "You know that. But yes, I am hoping to hear that he and the others are still safe. I'm worried about them."

"So am I," Zach agreed. The house they were staying at was in a busy Los Angeles neighborhood. It looked like most other houses, but it had been remodeled with extra security features, including an elaborate alarm system, bulletproof glass, and strong doors with secure locking mechanisms. And it had a computer room with state-of-the-art equipment. They didn't have to use Frank's small laptop as long as they were staying here.

They went into the computer room, where they sat down side by side and booted up one of three computers. They soon accessed Bria's account. As Bria suspected, there was a message from Walt. There was also one from Sheriff Rutger.

"Which do you want first?" Zach asked.

She grinned at him. "Let's open Walt's first," she said.

"You really do miss him, don't you?" Zach asked half jokingly.

"Who did I ask to come help me?" she asked, her eyes focused on his.

No further words on the subject passed between them.

"Open it," he said softly, and she pulled her eyes from his.

Walt's message was short. He told Bria that he and Sage were both safe and that the sheriff had worked out a safe place for them to stay. Then he wrote that he hoped she was also safe and expressed his desire that this nightmare would soon be over. He also said that Sage wanted him to say hi to them.

Bria let out a small cry of alarm as they began to read the sheriff's message. She grabbed Zach's arm, and he looked up from the message. He suspected that his face mirrored hers. This was horrible. "I wish your father knew about this," Zach said in a shaky voice.

"I'm just glad that Bishop Rutger and his wife are both okay," Bria said, her eyes misting up.

"The Lord is watching over them just like He's watching over us," Zach said as he pulled her close to him. "They are good people. We're lucky to have someone of his caliber as sheriff."

She nodded her agreement. "Because of him, two of the terrorists are caught." She was thoughtful for a moment. "I wonder if Dad knows the guys the sheriff caught."

"He may," Zach said. "Although, like he said when we were getting ready to leave the Mirage, he doesn't know all of them. Your dad is a brave man. I can't believe he's doing what he's doing."

"He's doing it to save innocent lives," Bria said, leaning her head against his shoulder. "I just hope he can succeed."

"We've got to believe that he will," he said.

"There you are," Patty said a moment later.

Zach removed his arm from around Bria as she lifted her head from his shoulder and looked sheepishly at her mother.

"You two look like you have seen a ghost," Patty said. "What's the matter?"

"We're checking e-mails. You've got to read this one from Sheriff Rutger," Bria said. "It's horrible."

Patty's face went white as she read. "They tried to kill Bishop Rutger and Myra," she said, shaking her head in disbelief. "What horrible people they are. I just pray that your father will find a way to stop them for good. I live in fear every moment that he's gone."

Bria stood and put her arms around her mother. The two women wept quietly. Zach slipped from the room, leaving them to comfort one another.

Chapter Sixteen

One at a time, the attorneys for Janie, Rex, and Jay advised their clients not to take the polygraph tests. Sheriff Rutger had no choice but to call off the remainder of the tests. He was now certain that the three of them were hiding something, but what? The probability that the dead harmonica-playing agent was the killer was high, but there was no way he could justify closing the case considering the lack of cooperation from these three persons of interest. His hands were tied until he could find more evidence.

Several days passed. The investigation stalled. The two men who had tried to bomb the sheriff's home obtained lawyers who made sure they kept their mouths shut. Federal charges were filed, and the men were kept isolated in jail.

The sheriff's wife stayed out of town while he lived out of his office, although he did relax his self-imposed exile from home and spent more and more of his free time there. No more threats came, and he entertained the hope that he had the men responsible for the threats in custody.

One week following the bombing, however, the threats started anew. But they were different. The sheriff received a note in the mail that was unsigned, had no return address, and was typed on a single sheet of white paper. The envelope was stamped Salt Lake City. When his secretary dropped it on his desk, he felt the old familiar fluttering begin in his stomach.

He opened it and read,

You are holding two innocent men in jail. They are working for the people of America. You and your kind are the enemy. Turn them loose immediately or suffer the consequences.

That was it. Even though no names were mentioned, there was no doubt that it referred to the men who had tried to kill him and his wife. There was no way they were being turned loose, but maybe they did need to be secretly moved to a larger, more secure facility.

Marlon Sessions tapped on the frame of Lee's open office door and peered in.

"Come in, Marlon," he said wearily.

"I understand that you have a suspicious piece of mail," the chief deputy said.

"Yes, I'm afraid so," Lee said as he signaled for Marlon to come in and shut the door behind him.

They read and discussed the note, and Marlon agreed with Lee that they should try to move the men as quickly and quietly as possible. By noon, with the help of federal authorities, that had been accomplished. But that did little to ease the tension that the sheriff and his officers were feeling. Even though the prisoners wouldn't be easily found and would almost certainly not be busted free, it didn't change the matter that the threat had addressed. They were not turned loose, and consequences would likely follow.

Every police officer in the county and beyond was put on high alert. All vacations and special days off were canceled. The state sent in additional officers to provide security to the jail and the sheriff's home and to just be visible to the public. The deadly waiting game was on.

* * *

Rich called the phone Patty and Bria were sharing. He did so from a cheap, throwaway cell phone.

"Put this on speaker," Rich said when his wife answered the phone.

"Is there a problem?" she asked as soon as she had complied and laid the phone on the table where they were gathered around, nerves on edge.

"I don't think so," he said. "In fact, I think that I'm making progress. However, there is one interesting thing that came up, and that's what I'm calling about. I've been told that interest in you guys seems to have faded away. I think the thugs realize that you don't know anything about whatever it is they are concerned about. This was not my decision, but you no longer have anyone watching your location."

"What!" Bria screamed. "We need someone."

Zach took hold of her hand. "I'm here," he whispered.

She nodded an acknowledgment and leaned against him as Rich responded.

"Resources are tight," he said. "My bosses feel that we need to use them elsewhere. So I'm just calling to tell you guys to be doubly careful, although I'm quite certain that you are in a safe place."

The call ended shortly after that.

"It's been over a week since Rich left," Patty said shortly after the call had ended. "We are getting on one another's nerves. We can only watch so much TV, read so many books, and play so many games. I think we need to get out of here for a while."

"We don't have a car," Bria said. "There is still food in the house."

"We need milk and eggs and could use some fresh fruit," her mother reminded her. "But it's not just that. I think we need some physical activity. We should go to the beach or a zoo or a museum, something like that."

Zach couldn't have agreed more. Being cooped up was driving him nuts. He was used to being busy.

"That sounds good to me," he said eagerly. "We can get a cab or even rent a car. Or we can go on the Internet and check out bus routes. I'm sure there's a way we can go somewhere and still get back in reasonable time."

He looked at Bria, who smiled and stopped wringing her hands.

"Let's do it," she said with some enthusiasm. "I vote for the beach. We don't have to go swimming, but we could just walk and look at the ocean. I'd love that."

"Then it's agreed?" Patty asked, smiling. "Let's see about the buses. I think that's a great option. We have money and can do that easily enough."

Zach thought about the money he still carried in his shoes. He hadn't touched it. Rich had left them with some cash, but Zach was still glad he had some money in reserve.

An hour later they were out the door and into the warm Los Angeles day. It was smoggy, but they all felt like escaped prisoners. The three-block walk to the closest public bus stop was refreshing. They kept close watch about them, but the news that Rich had given them about the terrorists losing interest had lifted much of the burden they had carried for so many days.

* * *

Rich Phillips could not believe what he was hearing. Kerry Sunger had just called his cell, the one only used by members of the organization.

"GR," he had just said, "I need to meet with you alone." That had not happened before, and it seemed strange. It could either mean that he was deeply trusted or that he was in deep trouble. Rich had nerves of steel, but those nerves were on edge as the terrorist leader went on. "You and I need to talk. There is someone I don't trust in the organization. I'll meet you in Las Vegas tomorrow morning. Let's both fly in there and connect at the airport."

After spending a night of worry, Rich arrived at the airport. Kerry had arranged to meet him at the Avis car-rental desk. Rich was totally alert but still slightly on edge. The last thing he wanted was to walk into a trap. Too much depended on his success in this highly critical undercover assignment. There was his family to think about, too. His love for them knew no bounds.

He observed the desk from an obscure position for several minutes. He was trained, skilled, and well-practiced at this sort of thing. The same could not be said of Kerry Sunger. He and his group were filled with hate and misplaced ideals. They were violent but sloppy when it came to covert operations.

This was reinforced to him as he watched Kerry approach the desk a few minutes later. He did not watch his back the way Rich did, seemingly thinking that he was invincible. It would have been easy for Rich to slip behind him and do whatever he wanted before Kerry could react. He watched for a moment more. Kerry was casually looking around, but he was also busy at what appeared to be the business of renting a car.

Finally as satisfied as he possibly could be, Rich approached him, walking easily and smiling.

"Hello," he said, making Kerry turn his head quickly. "I see you beat me here."

"I didn't see you, GR," Kerry said.

"I barely got here," Rich lied. "My plane was a little late. Sorry."

"It's okay," Kerry said, appearing relaxed now. "I'm getting us a car. We're going down to the strip."

He didn't say why, and Rich didn't ask. A few minutes later they were on their way. As Kerry drove he began to talk. "Rich, have you noticed anything about Harrison Bagshaw that makes you wonder about his loyalty to the organization and our cause?"

Rich felt the tension in him rise. There was no way to know what Kerry was thinking or what kind of answer he expected. "I'm not sure what you mean. He has a lot to say."

"Exactly," Kerry said. "Too much at times. It makes me wonder if he's acting."

"I hadn't thought about that," Rich said cautiously. "Has he said something in particular that worries you?"

"Not exactly, but I have reason to believe there is someone in the group who's infiltrating us. I'm just trying to figure out who it is," he said, looking over at Rich as he spoke.

Rich said nothing as Kerry merged onto the freeway. Once he was safely in the flow of traffic, Kerry continued. "I've thought about it a lot. Something about Harrison bothers me. He's the only one I don't feel totally comfortable with. I was just wondering if you felt the same. He wasn't with us when we bombed those places last year, and the way he appeared and joined us makes me uneasy now that I have reason to doubt him."

"I'm new, too," Rich pointed out, hoping he sounded casual. "I hope you don't distrust me because of that."

Kerry again looked over at him, shaking his head. "Being new isn't the issue. You are solid as far as I'm concerned, and the others agree. Anyway, what do you think; could Harrison be a mole?"

"I suppose so. Do you want me to get a little better feel for him?" Rich asked.

"That was exactly what I was going to ask you to do. Where both of you are newer, I thought you would be the best person to gain his trust."

"I'd be glad to," Rich said. "The last thing we need at this point is someone from the inside screwing things up for us." He tried to make his voice sound deadly.

"Now, let's you and I have a look at one or two of these casinos. I'm thinking that we might get the attention of the people if we do something big, really big. And I have an idea how we can do it," Kerry said.

Rich avoided looking at him, afraid that he would have a hard time keeping the shock he was feeling from appearing in his eyes. And he carefully controlled his voice as he said, "Casinos. A waste of resources in more than one way, not to mention the electric pollution they generate. Filthy places."

"Exactly. My thoughts exactly."

"Plus, they're always crowded—always busy. You may be on to something."

"Yeah, I think so. We took out an enemy agent in one of them, and that got me thinking. Apparently we have to make a bigger impact before they take us seriously. I thought the things last year would do it, but I was mistaken," he said as he glanced over at Rich.

Rich hoped he had his true feelings totally under wraps as he let Kerry catch his eyes. The look he saw in the depths of the terrorist's dark brown eyes was terrifying. This man was insane! He didn't care who was hurt or killed as long as he accomplished his goals. Rich was certain he was mentally unbalanced. He wondered what in the world might have caused this man to go so far in his bizarre quest to obliterate pollution and its effects on the environment.

"How much more time are you going to give them?" Rich asked. "It seems to me like you've been pretty generous."

"Way too generous, GR," Kerry said, his voice rising as the emotions in him began to froth. "You know they killed my wife, GR. Lung cancer is an awful way to die. I watched her suffer for two years before she was finally taken away from me. How many others will they destroy before we can stop them?"

Rich was absolutely stunned. This man had totally lost it in trying to carry out his personal vendetta. He composed himself before he said, "There's no other way, Kerry. When will we strike?"

"We're going to act soon. After you and I scope some places out, we'll make a decision. I have the materials we need collected. We're going to blow some places clear off this planet."

Rich needed more specifics, so he prodded the man on. "We need several targets," he said.

"Yeah, and big ones," Kerry agreed. "The bigger they are, the clearer the message."

By the time they had parked the rental car, Kerry had talked a lot, and Rich had taken it all in, as had the little recorder he carried deep in his pocket. If what Kerry was proposing was actually carried out, it would spell disaster of the greatest magnitude. This madman and his followers had to be stopped. From what Kerry had said, the trip today was mostly to decide which casinos to plant a series of bombs in. The decision had already been made that at least one of them was going to be destroyed. Rich was sick at the thought of all the innocent people who might be hurt or killed at the casinos.

That was not all, however. A power plant in Huntington, Utah, was slated to be destroyed and a couple of coal mines shut down with irreversible damage. And if Kerry wasn't hallucinating or deliberately trying to mislead Rich, he already had the supplies on hand to create the bombs. Things were going from bad to worse. It was time for the federal agencies to step up their efforts. With a little more evidence, perhaps Kerry and some of the others could be taken into custody. However, Rich had to know the exact targets and specific dates. Also, he absolutely had to know where the explosive devices and materials were being stored.

Kerry didn't give him all that information, but he was with Kerry when the terrorist leader decided to target the Mirage. They obtained a map of the casino floor, and Kerry marked the spots where he calculated bombs would do the most damage.

"We'll use a series of bombs," he said with excitement. "They will be planted in advance with a remote detonation and will be linked to trigger simultaneously. It will be beautiful."

* * *

"Let's go back to the beach today," Cody said. "That was fun."

"Yes, and relaxing," his mother agreed. "I don't see why we can't, do you?" she asked Zach.

Bria had gone to her room right after lunch, and he hadn't seen her since. "I think we can. It was nice just getting out and about," he agreed. "I know it was good for Bria. It was nice to see her laugh again. She hasn't done much of that lately."

Patty's face clouded. "I've been worried about Bria," Patty said. "This is rough on all of us, but it seems to be especially so on her."

"I'm sure she's worried about your husband. She lost him once, and she's scared to death of losing him again," Zach said. "I think that's what's bothering her the most."

"Then we should go out again," Patty said with finality. "We'll all worry less if we are busy. I'll go get Bria."

When Bria emerged from her room, her eyes were red, but she was smiling. "I'm ready to go again," she said lightly.

* * *

"I'm still worried about what Calvin Portman might have said to those young people in Utah," Kerry said as he and Rich drove back to the airport. "I'm sure he leaked information about our targets in Utah. The man was an idiot, and I've got to make sure we are not compromised."

Knowing this affected his family and Zach, Rich tried to keep his composure as Kerry looked directly at him. This was the exact opposite of what he'd heard and passed on to his family.

"I didn't know Calvin," Rich said, keeping his voice even.

"No, but Harrison did. In fact, it was Calvin who first introduced me to Harrison. That's another reason I don't trust Harrison." Kerry's voice began to take on the frantic edge that worried Rich so much. "It's best that Calvin is dead. I think Calvin told those hunters things that they might have told the authorities. And someone, one of our own, is communicating with that sheriff in Duchesne." When he looked over at Rich, his eyes were blazing.

"Harrison?" Rich asked.

"That's what I think," Kerry confirmed. "The sheriff should have been dead. It was a perfect plan. But he knew they were coming. There's no way he could have avoided being blown off the planet unless someone warned him."

Rich nodded in agreement when Kerry again looked his way. He was guessing, but he thought it might be a good guess, so he risked it.

"And because of that, two of our best bomb makers are in custody."

"Exactly!" Kerry thundered, pounding his fist on the steering wheel. The car dipped into the oncoming lane for a second. Horns honked and cars swerved. Kerry made it back into his own lane without crashing, but it was way too close for Rich's comfort. He wisely said nothing about it.

"We are going to get them out, and that sheriff is going to wish he'd let them go when we asked."

After a period of silence, Kerry said, "I'm going to give Sheriff Rutger one more chance. Maybe he'll be reasonable. If not, he can only blame himself for what happens next."

Chapter Seventeen

A call was transferred to Sheriff Rutger's office. The caller had refused to identify himself, but Lee's secretary had informed him of the call, and he'd told her to send it through.

"This is Sheriff Rutger," he said.

"You are running out of time," a man warned. "Turn them loose or you will die and so will a lot of others, including your wife and daughter."

There was a click before Lee could say anything. He stared at the phone in his hand as he felt a shiver pass through his body. He had to warn Myra and Judith. He picked up the phone and made a call.

"Get out of there," he told Myra when she came to the phone. "Take Judith and the family and leave. Do it now."

"Lee, you're scaring me," she said.

"That's because I'm scared," he admitted. "They know where you are. And they just threatened you and Judith."

"Where should we go?"

"I don't know. Just leave. I'll call you back when I figure something out," he said.

When he hung up the phone, he was in a cold sweat. His secretary looked in on him.

"Get Marlon and Andrew," he said before she could say a word. She turned and left quickly. Lee picked up the phone again. He called Agent Crooney. "We've got to talk," he said. "Things are getting worse."

* * *

Waves rolled gently onto the beach. Cody squealed with delight as he rushed into the water until he was up to his knees then ran back. The beach was busy that afternoon, and people were everywhere. The Phillipses and Zach were enjoying a good swim.

They swam, sunbathed, and swam some more. Their cell phones were buried in a pile of clothes and towels a short distance from the water, so when Rich called to tell them about the impending danger, they couldn't hear the ringing. They'd also left their pistols at the house that afternoon, feeling safe and not wanting to pack them to the beach.

* * *

Rich was almost beside himself. Once he'd landed in Phoenix to find and meet with Harrison, he'd located a pay phone and tried to call Patty. When she didn't answer, he tried Zach's phone. When that didn't work either, he waited, found another pay phone at a convenience store, and tried again with the same results. He prayed that something had not already happened to them.

He had to wait until after he'd met with Harrison to try again. That had taken a couple of hours. He hadn't expected to learn anything from Harrison. Rich was the mole, not loudmouthed Harrison, as Kerry suspected. The time was not a complete waste, however, for when he brought up the topic of Calvin Portman, Harrison got angry.

"I can't believe he let himself get killed," Harrison said. "He's the one who got me involved in this thing. He was passionate about saving our planet. If anyone ever figures out who killed my nephew, I will personally see to it that he dies."

It was dusk in Phoenix by the time Rich was able to make another attempt to reach his family. His results were the same. It would be getting late in Los Angeles soon. In desperation, he called one of the FBI agents who had helped him place his family in the safe house. He asked him to check on them to make sure they were okay.

By the time he got a call back from the agent, it was almost dark in Phoenix, meaning that darkness was not far away in California. He was dismayed and extremely worried when he received the report that they were not at the safe house. Anxiously, he tried the phones again, but there was still no answer.

* * *

"They've got to be here somewhere," Bria said, her face distraught. "We left them right here when we started swimming."

They'd been looking for their clothes for close to an hour. Everything was missing but their shoes and towels, which had been tossed aside but not taken. They had traipsed up and down the beach, but the only thing they'd found had been Cody's shirt.

"Someone stole them," Zach said.

"They took our cell phones," Patty said anxiously. "We have more clothes at the house, but what if we need our phones?"

"Maybe tomorrow we can go buy one," Zach suggested. "We'd at least have something to use in an emergency. And we do have the computers. We're not completely cut off."

"I'm scared," Bria said. "We can't even call the cops."

Zach said, "I'm glad we left our guns at the house. At least we still have them."

"It's all my fault," Patty said miserably. "We should have gone to a museum or something today."

"But this was fun," Bria said. "Even though we have to catch a bus in our swimsuits now," she added as she looked down at her bare legs in embarrassment.

"And without any money," Patty reminded them. "We even lost our IDs."

"Not to worry," Zach said. "We never used them anyway, did we?"

"No," Patty admitted.

"And they aren't who we are," he added.

"That's true. But we do still have Cody's. I didn't bring his. But I suppose that someone can get us new ones if we need them," Patty said.

In spite of her mother's attempt to be hopeful, Bria looked even more worried. "We are going to have to walk back. I don't care about just having my swimsuit and sandals on, but that's a long way to walk. It'll take hours. Do we even know how to get there?"

"I have a solution," Zach said, as he took off one of his shoes and held it up with a flourish.

Bria didn't see the humor. "What are you doing?" she asked with a frown.

"I am an Eagle Scout," he said as he reached into his shoe and worked his fingers for a moment. "I'm always prepared," he added as he displayed a fifty-dollar bill. "This should at least get us back to the safe house."

For a second, Bria looked quite startled, and then she threw her arms around him and hugged him tightly. "Zach, you're great," she said as she pulled back from him.

"I have another one in here," he said, displaying the shoe again. "Is that worth another hug?"

It was worth three—one from Bria, one from Patty, and one from Cody. It even earned Zach a bonus, a slightly lingering kiss on the cheek from Bria.

* * *

Rich was standing beside a pay phone, waiting for a call from the FBI agent about what he found at the safe house. He was so intent on receiving the call that he was surprised when he felt the vibration of his cell phone in his pocket. He shook both hands angrily before composing himself and pulling it from his pocket.

"GR, this is Kerry. How did your meeting with Harrison go?"

"Okay, I guess," Rich said as he moved away from the pay phone and concentrated on how to answer Kerry. "He's pretty upset about Calvin. In fact, he's furious. He says he'll personally take care of whoever killed him. By the way, did you know that he is Portman's uncle?"

As Kerry spoke again, the phone in the booth began to ring. Rich was far enough away that it was faint—Kerry wouldn't be able to hear it. But Rich couldn't answer it. He clenched his jaw in frustration as he listened to the terrorist leader say, "I didn't know that, but I don't care. Is he the mole?"

"I spent a long time with him this evening," Rich said. "He could be, but I'm not sure. To listen to him talk, he sounds as devoted as they come."

"Yeah, he always has talked right." Kerry grumbled. "I was hoping you could pick up some vibes."

"I'm sorry, Kerry. I tried. I just don't know. I'll try again if you like."

"No, let me think on it," Kerry said. "I'm inclined to push him back and keep him out of the loop. I don't know if I want to take a chance on him."

"That's smart," Rich said. "If nothing else, he's so bent on revenge that it could make him unreliable. It's already caused him to lose his focus."

"Good thinking, GR," Kerry said.

"Thanks. By the way, did you get the plan for the Mirage detailed on your computer like we discussed?"

"I did. I also have one on the power plant in Utah. I've got a couple more to do, and we'll be ready to make our move. But I need those men out of jail in Duchesne first. That'll happen tonight. Should be easy," he bragged. "I'll be in touch."

Rich walked slowly back to the pay phone as he returned the cell phone to his pocket. He'd missed the call he'd been waiting for. He didn't know if the FBI agent would try again, but he stood near the phone, determined to wait for a while just in case he did. As he waited, he paced, pulling on his beard and running his hand repeatedly through his hair.

There wasn't much time. He had to get the federal forces ready to move. But first he had to make sure his family was safe. He also needed to get a warning to Sheriff Rutger to be especially alert tonight. Rich's gut ached.

* * *

The sheriff felt that for the time being his family was safe. They'd joined the Hinshaws in the safe house in the Salt Lake area. Security was tight there. For now there was nothing more he could do for them. He stayed at the office. There was a strong law enforcement presence around the public safety complex and throughout the community. Agencies from around the state had generously responded to his need. A call from Jim Crooney revealed that some kind of attack might be made on the jail that night, which had the sheriff and all of the officers under his command on high alert. Crooney himself flew in to assist the sheriff. And now since the sheriff was so deeply involved in this mess, Crooney felt he deserved to know exactly why the Phillipses were such a target in the first place.

When he arrived, he asked if he could have a moment with Lee. What Crooney shared with Lee once they'd closed the door left the sheriff stunned. The agent who'd tipped Crooney was a man well-known to Lee. So the drowning had been faked. That explained a lot.

Two-man patrols and stationary units were assigned to drive throughout the town and keep a close eye on the community and the jail complex. Other officers were placed in other key positions. Late that night, one of the patrol units spotted two vehicles with out-of-state plates coming into town. Each appeared to have two individuals in it. The officers followed the two vehicles, thinking they were going to just go right through town. When they turned north on SR 87, they called it in. Others observed them as they proceeded north one mile and then turned on the county road that led to the jail complex on Blue Bench. Obviously, whoever was behind this didn't know the two jailbirds had been moved.

The cars split up as they approached the corner by the jail. One went north, slowly passing the west side of the jail while the other stayed on the south side. They each passed the building, turned around, and came back again. The sheriff and Agent Crooney had had enough. Lee ordered that the cars be stopped.

A roadblock was hastily set up at the bottom of the hill west of the jail in front of a large pile of crushed gravel, where the drivers wouldn't see it until they turned onto the top of the hill. At that point, other patrol units were positioned to move in and cut off their retreat. The two cars were close to each other as they came around the bend at the top of the hill and started down. Suddenly, they braked and spun their cars around, accelerating rapidly back up the hill.

As planned, their retreat was blocked. The units from the road-block moved on them until the two out-of-state vehicles were pinned in by a dozen police cars. In seeming desperation, they turned off the road and tried to escape to the south through the sagebrush that grew there. Four-wheel-drive units pursued them until the two cars became hopelessly stuck in the brush. The four occupants of the cars burst out and opened fire on the approaching police vehicles.

A hail of police gunfire erupted, and the four men collapsed near their vehicles. At that same time, another vehicle, a van with blackened windows and Colorado plates, turned off Main Street and headed north on SR 87 at a high speed. It was pursued by one of the few remaining patrol units on Main Street. When it also turned off the highway and onto the county road, four police vehicles converged on it. Sheriff Rutger himself drove one of them, accompanied by Agent Crooney. The gunsmoke had barely cleared from the first shoot-out when the next one erupted. The back door of the van burst open followed by an eruption of gunfire. The return fire was withering when the van suddenly blew up, shooting flames a hundred feet into the air and scattering bits of metal, glass, and bodies hundreds of yards in every direction.

* * *

Kerry Sunger sat in stunned silence, his phone in his hand. He'd been talking to one of his men in Duchesne, Utah, when the man had suddenly shouted that they were in a police trap. Kerry had ended the phone call and dialed another of his men, who had been just a few miles behind the first cars, and ordered him and the guys with him to back up the others.

"There can't be many cops; it's just a Podunk town. Take them out!" he screamed.

The last thing he'd heard was the driver of his van shouting that they were surrounded.

"Open fire!" he commanded. He heard gunfire through his phone and an especially loud bang . . . and then nothing.

After shaking off the shock, he tried the cell phone numbers of every man in the three vehicles. There was no response. He cursed and hurled the phone at the wall. He sat, his head in his hands, for several minutes. Then he slowly rose to his feet, found another phone, and punched in a number.

"Hello," said Harrison Bagshaw.

"Harrison. This is Kerry," he said as he paced angrily back and forth in his Denver office.

"What's the matter? " Harrison asked.

The terrorist leader cursed and said, "We've got a mole, I tell you. You say you don't think it could be GR Roper. I'm sure it is."

"He's devoted to the cause," Harrison argued. "I told you earlier that he and I talked today. GR is ready to do whatever you ask him to."

"I wanted to believe it, Harrison," Kerry said, cursing. "But I'm having my doubts now. He's almost as new to the organization as you are, but I'm not sure of his background. It seemed to check out, but I don't have a good feeling about him. And he knows a lot about our plans."

"Has something happened to make you think this?" Harrison asked.

"I'll say. I think we just lost eight good men in Duchesne, Utah. There was a shootout, and I'm afraid that the bombs in the van might have gone off."

"What were they doing there?" Harrison asked. "That's where my nephew got killed."

"I know, and it's also where two of our people are sitting in jail. I sent men to get them out. They are my two best bomb experts, and I need them back. It's a tiny town with only a handful of cops. The sheriff isn't very smart, and it should have been easy for eight men to get them out and get away, but it didn't work. Someone tipped them off, and I'm thinking it was GR."

"What do you want me to do?" Harrison asked.

"He's in Phoenix with you. At least he's supposed to be. Call him and tell him there's something you need to discuss with him. If you learn anything that makes you think he might be a mole, waste him. I don't think he'll be of much use to us at this point if I am wrong," Kerry said darkly. "So get on it. Call me back. If you have to eliminate him, let me know when it's done."

* * *

As near as the officers could tell, four men had died in the exploding van. One more had received fatal gunshot wounds, while three were badly wounded. Three officers had also received gunshot wounds, and one had been burned by a piece of flaming shrapnel. Sheriff Rutger was among the wounded. Marlon Sessions, assisted by Crooney, took over command of the scene when the sheriff and the other wounded men were taken to the hospital in Roosevelt.

Concern over more terrorists showing up caused the already tight security to be heightened. More officers were rushed to the area, some coming by plane from Salt Lake City. Bomb experts and a score of federal agents also descended on the small town.

The investigation was almost certain to take hours and even extend into days. Sheriff Rutger had resisted being taken from the scene, but he was injured badly, and there was no choice. On the way to the hospital, he drifted in and out of consciousness. His phone began to ring once while he was awake, but he was helpless as he tried to get to it, losing consciousness once again.

Chapter Eighteen

As the bus rolled along, Zach suddenly remembered that the keys to the safe house had been in their clothes. He was leaning forward, intending to mention it to Patty, when there was a sudden, grinding crash. He was violently thrown into the seat in front of him. The bus tipped dangerously, and Zach began to slide into the aisle.

"Zach, help me," little Cody cried as the boy slid beside him. Screams filled the bus, and dust flew as the bus settled back onto its wheels, bounced for a moment, and then became still.

"I'm right here, Cody," Zach said as he quickly checked the little guy out, relieved that he seemed to be okay. Cody clung to him, crying, while Zach rapidly made sure he himself hadn't suffered anything worse than a few bruises. Then he got to his feet and made his way to the seat in front of where he'd been sitting. Bria and her mother, who had also been thrown from their seats by the force of the impact, were shaken but otherwise okay.

Two hours later they found themselves seated with their towels wrapped around them in a police station. They learned that the car that had hit the bus head-on had been stolen. The thief had been critically injured, but there were only a couple of passengers on the bus who needed medical attention. All the passengers but the Phillipses and Zach had been sent on their way when a substitute bus arrived. A lack of ID had raised concerns with the cops, which led to their current situation.

They had debated trying to call Rich Phillips but had decided against it, not wanting to cause him undue worry. But they had called the sheriff's department, only to learn that things were in chaos there. When

Zach told them that they had to speak with the sheriff, the woman on the phone finally gave him Lee's cell phone number, but she said that he probably couldn't answer it. She'd been right; no one answered his phone.

Zach called the sheriff's office again and asked to speak to the chief deputy. The woman on the phone told him that it was impossible. The chief deputy was busy.

"Tell him it's Zach Barlow calling, and it's urgent," he said.

There was a prolonged silence, and then the woman asked him to hold. He sat on hold for five minutes while a big L.A. cop stared him down. When Chief Deputy Sessions finally came on the line, his first words were, "This had better not be a hoax."

"It's no hoax," Zach said. "I need someone to verify my identity and that of the Phillips family." He then quickly explained about the wreck and that he'd tried to reach the sheriff and couldn't.

"Just a minute," the chief deputy said. "There is someone else here who needs to speak with you. Hold on."

Puzzled, Zach waited. A moment later, a man said, "Is this Joe Sowers?"

Zach hesitated for only a moment before saying, "Yes, and who are you?"

"I'm Special Agent Jim Crooney of the CIA. Tell me what's happening."

Zach explained and then asked with trepidation, "Is something wrong with the sheriff?" Patty and Bria eyed him with concern.

The agent hesitated and said, "He's going to live, but yes, he's been shot. It's been a rough night here. Now, let me talk to an officer there. I'll see that you are taken care of."

Their immediate problem was solved. In less than thirty minutes, an FBI agent showed up and introduced himself as Special Agent Drew Esker. He was just over six feet tall and filled out his dark blue suit with bulging muscles. His friendly presence was reassuring to Zach.

"I can vouch for these folks," he told the two officers who had been watching them like hawks. "They will be coming with me."

When they were in Drew's black Crown Victoria, he said, "Looks like you folks have had a run of bad luck."

As they rode to the safe house, they explained what had happened to them. "You should be okay now," Agent Esker said after he'd unlocked the front door and handed Patty a key to replace the one that had been stolen. We'll have the locks changed in the morning."

As a precaution and before he allowed Zach and the Phillips family to enter, the FBI agent walked through every room in the house, opening all the closets and inspecting inside. He checked every window and door and even looked behind and under the furniture. When he'd finished, he said, "Looks good." He handed Patty a business card. "The house phone here is working fine, so call me if you need me. I'll answer this cell phone anytime, day or night."

After Agent Esker had gone, they relaxed for a minute—but not for long. They had a lot more to worry about. They wished there was a way that Rich Phillips could call them, but Patty didn't think he had the number of the safe-house phone. They also wished they could learn more about the condition of the sheriff, and they wondered if they were really safe in this place. Zach was especially nervous, feeling responsible for all of them.

* * *

When the cell phone in his pocket began vibrating, Rich Phillips groaned. He tensed when he heard the voice of Harrison Bagshaw. "GR, Kerry needs for you and me to get together and talk some things over and then get back with him. It's almost time to act, he says. When can we meet?"

"It's late," Rich said, his mind and body both exhausted. "Let's make it first thing in the morning. You name the place."

"No, it has to be tonight. You know Kerry," Harrison said with a chuckle. "When he decides it's time to do something, nothing stands in the way."

"It's been a long day, Harrison," Rich began again.

"This can't wait," Harrison interrupted.

"I was just going to say that even though it's been a long day, if we need to get together, that's what we'll do. The cause is greater than either of us," Rich said as his mind began to churn. Something smelled rotten.

"Great," Harrison said. He named a location, and Rich agreed to be there.

He hadn't been off the phone long when it vibrated again. "GR," a familiar voice said, "things are not always what they appear to be."

It was a code phrase that had been developed for the current operation. He instantly recognized who was calling. "It's a mirage," he said, completing the code.

He closed the phone and dug another out of a bag in the closet of his room. He punched in a number and waited as the call went through. "Rich, I'm glad I got through to you," Agent Crooney said.

"I was about to leave. Is there a problem?" Rich asked as he began to pace his small room.

"First, your family is safe," Jim said.

Rich heaved a sigh of relief. "Thank goodness. I've been worried sick. Sunger is still after them. I've been trying to warn them, but I've run into one problem after another. Where are they?"

"At the safe house here in Los Angeles."

"Is anyone with them?"

"No, does there need to be?"

"Yes. Get someone there as soon as you can," Rich said urgently. "Why couldn't I reach them?"

Jim explained what he'd learned from the FBI in Los Angeles. "Their cell phones are gone, and except for the boy, they have no ID," he concluded.

"Get someone over there, then call me back on this phone," Rich said. "And do it quickly."

He didn't want to be late for his meeting with Harrison, but he needed to make sure things were secure with his family. Jim called him back in ten minutes. "They are getting someone on the way," Jim told him. "You need to know that there have been some major things happening in Duchesne."

"What?" Rich asked with a furrowed brow. "I did call and warn that an attack was possibly planned."

"You don't already know what happened?"

"No, should I?"

"I just thought that you might have heard something through your contacts within the organization."

"No, but I'm going to meet one of their people as soon as I hang up. Maybe that's what it's about," Rich said as he wondered what else had happened in his sleepy little town.

Jim briefly explained what had occurred. "I was there," he said. "I saw it all. These guys are desperate. And it seems the ones the sheriff arrested must be important to them. They lost eight men trying to get them out. I'm glad you warned them, or it could have been worse for our people."

"I've got to go. Is the sheriff going to be okay?" Rich asked.

"He's in surgery, but the prognosis is good," Jim said.

"Alert the director. We may need to make some arrests soon," Rich said. "I think they're starting to get frazzled, and that's dangerous with people who are as volatile as the ones I've been working with. And just in case," he said, "some backup tonight might be helpful to me. I'm worried that I might be walking into an ambush of some sort." He gave Crooney the location of his planned meeting with Harrison and disconnected.

He left his room at a run, increasingly sure that Harrison was up to something. He had a forty-five-minute drive to the meeting place. He could only hope that was enough time for Jim to mobilize backup from the CIA and the FBI.

* * *

Zach didn't like the feel of things that night. He was nervous and couldn't sleep. He got up and prowled around the safe house for several minutes. When he returned to his room, he put his clothes on and grabbed Frank's 9mm pistol. The FBI agent who had left them at the house had told him to be very careful. Zach decided that he was going to stand watch while the Phillips family slept. He could sleep in the morning when they were awake.

The blinds on the bulletproof windows were drawn. He peered through the one in the living room and watched outside for a moment. Then he walked to the back of the house where the kitchen was located. He parted the blinds just enough to peek through. The floorboards creaked behind him, and Zach swung around.

Bria was staring at him from the doorway.

"What are you doing?" she asked.

There was very little light in the house, so he had to squint to make out the features of her face. "Just checking things," he said, trying to sound nonchalant.

"Why? Aren't we safe here?"

"I think so, but I want to be sure," he said as she walked toward him, her bare feet making only the slightest sound on the hardwood floor. He let the window blind fall back into place and stepped toward her. "I think we are, but after such a difficult evening, I'm not taking any chances."

She stepped close. "Thanks for being here, Zach," she said softly. "I feel safe with you."

He didn't say anything as he studied the shadowy contours of her body in the dark room. She reached out and touched his arm. It sent electricity through him. He put one arm around her back and pulled her gently closer to him. She looked up at him. His heart was racing. He gently cradled her chin in his palm.

The only sound in the room was the ticking of a clock in the living room. He slowly bent down, and their lips met. For a moment the touch was very soft, then she leaned into him, and the kiss became deep and passionate. When they finally drew apart, she dropped her head against his chest. He could smell the sweetness of her hair. Both of his arms encircled her slender waist, and hers moved around him. The softness of her against his muscles was breathtaking.

There was a click at the back door. In the silence of the room, it hit Zach with the force of a rifle shot.

"Get down," he whispered frantically. "There's someone here."

Bria didn't need to be told twice. She dropped to her knees, and he dropped beside her. Together they slipped backward toward the living room. They heard a click again, and then Zach was sure he saw the kitchen door opening. He pulled Frank's gun from his pocket as he continued to back up, his body touching Bria's as they moved together. They found and slipped through the door and around the corner.

He leaned next to her ear and whispered, "Stay down," his eyes never leaving the kitchen door.

Zach touched Bria's arm reassuringly before sliding slowly forward again. He entered the doorway just as a dark figure slipped through the kitchen door. He could see the silhouette of a pistol extended in front of the intruder. He held his breath and didn't move except to bring his gun up and aim it at the center of the figure now framed in the doorway.

The man's gun swung slowly one way and then the other. Zach swallowed hard, preparing to act. He waited until the silhouetted gun was pointing at a ninety-degree angle away from him. His finger tightened on the trigger, and he said, "Drop it."

Before the gun had swung all the way back toward him, Zach pulled the trigger. Flame shot a foot from the end of the barrel, and his hand bucked. The figure in the doorway flew backward, hit the wall, and slid to the floor. There was another shot and then another from somewhere outside. Zach didn't know what that meant, but he slipped back and reached for Bria. His hand touched her cheek.

He still held the gun forward while he looked over his shoulder. There was no movement. Then he heard someone at the backdoor. He tightened his grip on the pistol. "Zach, is that you? I'm Special Agent Drew Esker with the FBI. We met earlier. I think we have them all."

Zach recognized the agent's voice. "It's me," he said as relief poured over him like a bucket of warm water. He felt one of Bria's arms come across his back.

"I'm coming in," Agent Esker said. "My partner is outside."

Just then a bedroom door opened, and Patty Phillips said, "Zach, are you okay?"

"I'm fine, and so is Bria. What about Cody?"

"He's with me. When I heard the first shot, I ran to his room and kept him quiet," she said with a shaky voice.

Zach stood and turned the light on as the familiar face of the FBI officer appeared at the backdoor. Bria stood too, leaning heavily into Zach. She didn't say a word as they moved together into the kitchen, trying not to look toward the doorway and the awful scene before them. Although, thankfully, Zach hadn't killed the man, his shot had created a nasty wound.

Bria's mother turned on the living room light, and with her son, she hurried over and threw her arms around Bria.

Within minutes the street in front of the house was filled with flashing red and blue lights. Special Agent Esker looked apologetically at the family. "We'll move you tonight but not until we do some preliminary work here."

Zach sat on the sofa near Bria. Beside them, Patty held her son tightly as they waited. Camera lights flashed both outside and inside the house. A couple of detectives asked them dozens of questions. They inspected Zach's gun but did not attempt to take it from him.

Finally, Agent Esker came in from wherever he'd been outside. "I'll take you folks someplace else now," he said. "Get your things."

Once they were in his black sedan, the FBI agent said, "It appears that someone was at the house while you were gone today. The back-door lock had been rigged. I'm kicking myself for not checking it more closely before I left you."

"We're just grateful you showed up when you did," Patty said.

"It seems to me like you had a pretty good man protecting you." He looked over at Zach as they sat at a traffic light waiting for it to turn green. "You should consider a career with the FBI. You were pretty cool under pressure. I guess you might also consider the CIA, like Bria's father, but I would recommend my agency." He grinned. "We compete a lot as agencies but when the chips are down, as you have seen, we work closely."

"I appreciate what you've done for us," Zach said. He chuckled. "But I think I'll stick to breaking horses, wrangling bulls, and roping calves. It's a lot safer."

Chapter Nineteen

Harrison Bagshaw seemed on edge when Rich met him that night in a remote area not far from the Phoenix Zoo. Rich was tense himself as he glanced toward the shadowy trees and huge rocks that surrounded him and Harrison.

"What does Kerry have in mind?" Rich asked. "I was with him just this morning, and I thought I knew about our next plans."

"Kerry says we've got to step up the pace. Things aren't going as smoothly as they should be," Harrison said. "For some reason he's worried about what's happening in that little town in Utah, the one near where my nephew was killed." He creased his brow as if in thought.

Rich wasn't fooled, but he played along. "You mentioned it earlier today. What's the name of that place?" he asked.

Harrison shook his head and turned away from Rich. "I can't remember," he said. "It's a strange name. Anyway, we lost more men there tonight, and Kerry is enraged over it. He's wondering how the sheriff up there is able to anticipate every move we make."

"That is hard to understand," Rich said with a shake of his head. He pulled a face and added, "I can't think cops in a tiny, out-of-the-way place like that would be smart enough to be ahead of guys like us."

"The sheriff is an idiot," Harrison said. "He should have already arrested the kid that killed Calvin."

"So it was a kid?" Rich asked.

"Sure it was," Harrison said. "It might have been the Phillips girl. Could have been a young guy named Zach. They both ran, and that's all the proof I need. They were both involved. I'd bet on it." His angry face began to relax.

"But the sheriff up there hasn't figured that out? Is that what you're saying?" Rich asked.

"He's a fool. He's no match for Kerry. Neither is the guy who's ratting on us to him," Harrison said, his eyes squinting as he looked at Rich, confirming Rich's suspicions that this man, and thus Kerry, suspected him. Yet he had been fairly certain that Kerry had been very suspicious of Harrison earlier.

"If it was the Phillips kid and her friend, I guess I won't get my revenge personally," Harrison said. "Kerry said they'd located them and were going to take care of them tonight. It should already be done."

There was a tight twist in Rich's stomach. He had no more time to waste—he had to get in touch with someone right away. Looking at Harrison, he let the anger that was boiling inside him show. He suddenly felt certain that this was indeed a setup. There could be more of Kerry's people hiding in the shadows. He prayed that if there were, the backup he'd requested was on its way for him as well. "You might be interested in knowing that Kerry asked me to let him know if I think you are the mole," Rich said, even as his eyes roamed the darkness about him. "You've let your cousin's death cloud your judgment. I think maybe you aren't to be trusted anymore. You are a mole."

"You are!" Harrison screamed at him as he stepped back and reached inside his pants pocket.

Rich saw movement behind Harrison and dove for Harrison's feet just as a barrage of gunfire erupted. Harrison struck the ground hard, the gun he'd grabbed flying from his hand. Rich felt the sting of sand as bullets kicked it into his face. His own gun was in his hand within seconds. He rolled to his left, ignoring Harrison, who wasn't moving at all. Gunfire continued sporadically.

Several bullets struck near Rich. He stayed close to the ground as he crawled rapidly toward a large rock a few feet away. He caught glimpses of muzzle flash from several directions. He didn't dare fire his gun because he had no way of knowing who were terrorists and who were federal agents. He was pretty sure that there were several of both out there now.

Once he reached the rock, he used it as cover. The gunfire died away. He could see Harrison lying unconscious as sirens sounded in the distance.

Rich stayed put as he waited, not wanting to draw gunfire in case some of Kerry's henchmen waited to snipe him. In a matter of minutes, law enforcement officials had surrounded the area. The sound of voices drifted to him as officers seemed to move in on his position. Two uniformed policemen approached and checked Harrison.

There was a flurry of activity as he heard one officer shout that this man was dead, riddled with bullets. In a moment, more officers joined them, including two men in dark suits. One of them called Rich's name.

"I'm over here," he said, not moving until flashlights illuminated him. Then he slowly got to his feet, leaving his gun on the ground and keeping his hands in sight. "I'm not hit," he said.

As the host of federal, state, and local officers came to the scene, ambulances arrived, and two men were hauled off in them. Rich was shocked to learn that the agents who had come to back him up had not shot Harrison. He'd been killed by his own people. But Rich's concern was not in what was occurring here. He was thinking about Kerry and wondering what else he might be up to.

No one except for Harrison and one of the ambushers, another member of the Earth Militia, was dead. The two terrorists who had been taken by ambulance were both severely injured. Rich made sure the local officials knew that those men must be kept from communicating with anyone. He was allowed to leave the scene, and he hurried back to his room in Phoenix. There, using his secure phone, he began to make calls. The first one was to his supervisor, Jim Crooney.

"What's the situation with my family?" he asked urgently.

"They're safe," Jim told him. "There was an attack, but the FBI had agents near enough to intervene. However, it was not before Zach Barlow took action on his own. Frankly, from what I'm told, he may well have saved the lives of your family."

Rich absorbed the news with shaking knees, but then, professional that he was, he turned his attention to the threats he feared were imminent. "I think we'd better arrest Kerry Sunger ASAP," he said. "I think he's shortened his timetable for attacks. The last I knew, he was flying to Colorado."

"Get me an address," Jim said. "I'll get things moving there. What other locations do we need to be concerned about?"

"I suspect that since he's lost a number of key people, he might be scaling back his attacks, but we can't count on that. The targets I know about include the coal-fired power plant near Huntington, Utah. The mines in that area are also in danger, but I don't have specific information on which he might have mapped out plans for. Every mine in the area needs to be alerted.

"There's also another mine in West Virginia that Kerry spoke of," Rich said. "Just a second, and I'll get you the name of it. While I'm looking in my notes, the Mirage Casino in Las Vegas is a target. Sunger has specific plans on where he wants to place bombs—they are on his computer. I know pretty much where those are since I was with him when he scoped the casino out." Rich found the name of the mine in West Virginia and gave it to Jim.

"Okay, I'll contact the director now, and we'll get things in motion. I'd like you fly to Vegas and coordinate the efforts there. You will have agents from our agency as well as the FBI and Las Vegas officers working with you," Jim said before disconnecting.

Rich was exhausted to the bone, but he had no time to rest. He had the feeling that Kerry Sunger was already getting the Earth Militia in motion and that he would inflict as much collateral damage and death as he could as quickly as he could achieve it.

He made the earliest available flight reservation to Las Vegas before packing his bags. He considered cutting his hair and shaving his beard but decided against it. He might actually encounter some of the people he'd been with during the months he'd been undercover. If Kerry hadn't already blown his cover to other members of the group, it might be valuable later.

* * *

As the sun rose, the shootout scene in Duchesne was still swarming with officers. Chief Deputy Sessions was directing much of the work. Sheriff Rutger, who was out of surgery and resting comfortably, was anxious to get back to work.

Marlon told him that he needed to heal first. "I'll take care of things here," he said.

"What about the men in custody? I think it's time we put some pressure on them," Lee said.

"CIA and FBI agents are working together on that," Marlon responded. "They think that more attacks are imminent. Crooney is using your office to make contact with agencies across the country. Agent Phillips survived an ambush this morning. Apparently his cover was blown. And one more thing: Zach Barlow shot and seriously wounded a terrorist in L.A. at a safe house there. Others were also taken out by FBI agents at that location. Fortunately the Barlow kid and the Phillips family are safe."

After he hung up, the sheriff winced and resettled himself in his bed. He had another call to make—he had to be sure his wife and family were safe.

* * *

Rich got an informative call just minutes after he landed in Las Vegas. The apartment Sunger was living in had been raided and searched. Sunger was not found, but a computer was seized and was being examined. FBI and CIA agents as well as state and local officers from Nevada had been alerted and were told to meet with Rich, where they could make plans on how to protect the Mirage.

He directed that meeting an hour later, and assignments were made. Rich personally went to the strip, where he began watching for anyone he might recognize from the terrorist group.

He still carried his terrorist cell phone just in case anyone there, most notably Kerry Sunger, tried to contact him. He even thought about attempting to call Kerry, but he was afraid that might alert him. Kerry had to be worried when he didn't hear back from the men he'd sent to kill Rich and Harrison in Arizona. But knowing the volatile nature of the man's personality, Rich knew that he would not withdraw and wait. He would order violence now and in whatever ways he could.

* * *

It was ten o'clock when Zach got out of bed at the hotel where he and Bria's family had been relocated a few hours earlier. He stretched as his feet hit the floor. He hadn't slept much and was still tired, but he was anxious to boot up Frank's laptop to see if anyone had tried to reach him. He also hoped to learn something about what was happening in Duchesne.

He was troubled in a way that he'd never been before. *He had shot a man.* The man was alive, but it still distressed him greatly. On the other hand, he knew that had he not done so, he and the Phillipses might not have survived.

As the computer was booting up, he ran his electric razor across his face. His mind was in turmoil, bouncing from one thing to another, finally settling on the murder of Caden Pendleton. Someone had shot him with Bria's rifle. And that someone could be one of the young people he had invited on the hunt. One by one he thought about them. As he did, he concluded, as he had so many times since that ill-fated day, that none of them was capable of murder. And there was always the mysterious harmonica player, a missing CIA agent. What role, if any, had he played in the killing? And what was it that Frank had tried to tell him as he lay dying on the casino floor?

He and Bria had talked it all over several times in the days they'd been sequestered, but they didn't have any answers. As he sat staring at the computer, he came to a decision. He wasn't a cop and shouldn't try to do the cops' jobs for them, but he found himself wondering what it would hurt if he were to go home and personally begin to visit with his friends, one on one. Maybe, in an unofficial capacity, he could learn what Sheriff Rutger and his deputies had been unable to.

The computer was booted up, and so Zach turned his attention to it. He searched first for news of Duchesne. There was plenty. More people had died there, people who had, according to reports he read, gone there intent on inflicting more damage to the sheriff and his department. It was pretty clear that none of the reporters had any idea what was really happening. They mentioned federal officers but concluded that they were there because of the attacks against Sheriff Rutger.

One theory emerged in almost every report Zach found, and that was that everything was somehow connected to the murder of Caden in the mountains above Moon Lake. Zach's own disappearance, as well as that of Bria and then her mother and brother, were all considered to be felonious acts committed by friends or accomplices of the dead man. Not one report could explain the death of the second man whose body had been taken from the mountains and whose identity had not been released to the press. The prevailing theory was that he was a lone hunter who'd fallen from a cliff.

The sheriff, Zach learned to his relief, was resting comfortably in the hospital in Roosevelt and was expected to make a full recovery. In the meantime, tight security was in place at the hospital. There was also speculation on the location of Zach's friends and fellow hunters. All were being protected, it was assumed by the press, from people who wanted to avenge the death of Calvin Portman.

When he couldn't find anything else of interest, he opened his e-mail account. There were a bunch of messages.

He opened one from his mother first. *Zach, if you get this message and you can, please let us know how you are. We are worried sick about you. So much has happened here. With all our love, Mom and Dad.*

Zach wasn't going to let them worry more if he could prevent it. So he hit reply and typed,

Dad and Mom, I'm fine. You don't need to worry about me. I'll be home soon, and I'll explain what's happening. If you see Sheriff Rutger, tell him my prayers are with him. I'm sorry I left you in such a bind. I thought Walt would be able to help. I promise that I'll be back soon. But don't mention that to anyone, not even to the sheriff. Other than you guys, I don't want anyone expecting me. Love, Zach.

He read it over and then hit send before he could change his mind.

There was a tap on the connecting door between his room and Bria's. Bria met him with a tired smile when he opened the door.

"Hi," she said shyly. She must have been recalling the kiss they had shared just before all the craziness the night before. He certainly remembered it and wondered what it might mean.

Their eyes met, and she said, "We are going to order some breakfast. Would you like some too?"

"That would be great," he said, his eyes lingering on her face. She stepped toward him, but he retreated. A repeat of the kiss was not a good idea right now. She looked hurt, but simply asked what he'd like to eat.

"A stack of hotcakes, a couple of eggs over easy, and a glass of orange juice," he said.

"Okay," she replied, and stepped back into her own room.

Impulsively, he reached out and touched her cheek. Then he smiled and said, "Thanks, Bria."

"No problem," she said, looking past him. Her expression changed, and he knew she'd seen the open computer. "Have you heard from anyone this morning?" she asked.

"My parents. They're worried, to say the least," he told her.

"Why don't you tell them you're okay?" she asked.

"I already did that," he admitted. "But I didn't tell them what's been happening or where we are."

She reached up and took hold of his hand. Her hand was soft and warm. For a moment, neither of them moved as they looked at each other.

Patty Phillips called out, "Bria, what should I order for Zach?"

The moment gone, Bria gave Zach a fleeting smile before telling her mother what he wanted for breakfast. Then she added, "I'm going to check my e-mails real quick."

Zach nodded his approval, and they went over to his computer. "It looks like you weren't through yet," she said as she glanced down. "You finish, and I'll wait."

He sat down and scanned through the messages. He deleted several and then opened one from Walt Hinshaw. Before he started reading, he looked over at Bria, who was kneeling beside him. She smiled, but neither of them said a word, and he began to read.

After finishing, he said, "He wants to go home. I don't blame him."

"Neither do I," she said. "I feel exactly the same way."

"Me too," Zach agreed.

"What are you thinking about?" he asked as he noticed Bria's distant look.

"At least you guys have a home to go to when this is all over," she said.

"I'm sorry, Bria. Your folks will find another one," he said awkwardly.

She smiled then said, "I don't think it will be in Duchesne. But at least I have my dad back. We can start over as a family." She looked down at the computer. "Do you have any more you need to look at?"

He scanned down through them. "I don't think so. I'll trade you places so you can check yours."

Bria also had one from Walt. "I'll step away if you like," Zach said. "I don't want to—"

"Zach," she interrupted firmly, "do you remember last night, just before that guy came to the door?"

"How can I forget?" he said uncomfortably.

"Did it mean anything to you?" she asked, her eyes narrowing.

"Of course it did," he said defensively.

"Nothing like that will ever happen with Walt," she said. She checked the e-mail from Walt.

The message said,

Bria, I hope you are okay. I'm going nuts. I want to go home, but I don't dare, especially after what happened to Sheriff Rutger. Do you know about that? You probably do. I wrote to Zach. Is he with you? I hope that we can all go home soon. And I hope that the sheriff gets better and can figure out who shot Caden. It wasn't me or Sage. And I know it wasn't you or Zach. I don't know about the others. They're being weird. They know something. They won't even take the lie-detector test. Please, if you get this, tell me if you guys are okay. Walt. Oh, Sage says hello.

Bria looked up at Zach and grinned. "Should we tell him that *we* are okay?" she asked.

Zach chuckled. "Yeah, go ahead."

Chapter Twenty

A warrant had been issued for Kerry Sunger, but he was still at large. He had not come back to his Denver apartment. His disappearance worried Rich, making him wonder if Kerry would personally show up in Las Vegas. With that in mind, he decided to change his appearance. Rich found a barber on the strip, and, in a matter of minutes, he had shed the image of GR Roper. Special Agent Rich Phillips was back. He looked in the mirror after the barber was finished. He hardly recognized his old self. It felt good. But now he also needed different clothes. He accomplished that in the next half hour and returned to the Mirage, where several agents and officers were on duty.

The day wore on, and he hoped that he was wrong about the attack moving forward on the Mirage ahead of the schedule he and Sunger had discussed. But when he spotted a familiar person walking through the front doors, he realized with a jolt that he'd been right. Sylvia Morris stopped and looked around once inside. She pulled a piece of paper from her oversized purse. Rich, from his position, couldn't tell what it was. He pointed her out to an agent who was standing just a few feet away. The agent walked slowly past her and then returned a minute later.

When he told Rich that it was a map of the Mirage, Rich said, "Let's arrest her. That's probably a bomb she's carrying."

Rich stepped in behind Sylvia while his colleague approached her from the side. She had started to walk again, and the two agents moved quickly. Sylvia's long, blonde ponytail swung back and forth as she picked up speed. She was nervous and kept looking around but hadn't yet looked directly behind her. Rich was almost to her when she suddenly looked back over her shoulder. When her eyes met Rich's, there was a moment of confusion on her face. But just as he reached her, Sylvia recognized him. She started to run, but Rich grabbed her ponytail, snapping her head back. The other agent grabbed the bag with one hand and then reached for her arm with the other. She began to struggle, but Rich pulled hard on her hair, and she fell backward. He pulled out a pair of handcuffs and forced her hands behind her back as she began to shout for help. Rich snapped the cuffs closed and then produced his ID, flashing it at the growing crowd and saying, "We are federal agents. This woman was about to rob the casino. Stand back."

"GR, you traitor!" she cried as two additional agents led her away.

"Don't let her talk to anyone," Rich ordered. "Isolate her. Sorry, folks," he said, addressing the crowd that the arrest had attracted.

Once she was removed by a pair of FBI agents, Rich and a local officer borrowed an administrative office and looked into the bag Sylvia had been carrying. There was a rectangular package inside. It was about eight inches long, six inches wide, and three inches thick. It was neatly gift-wrapped, but nothing was written on it. It was solid and quite heavy.

The local officer looked at Rich with worry on his face. "A bomb?" he asked.

"Probably," Rich agreed.

"Our bomb squad is standing by," the Las Vegas officer said. "Get them in here," Rich ordered.

A bomb-sniffing dog was brought into the room, and almost instantly, it keyed in on the package. "It's an explosive device," the handler said. "This dog never makes a mistake. I'll get it out of here and take care of it."

As soon as the bomb was removed, Rich met with the hotel manager and two assistants. "We just removed a bomb from the hotel," Rich said. "There may be more."

All three had been informed earlier of the potential danger, but even though they'd had advance notice, they looked at him like he was nuts. "That's impossible," one of them said. "No one would—"

The local officer cut him off. "This is real," he said sternly. "There are some crazy, misguided folks out there who, for reasons of their own, want this place wiped off the map."

"What do you want us to do?" the manager said as worry replaced his disbelief.

"Get everyone out of the casino," Rich said calmly. "We have the place surrounded with officers at every point of entrance, but that's no guarantee that someone won't find a way to get a bomb in here and detonate it."

"We might cause a panic," the manager said. "People could get hurt leaving."

"People could die if you don't make an announcement. I'll word it in a way that will cause the least amount of panic."

They agreed. Rich wrote out what needed to be said, handed it over, and said, "Everyone needs to hear it. Every guest, every employee, everyone! Get it done now."

Rich resumed his position near the main entrance, hoping that the FBI could get more information from Sylvia to aid them in stopping more destruction or loss of life. In the meantime, they could only proceed as planned.

It was about five minutes before an official voice reverberated throughout the huge building. "It has become necessary to have everyone leave the casino. There is no need to panic. Move toward the nearest exit. Please proceed in an orderly fashion. Once outside, police officers will direct you to a waiting area. Please begin the evacuation now." The usual loud noise hushed, and the announcement was repeated. Shortly after the announcement, a bomb-sniffing dog pointed out a man with a briefcase near a back entrance. He was promptly arrested and whisked away. Minutes later, another was arrested at a different entrance. Rich then recognized a young man who entered from a side door and walked right past his position and against the surging crowd of evacuating patrons. Another dog keyed on the man, and he was arrested without Rich needing to step in. The man was dragged away cursing. The duffel bag he was carrying was rushed out by bomb squad officers.

An FBI agent in Denver called Rich a minute later. "Agent Phillips," he began, "we have hacked into Kerry Sunger's computer."

"Is there anything in there that will help us?" Rich asked. He couldn't believe how smoothly things had gone so far.

"Yes, we retrieved a document that shows where he'd planned to plant the bombs, both in the casino and at other locations in the hotel. Plus we've located the site where Sunger keeps his explosives. We plan to raid the place as soon as possible."

"Can you e-mail it to me right now?" Rich asked urgently. Upon receiving a positive response, he gave the FBI agent his e-mail address.

Leaving another CIA agent in his place, Rich worked his way against the throng of evacuating people back to the same office where he had met with the casino officials. He opened the e-mail on a borrowed computer and studied the plan for a moment before coordinating the search from there.

It was dangerous work, but getting the casino totally evacuated was going to take a while. A lot of people were leaving the building, but more were not cooperating. One stubborn man demanded an explanation of why the evacuation had been ordered. When the casino manager told him that he couldn't do that, the fellow said, "Then I ain't leaving," and began shouting at others to follow his example.

Rich was contacted, but he didn't have time to argue with anyone. He was busy sending officers to various locations throughout the huge building. He turned to a local officer and said, "You go tell him to leave. If he refuses, arrest him. Arrest anyone who resists."

"You've got it, Agent," was the response.

Arrests were made, cooperation picked up, and the casino was almost empty. Every location on the list was checked, but they only found one bomb. In the meantime, two more terrorists were caught carrying small bombs while trying to make their way into the huge building.

Just when Rich was thinking this was too easy, his worst nightmare occurred. There was a massive explosion someplace inside the casino. A device had been missed. People who had not yet gotten out panicked. They began to scream, push, and shove. Officers swarmed in, attempting to calm the crowd to avoid having people trampled.

Rich didn't have any time to inquire on what was happening at the locations outside of Las Vegas that Sunger had planned to bomb.

He felt sick as paramedics and firemen arrived and began to rescue victims while attempting to stop the fire that the bomb had started.

The fire department chief personally reported to Rich an hour later, after the fire had been contained. "The bomb was located in one of the kitchens," he said.

"No kitchens were on the list," Rich said, shaking his head in despair. "I guess someone made his own plans. Do you have any way of knowing how many people were injured or killed?"

"No exact count yet," the fire chief answered. "But it appears that we got lucky. The kitchen was pretty well emptied before the device was detonated. And since you had forewarned us, we were close enough to prevent the fire from spreading badly."

It wasn't until later that Rich learned that there had been a couple of fatalites and several injuries. The worst had been thwarted, however, and Sunger's organization had taken a beating. But Rich and other officials did not relax for a moment. There was no telling where Sunger would strike next, and it made Rich sick to know they hadn't found him yet.

* * *

Every location that Rich remembered being mentioned during his months undercover was monitored. Only one location in addition to the Mirage produced results. Two men were arrested as they attempted to drive a rental truck full of explosives into the power plant near Huntington, Utah. Pictures of every person arrested were sent to Rich over the next twenty-four hours. He looked at them and compared them to the list he'd compiled over the months. Many of them he recognized, and in every instance, they were the more fanatical members of the Earth Militia. One face did not appear in any of the photos—that of Kerry Sunger. Rich and his colleagues had to find out what his next move would be before things got worse.

In an attempt to protect Rich, the authorities in Phoenix released the names of *four* men as having died in the attack on Rich. There were only three who *actually* died, including Harrison Bagshaw and one of the men who had originally been taken to the hospital. But the name of GR Roper was included on the list. The hope was that Sunger would think that the man he suspected to be a mole was dead.

The names and pictures of the others whom Rich had secretly photographed and cataloged were sent to law enforcement agencies nationwide. Many terrorists were still at large, and Rich, knowing of their unreasonable fanaticism, warned his colleagues to be vigilant. Kerry would be marshaling his forces and attempting to recruit new fanatics.

For the time being, however, Rich knew he had more important things to do. The close call his family had had in L.A. made him decide that even with the terrorists still at large, he was going to spend some long-overdue time with his family.

* * *

Sheriff Rutger was in a great deal of pain when his secretary phoned to say that a CIA agent had called and said he needed to talk to him, that it was very important. Even though he was in a lot of pain and he was unable to physically participate in the work, he told her to have him call his cell phone.

Ten minutes later, Rich Phillips made that call. "I'm sorry to bother you, Sheriff, and I hope you are recovering well," he said.

"I'll get there," Lee said with as much good humor as he could muster. "Congratulations on your work in Las Vegas. It sounds to me like you have about wiped out the terrorist threat."

"That's why I'm calling," Rich said. "It's not over yet. A man by the name of Kerry Sunger is the mastermind, and he is still at large. As far as the world knows, and hopefully as far as he knows, I am dead, but I'm not about to underestimate the man. I've spent enough time with him that I have a pretty good feel for how he thinks. He's dangerous, and, if nothing else, he will try to get revenge on me and possibly on you. You need to keep your people on high alert until we capture Sunger."

"I appreciate your concern, Rich, and I will do as you suggest. I don't need more trouble here," Lee responded. He contemplated for a moment the death of the terrorist who'd brought much of this trouble into his area. He still didn't know for sure who had killed Calvin Portman. He almost mentioned that to Rich, but then he decided against it since Bria still had to be considered a person of interest in the case. So he thanked him for his call and said, "Will you keep me posted on any developments? I can't get around much yet, but I'm still the sheriff here, and I am in constant contact with my officers."

After Rich was off the line, Lee laid back in his bed, deep in thought. Even though Portman had been one of the terrorists, he had still been shot and killed in his jurisdiction. He hoped it might have been the Agent Boyd Swift, Rich's CIA colleague, whose body had been found a mile from the young hunters' camp. But he didn't know that for sure, and until he did, he had an open murder case on his hands. Some of the young hunters were hiding something, with the help of their attorneys. Somehow, he had to find out what they knew. Kerry Sunger's capture might be the final goal of the CIA and the FBI, but Lee's final goal was solving a homicide.

* * *

Without saying anything to Bria or her mother, Zach had arranged with his parents to buy himself an airline ticket home. That done, he was to leave early the next morning.

There were several reasons for going home now. For one, his father needed help on the ranch. It also appeared that not much progress was occurring on the murder investigation. The sheriff was still in the hospital, and according to Walt, the others were still in hiding. On advice of their attorneys, they still hadn't taken the polygraphs. Zach thought it might be a good time to see if he could get the other hunters to talk to him.

It had been a couple of days since he'd told his parents that he was going to come home, and he had decided not to wait any longer. His mother had enthusiastically gone to work on the arrangements. Zach had enjoyed being near Bria, but it had become too much of a good thing. Being confined to their rooms was nerve-wracking, and tension had built between the two of them. He had to get out so that he could think clearly. He had to know if being with Bria twenty-four-seven had clouded his judgment regarding her. He'd heard that patients sometimes fell in love with their doctors and the rescued with their rescuers. Was his relationship with Bria like that? He liked her and thought she was a beautiful girl, inside and out, but he didn't know if he wanted to get serious yet. With all that had gone on recently, he hadn't had time to think about much except Bria and her family, but now that he was headed home, thoughts of seeing Sage brought him a feeling of anticipation. He knew he had to be careful with his feelings, and Bria's. He didn't want to hurt her by leading her on if things didn't work out. He dreaded breaking the news to her, but he felt strongly that he needed to do it. And it had to be done before he went to bed that night.

Early that evening, as he was working up his courage to explain his plans to Bria and Patty, Rich showed up at their hotel. Clean-shaven and with his hair short and neatly combed, he looked the way Zach had remembered him. Bria flew to him and threw her arms around his neck. He held Patty close after that and hugged his son and mussed his hair. Zach retreated to his own room while the family enjoyed some time together. Later, Rich invited him to join them for dinner at a restaurant in the hotel. They enjoyed their meal, but the Phillipses were so excited to be together that Zach felt uncomfortable and out of place. He participated in very little of the conversation.

After dinner, Rich offered to take them to a movie. "There is still danger out there, but I'll make sure we're okay. I'm sure all of us could use a distraction from the pressure for a few hours," he said.

Everyone was excited but Zach. He begged out of it. "You guys should go as a family," he said firmly. "I'll stay here."

Bria argued, but his mind was made up. He'd hoped to have a few minutes alone with her so he could explain his plans, but it didn't work out, and his flight was scheduled for six in the morning. He had to be at the airport at four. He wrote a note and left it on Frank's computer, along with Frank's 9mm pistol and his own little .22. He couldn't take it on the plane, and anyway, he didn't want to have to shoot anyone again—ever. The computer and 9mm were the property of the CIA, and he knew that Rich would take care of them. He went to bed early, his alarm set for three in the morning.

He made sure that his half of the connecting door was not locked when he left at three thirty to catch the cab. He was going to miss being around Bria, and yet he was also looking forward to not being confined with her and her family any longer. He hoped she'd understand. Most of all, Zach looked forward to getting home and working on the ranch. He needed to be out and about, working up a sweat, and trying to wipe away at least some of the tension he'd been experiencing.

His folks met him at the airport in Salt Lake City, and after an emotional reunion, they headed for Duchesne. They visited most of the way as he told them those things that he could about the events that had occurred while he'd been gone.

* * *

Zach hadn't joined them for breakfast like he had the past couple of mornings. "Put yourself in his shoes," Patty said as Bria pouted. "He probably feels uncomfortable; that's only natural."

"Your mother's right," Rich agreed. "But since I'm back, I'll bet he'll be glad to get out of the hotel for a little while and do something with us."

Bria was wringing her hands. "Maybe," she said. "Or maybe he's sick of being around me."

Her mother smiled. "I doubt that, dear. But you have both been a little tense with each other the past couple of days."

"I'm sure this has been hard on him," Rich said. "I'll go talk to him for a little while. There are some things I want him to know. And I'll invite him to go with us later."

"Thanks, Dad," Bria said. "I love you guys, but I also have enjoyed being with Zach."

"So I've noticed," Rich said as he tapped on the connecting door. When there was no answer, he tried pushing on it and it swung open.

"Zach," he called. "Are you up?"

The room was dark, and there was no answer. With a look of concern at his wife, he stepped into Zach's room. He reappeared a moment later.

"He's not here," he said. "His stuff is gone, everything but his .22 pistol. He left a note on Frank's computer. It's folded over and addressed to you, Bria," he said as he held it out to her.

With her hands shaking and her eyes brimming with tears, she took the note and went into Zach's room, where she could read it in privacy. She sat down on the sofa and turned on a lamp. She slowly unfolded the note as a cold dread crept over her. It was addressed, *Dear Bria.* It filled most of the page, but the first line was all it took to start her heart pounding.

It seemed an eternity before she could make herself read beyond the first line, in which he had stated that he'd gone home. When she finally did, it made sense to her mind, but it confused her heart. When she read, *I wanted to tell you in person last night, but there wasn't a chance,* she dropped her hands into her lap and let her tears fall. The last line brought her a little comfort. He wrote, *I'll keep in touch. Check your e-mail when you can. I will miss you Bria, but I think we need a break from each other. Anyway, I'm needed at home. Take care of yourself and your family. Love, Zach.*

She cried some more, her tears dropping on the note in her hands. A hand touched her shoulder, and she looked up. Her father had come in so silently that she hadn't even heard him. "Are you okay, sweetheart?" he asked.

She stood up and turned toward her father and shook her head. She fell into his open arms. He held her like that for a long time, stroking her hair and kissing her on the top of the head. After she was finally cried out, she pulled away from her father and said, "Dad, I think I love Zach. I can't stand the thought of not knowing when I'll see him again."

"You have your mother in you, Bria. Think what I've had to put her through the past few months. You can do it if it's important enough to you. And you will be a lot stronger for it," he said softly.

"What if he decides he doesn't want to be with me?" she said. "That's what I'm afraid of."

"I can't help you there," Rich said. "Deep and lasting love only comes after there are some rocky times. Don't give up on him, but also, Bria, don't push him. He has other worries, and until he gets them taken care of, you need to give him his space."

"I don't want to lose him, Dad," she said.

"Is he yours to lose?" he asked.

Shocked, she looked at her father again, her eyes wide.

"Did he tell you that he loves you?" he asked.

"Not exactly," she admitted.

"Not exactly or not at all?" he pressed.

"He wrote this," she said, holding the tear-dampened note and pointing at the last two words Zach had written.

"That's not the same thing," her father said. "Did he ever tell you that there was no one else and wouldn't ever be?"

"No, but we . . ." She stopped. "You mean maybe he doesn't feel like I do?" she asked.

"I don't know how he feels. And it sounds to me like you don't either. I can't promise you that there is a future for the two of you. Time alone will tell that. In the meantime, Bria, relish the time you've had with him. Maybe after you are apart for a while, you'll find that you don't feel as strongly as you do right now."

"I think I love him," she said.

"You *think*?" he said. "That's not the same as being sure. You have doubts." He took her in his arms again, and she felt the security he had offered since she had been a little girl.

"I love you, Dad."

"And I love you, dear. Come on, I'm taking a few days off. I need them. And I want to spend it with you and your mom and brother. We'll have a good time."

"When are we going to be able to go home to Duchesne?" she asked, fearing what his answer would be but hoping she was wrong.

He didn't answer, and when she drew back from him and looked him in the eye, she saw the answer there.

"We aren't going back," she said meekly as she felt her world slipping away. "Daddy, we've got to."

"We'll see," he said.

Chapter Twenty-One

For the first couple of days after getting home, Zach worked hard trying to catch up on the things that had fallen behind on the farm while he'd been gone. It was cool, but the early snow had melted, and it wasn't uncomfortable working outside. He fixed some corrals, chopped a big stack of wood for his dad's wood-burning stove, and winterized the farm equipment that they wouldn't be using until spring. He also worked with the horses, riding the colts he'd started to break in the summer. He got the watering troughs plugged in and made sure the heaters were working properly so the cows and horses would have water when the really cold weather came in a few weeks.

Every evening, he e-mailed Bria, but she didn't respond. His heart ached. He must have made her angry. But he knew it had been the right thing to do.

On Saturday night he went to the sheriff's house, having heard that he'd been released from the hospital that day. He'd been there longer than anyone first anticipated. His wife told Zach that he hadn't healed as quickly as the doctors had predicted.

Zach and Sheriff Rutger had a good visit, but Zach mentioned nothing of his plans to visit with Jay, Janie, and Rex. They were still gone—he already knew that. Walt and Sage were home now, but he hadn't seen or talked with either one of them. The sheriff told him that he would be back to work in a week or two at the most. He assured Zach that he felt like the worst of the danger had passed. Zach hoped he was right because he was ready for a normal life again.

On Sunday, a lot of people at church questioned him about where he'd been and what he'd been doing. He deflected the questions and left priesthood meeting a few minutes early so that he wouldn't have to keep answering questions. After dinner, he went to his room and checked his e-mail. There was still no response from Bria. Tomorrow, he was going to see if he could find where Jay, Rex, and Janie were. He was determined to talk to them. He also wanted to talk to Walt and Sage.

That afternoon, his mother called upstairs, "Zach, there's someone here to see you."

He headed down and was surprised when he saw Walt and Sage standing in the living room.

"Hi, guys," he said.

Walt shifted his feet, his head hanging. "Hi," he said without looking up.

Sage, on the other hand, caught Zach's eye. She looked beautiful with her shoulder-length blonde hair accentuating her blue eyes. But those blue eyes of hers looked sad, and she was nervously twisting her hands.

Moving toward him, she finally spoke. "Hi, Zach. I'm sorry."

"You have no need to be sorry," he said. "This is all my fault."

"Zach, it is not your fault!" she said firmly. "What you did, you did for us."

To his surprise, she threw herself against him, wrapping her arms around him tightly. Awkwardly, he put his arms around her back and returned the hug. Sobbing, she laid her head against his shoulder. As he held her, he was surprised at how good she felt in his arms. That bothered him. It was Bria he wanted in his arms. Wasn't it?

He looked past her at Walt, who was watching the two of them with wide eyes. When Zach caught his eye, he shrugged.

When Sage finally pulled herself away, she looked again into Zach's eyes. "I've been so worried about you," she said.

"It was something I had to do," he said. "I wanted to let you guys know, but . . . I couldn't."

"I know that now," she said. "I'm . . . we're . . . just so glad you're back. I've . . . we've missed you."

"It's good to be back," he said.

"Can we talk, or is this a bad time?" Sage asked.

"This is great," he said. "Let's sit down." He gestured to the sofa. Walt sat on one end, Sage sat in the middle, and Zach sat next to her.

Sage squirmed uncomfortably, tugging at a strand of her blonde hair. Zach watched her with interest. He wondered why he hadn't taken the time to get to know her better. She finally said, "I'm frustrated with Jay."

Not sure what to say at that unexpected statement, he nodded. "What did he do?"

"He said some rude things about you and was a jerk to Walt, too. I thought Jay was better than that."

"He's under pressure, just like the rest of us," Zach said. "Jay's a good guy."

"He's okay, but I'm still frustrated with him, not to mention Rex and Janie," she repeated. "Both Walt and I have tried to contact them, but they never answer their cell phones or e-mails."

"I haven't tried," Zach admitted. "But I'm going to."

Sage laid a hand on Zach's arm. "Zach, those guys know something about Caden's murder that they haven't admitted."

Zach pulled his head back in surprise. "How do you know that?"

"We don't *know* it," she said, "but Walt and I both *feel* it. If they didn't have something to hide, why wouldn't they take the lie-detector test?"

Zach took a deep breath and said, "Don't think I haven't had the same thoughts."

Sage went on. "When Jay fought Caden that day, I thought it was just because he liked Bria so much, but she never liked him. I think Caden and Jay must have had trouble before we ever went up there."

"So do you guys think Jay killed Caden?" he asked, looking directly at Sage.

She slowly shook her head. "He has a bad temper, but he'd never go that far."

"Then who do you think did it?" he asked.

"Maybe Rex," she answered hesitantly. "Rex was really angry over Caden losing your horse like he did."

"What about Janie?" Zach asked.

"She's mean," Sage said with a grimace. "She was way rude to Bria." She glanced at Walt and then added, "But she was also scared of Caden. And she detested him."

"How do you know that?" Zach asked.

"She said he made her skin crawl." She shivered as she said it. "He made mine crawl, too, but it was the way she said it that has me wondering."

"If she killed Caden, do you think that either Jay or Rex know it?" Zach asked.

Sage slowly nodded. "That's what I think," she said.

"All three are hiding what happened up there," Walt said, shaking a finger in the general direction of the High Uintas. "I think they're going to try to blame one of us."

"By *us* do you mean you two, or are you also including me and Bria?"

"One of the four of us," Sage confirmed.

"They say they think that Bria didn't do it, but they don't mean it," Walt said. "And when we were in the sheriff's office just after you disappeared, Jay said something about you running off because you weren't man enough to face up to what you'd done."

"Really?" Zach said with a frown. "Well, I suppose it could look like that. Do you think the others feel the same way?"

"We know they do," Sage said. "And it's not fair to you, Zach." There was a tenderness in her eyes that he hadn't noticed before.

"Are you saying that you think they're going to try to accuse *me*?" he asked, spreading his hands in disbelief.

"Yes," Sage told him. "Or they'll try to blame both you and Bria."

"They'll try to blame us too," Walt said.

"But you two passed the polygraph," Zach reminded them. "Bria and I have yet to take it."

"You'll pass. So will Bria," Sage said with confidence. "By the way, when will she and her mom and little brother come back?"

Zach faltered. "She . . . she . . ."

"Zach, isn't Bria coming back?" Sage asked.

He shook his head. "I don't think so."

"Did something happen to her?" Walt asked. "She hasn't answered my e-mails since you came back."

"She's fine. At least she was when I left them," he said. "She hasn't answered mine either," he added, hoping she really was okay.

Sage leaned forward and put both her hands on his. "I'm sorry," she said. And as he looked in her eyes, he knew she meant it. "I just want you to know this, Zach. Walt and I are here for you. We're in this together."

"I'll try to be here for you too."

Sage stood up. Walt and Zach did the same. "We better go now," Sage said. "Thanks for listening to us."

Sage impulsively threw her arms around Zach again. He held her tightly for a moment. When she stepped back, she leaned forward and kissed him lightly on the cheek. Without another word, she turned and headed for the door. Walt stood awkwardly for a moment. Then he quickly hugged Zach and said, "I appreciate you, Zach."

Sage had stopped at the door and was watching the two of them, her blue eyes misty. "When you want to talk, don't hesitate to call."

He watched them both until they were in their car. They'd been his neighbors all their lives, but he hadn't realized until just then how much they meant to him.

* * *

The past few days had been busy. Rich Phillips had taken his family all over Los Angeles. They had enjoyed each hour they'd spent together. And when Rich left L.A., he took them with him. They flew to Portland, where Rich told them they would be living for a while. They were given new IDs under different names. "For all anyone can know, I'm a businessman again," he'd told them before they left. "It's our hope that the terrorist leader believes I'm dead. Agents are actively looking for him right now, but I needed a break. One of these times we'll settle down and I'll take a big break. I'll find a different job. But before I can retire, I've got to see that the Earth Militia organization is wiped from the face of the earth."

"I hope that is soon," Bria had said.

"So do I," Rich had agreed.

Zach's name had seldom been mentioned in the past few days. But he had never been far from Bria's mind. However, she was trying to figure out how she was going to forget him. She had come to realize that her father was right; they needed to move on. Duchesne, though a bright spot in their lives for several years, needed to be in the past now. Even going to school in Utah probably wasn't going to be a reasonable option.

She booted up her computer that Sunday evening. There was a message from Walt again and another one from Zach. There was also one from Sage. She looked at the screen for a long time. With tears clouding her eyes, she opened Walt's. She tried to read, but it was all blurry. She wiped her eyes and tried again. He told her that he and Sage had been over to see Zach. That did it. She closed the message and shut off her computer.

They were part of her former life. It was time to move on. Bria Phillips no longer existed.

Chapter Twenty-Two

Zach didn't waste time on the telephone that Monday morning. It was too easy for people to shut you out on the phone. Instead, he was in his pickup. He was going to make a personal visit to each of the parents of Jay, Rex, and Janie.

He went first to Rex's place. His father was gone, but his mother was home and invited Zach in; however, she did not invite him to sit—they stood just inside the door.

"I'm glad to see you're okay," she said. "We've been worried about you. I'll bet it's good to be back." She didn't really look like she was happy to see him, but he pressed on.

"It really is," he said. "But I wish things were back to normal."

"So do we," Mrs. Lerner said with a firm nod and a stiff frown. She was a tall, severe woman in her early forties. She towered over Zach and looked down at him as she spoke. "Can I assume that since you are back now that it's safe for Rex to come home?"

Zach hadn't anticipated that question. He shifted nervously under the woman's gaze. "I feel safe enough," he said, thinking back on how closely he and the Phillips family had come to being killed a few days ago. "But I didn't ask the sheriff if it was safe. I just came because I was tired of running."

"Did I hear that the sheriff was also back at his house now?" she asked.

"Yes, he's home. I visited him yesterday."

"How's he doing?" she asked.

"He seems to be okay. I mean, you know, he's going to recover fully. But he had a close call," Zach said. "His injuries were worse than they thought at first."

"I don't understand what's going on, Zach. This whole affair is insane. Rex told his father and me about all the trouble Caden caused on your trip," she said as her eyes narrowed and she glared at Zach. "It would be better if you hadn't taken Caden."

"I couldn't agree more," Zach said, determined not to let her glare intimidate him. "I hadn't planned to, he just—"

"I know," Rex's mother interrupted. "Rex told me that the creep invited himself."

"Yeah, that's about it," Zach agreed.

"I guess I can't blame you, but it's sure caused a lot of people a lot of trouble," she said, her face still hard and accusing.

"I'm sorry. All I wanted to do was have a good time with some friends. I didn't know it would turn into this kind of ordeal."

"Well, it did, and now I think the sheriff believes Rex might have had something to do with Caden's death."

"He hasn't told me that," Zach said. "And I know Rex well enough to know that he's not like that."

"Of course he's not. But people in the community seem to think differently. The sheriff, injured or not, needs to get busy and get to the bottom of this," she said, her face growing harder by the minute.

"I'm here to see if I can get to the bottom of this myself. As you just said, it wouldn't have happened if I hadn't let Caden push his way in. I was hoping Rex would help me," he said.

"If you're serious, Zach, I'm sure he will. But I don't want him taking a polygraph like the Hinshaw kids did. Our attorney tells us that lie detectors aren't reliable."

"I didn't take it either," Zach said, hoping to get her more on his side. "And I don't want to, even though, like Rex, I don't have anything to hide."

"Are you saying you want to talk to him?" Mrs. Lerner asked, cocking a dark eyebrow.

"Yes, if I could. I'll go to wherever he's staying if I need to. I think he and I can figure this thing out," he said with confidence he didn't feel.

"Let me call him and see if he'll agree to meet with you," Mrs. Lerner said.

She left Zach standing while she exited the room. When she came back, she had a piece of paper in her hand. "Rex says to come. Here's the address where he's staying. Don't let anyone else see it. And as soon as you get there, give this paper to him. He'll destroy it."

Zach struggled to keep from showing his annoyance. He accepted the paper, looked at it for a moment, and then held it out to her. "There won't be any need for me to take it," he said as evenly as he could. "I've memorized it. Thanks for your time."

She accepted the paper and crumpled it in her hand. "He'll be expecting you," she said.

Back in his truck, Zach pulled out of the driveway and started down the street. He debated going to Janie's house next and then out to Jay's father's farm or just heading for Salt Lake and meeting with Rex. He finally decided to stop at Janie's first, even though he was anxious to talk to Rex. If Janie and Jay were both on the Wasatch Front, it might save him time in the long run. He stopped at Janie's house and rang the doorbell.

Janie's mother finally answered the door, appearing to be out of breath. She was short and heavy. A woman of close to fifty, she actually appeared to be closer to sixty.

"Zach," she said in surprise, "I thought you'd run off when things got too hot for you." She favored him with an accusing glare.

"I've been gone, but I'm back. I'm trying to see if I can't help figure out who killed Caden Pendleton."

"Well, it wasn't Janie," she said.

"I believe you," he said, hoping to soften the woman up enough to find out where Janie was staying. "I came to apologize for causing you folks so much worry."

"Saying sorry won't help my baby none," she said. "I don't know what you think you were doing dragging the poor girl into the mountains like that."

Zach tried to calm himself since the woman was clearly trying to get her digs in. He said, "I was hoping to get a chance to talk to her. Maybe we can figure out what happened and help the sheriff out."

"It's pretty clear what happened. You and that bratty little Phillips girl caused problems for the other kids," the woman said, drawing in deep, ragged breaths in the cool morning air.

"I'm sorry you feel that way," Zach said. "But that isn't true."

"Then why did you drag my baby up there?" Mrs. Thorne asked. "I mean, she ain't no friend of yours. And she was scared to death of that friend of yours who got killed. You had no business making her go on a trip with that . . . that felon."

"I didn't know he was a felon, and I didn't drag Janie up there. I invited her, and she accepted," he said defensively.

"Like she could tell the all-important Zach Barlow no," she said, her eyes blazing.

Zach was getting nowhere with Janie's mother, so he said, "I'd like to speak to your husband." Zach knew that he'd lost his job, which was one of the reasons he'd invited Janie in the first place. He really expected that he'd be home.

"He's out looking for a job," she said, leaning heavily against the doorframe and breathing deeply. "I'm tired. Why don't you just get. You've done enough damage."

Zach didn't say another word. He left before the angry woman could slam the door in his face.

Jay's mother wasn't home, but he found Mr. Kilpatrick in his barn working on a tractor. There were parts strewn all over the floor, and Jay's father was standing on the far side, tightening a nut.

"Good morning," Zach said, trying to sound cheerful while feeling anything but that after the reception he'd received at the previous two places.

"Oh! You scared me. I didn't hear you come in," Mr. Kilpatrick said as he stepped back, pulled a greasy rag from a back pocket, and wiped his hands on it—not doing a lot of good, that Zach could see. The rag was as black as his hands. But the sturdy farmer seemed satisfied after a moment and stuffed one corner of the rag back into his pocket.

"I didn't mean to startle you. I went to the house, but—"

"My wife's in town getting her hair done," Mr. Kilpatrick said as he circled the tractor so that he was standing on the same side as Zach. "Heard you were back," he said. "Have a good trip?"

Zach didn't detect any malice either in the man's voice or on his face. "Not really," he said honestly. "But there were some things I had to do."

"Well, if you feel safe coming back, then I think Jay should too," the man said, offering his hand to Zach then thinking better as he looked at it. "Guess I'm kind of greasy. So is it safe for Jay to come home now?"

"I don't know about that," Zach countered. "I don't know what all's going on."

"Guess none of us does. Sure is too bad about the sheriff. Hope he's going to be okay."

"I think he is," Zach said.

"That's good. I voted for him. Darn good man, he is. Too bad none of us knew what a no-good character that Pendleton guy was."

"That's for sure," Zach agreed.

The farmer's face grew serious. "I hope you don't think any of us are blaming you for what happened. I for one appreciate you inviting my boy to go with you. He was excited about it. Too bad it turned out the way it did, but it sure wasn't your fault."

"Thanks. I'm afraid not everyone feels that way. But I do wish I hadn't ever taken those guys up there," Zach said.

"Who would have ever guessed that Caden was such a bad one. I know he and Jay had some words, but those things happen. Jay was just defending that pretty little Phillips girl. He really likes her, and I don't blame him. He was excited when he heard she was going. 'Course, he wasn't quite so happy about Walt Hinshaw. The two of them are kind of rivals. Jay thinks Walt likes her too. He hopes when she gets home that he'll have a chance with her." The fellow smiled. "Oh, to be young again like you guys. Those were the days."

Zach smiled back. "If you say so," he said, not at all certain that he agreed.

"I sure do say so," Mr. Kilpatrick said with a chuckle. "By the way, where have you been, anyway?"

Zach had expected that question all morning. The last thing he was going to do was tell Jay's dad that he'd been with Bria.

"I was threatened," he said, not mentioning that the threats came later. "I just decided to leave until I felt like things were safer here."

"I can't say I blame you. That's what Jay should have done. Wish you'd taken him with you. This attorney we got for him is costing us a bit."

Zach smiled, not at the cost of the lawyer but at the thought of Jay being with him and Bria. That would have been something. "I should have thought of that," he said. "Anyway, I couldn't stay away longer. Dad needs help. You probably need Jay on the farm too, don't you?"

"I'll say. Work's not getting done with him gone."

"Do you think Jay would talk to me? I know he's probably mad at me," Zach ventured.

"Jay? Kid's got a temper. He might have said something that he shouldn't have, but he respects you, Zach," he said seriously. "And so do my wife and I. Your family are good neighbors—couldn't ask for better. Yes, I'm sure he'll speak to you. I'll see if his attorney will let him come home now."

"That's not necessary if you don't feel good about that. I'll go to wherever he is if that's okay."

"That would be great, but he's not close by. We sent him up to my brother's place in Twin Falls."

"Then I'll go to Twin Falls," Zach said. "All I'll need is an address or phone number. I'll head out today."

Zach knew that he might not get to talk to Janie, but at least Jay and Rex were willing to meet with him. Maybe he could figure something out, although he didn't have a whole lot of hope. But he felt like he had to try. He felt a twinge of guilt. Sheriff Rutger was a good man. Maybe he should talk to him one more time before he went to talk to Jay and Rex. He drove to his house.

Myra Rutger answered the door. "Zach, it's good to see you again," she said. "Lee is doing a little better today."

"Good. Is he up to visiting with me again?" Zach asked.

"Of course."

For a couple of minutes, Zach and the sheriff just chatted like they had the day before. Zach was nervous about bringing up his plans, but the sheriff gently forced his hand when he said, "Zach, you have something on your mind. Go ahead, I'm listening."

"I'm sorry, Sheriff," Zach said, "but there's something I want to do, and I don't want to do it behind your back."

The sheriff smiled. "You want to know who killed Calvin Portman," he said.

Zach nodded. "I'd like to visit with Rex and Jay," he said. "I know you and your deputies have talked to them, but I thought that maybe they'd talk to me if I approach them right."

The sheriff shifted in his bed, wincing as he did so. "They have lawyers. They won't talk to us now. They refused to take a polygraph."

"I'll take one, Sheriff," Zach said.

"Not right yet," Lee said. "I like your idea. But you don't know where they are. I don't even know."

Zach cleared his throat. "Actually, I do know. Their parents told me."

Lee smiled. "Then go talk to them, with my blessing," he said. "I just ask one thing."

"What's that?" Zach asked.

"If you learn anything that will help me, share it with me," the sheriff said.

Zach promised him, and in a few minutes he was back in his truck and driving home. He had his cell phone in his pocket, and his hunting rifle was under the seat in the back of his pickup. He packed a bag and then told his folks where he was going and what he was planning to do. "But please don't tell anyone where I am," he said. "Sheriff Rutger knows, but he wants to keep it quiet for now."

"Son, do you have to?" his mother asked, her face creased with worry. "I know you want to help the sheriff, but you just got back."

"I do," he said firmly. "But I'll be careful. I didn't think I'd have to be gone overnight, but Jay is a long way away. I have my phone, so we can stay in touch."

"Is there anyone who can go with you? I'd feel better if you weren't alone," his father said.

"Like who?" he asked.

"Walt, maybe."

"I hadn't thought of that," Zach said. He wanted to talk to Jay and Rex alone, but that didn't mean that Walt, if he wanted to accompany him, couldn't wait in the truck. "I better check with the sheriff, but I think he'll be okay with it."

After getting the sheriff's approval, Zach called Walt's home number. Sage answered.

"Hi, Sage, it's Zach."

"Zach, thanks for calling," Sage said, sounding cheerful. "What's going on today?"

"I'm going on a little trip. My folks think someone should go with me. It'll be overnight, but I'll foot the expenses if—"

"I agree with your parents," Sage said, cutting him off. "Were you wondering if Walt and I could go with you?"

Not really, he thought. "Yes," he said. It had never occurred to him that Sage would want to go. He wouldn't have called if he'd thought that.

"We'd love to. At least I would, and I think Walt would too. We're still a little nervous being home like this," she said, sounding more excited than a nervous person should.

"Are you sure it's okay with Walt?"

"Yes, he has a class tonight, but he's missed enough lately that I don't think one more will make much difference. What time are you leaving?" she asked eagerly.

"As soon as possible. I've got a long way to drive and a lot to do," he said.

Sage didn't ask what the trip was about, but she did ask, "Can we have half an hour? I need to comb my hair and pack a few things. And I'll need to find Walt. He went outside a few minutes ago."

"Sure, I'll pick the two of you up in thirty minutes, and don't worry about the expense. It's on me," Zach said, trying unsuccessfully to keep the irritation from his voice. It was not that he didn't like Sage; he just didn't want any complications.

"Thanks, Zach," she said. "I'll try not to be a bother, I promise."

Then he felt guilty. She was a good girl. He didn't want to make her feel bad. It would cost him more for an extra room that night, but it wouldn't break him.

He pulled up to the Hinshaw farmhouse in exactly thirty minutes. He was extremely anxious to be on his way. Walt was standing by the gate, a duffel bag in hand.

Zach stopped and jumped out. "Let's put it in the backseat with mine. There'll be plenty of room back there for Sage, even with the bags. Is she about ready?"

Walt got a funny look on his face.

"What?" Zach asked impatiently.

"I don't think she's going."

"Why? She sounded like she wanted to when I called," he said.

"She says she didn't think about having to have another room if she went. And she isn't working now, so she doesn't want to dip into her savings to pay for it herself," Walt said. "And I think she's embarrassed. She realized you were probably only calling to invite me."

For a moment, Zach thought about just getting in the truck with Walt and hitting the road, but he didn't do that. He was not one to intentionally hurt anyone's feelings. *Even the girl next door.*

"She can go," Zach said, heading for the house. "You get in the truck, I'll get your sister." he told Walt.

He rang the bell. For a moment he thought she wasn't going to answer it, and she didn't. Her mother did.

"Is Sage ready?" he asked with what he hoped was a warm smile.

"Didn't Walt tell you? She decided not to go," her mother said.

"Would you ask her to come talk to me?" Zach said. "I'd like her to go."

"Are you sure?" Mrs. Hinshaw asked.

"Yes. Please ask her to come talk to me."

A moment later, Sage came in, looking a little sheepish.

"You guys go ahead," she said. "I didn't realize that you were calling just to ask Walt. I'm sorry. I didn't mean to—"

"Get your suitcase, Sage," he said with a smile. "I want all three of us to go."

"But . . ." she began.

"Don't worry about the money, Sage. Go get your bag. Please. I'm not going without you."

"Are you sure?"

"Yep, I'm sure. Do you need help?"

She shook her head. "Okay, but I'll pay my own way. And I'll try not to be a pain."

"You're not a pain, Sage. And quit worrying about the money. Now get moving," he said, giving her a gentle shove.

He waited while she got her things. He felt guilty that she felt badly. He honestly hadn't intended to make her feel that way. She was back in a couple minutes, carrying a small suitcase. He took it from her hand and said, "I'll carry that."

She let him take it, and he opened the door for her. When they got to the truck, Walt was waiting in the backseat. That wasn't Zach's plan. He'd assumed that Walt would get up front with him and Sage would sit in the back. Another wave of irritation passed over him. But he shook it off, placed the small suitcase with the others, and circled the truck. He opened the passenger door and took Sage's hand, helping her up and into the cab. Then he shut the door and went back around to his side. He climbed in, glancing at Sage, smiled when she looked at him, and put the truck in gear.

Chapter Twenty-Three

Zach hadn't told Walt or Sage a thing about what he was up to. He was headed to an address in Sandy, but he couldn't let them know that; he'd promised Rex's mother that he would not let anyone know where Rex was staying.

As they were driving down Parley's Canyon, Zach said, "Sage?"

"Yeah, Zach," she said as her eyes met his.

"Don't you guys wonder where we're going?"

She smiled shyly. "I trust you, Zach. If we need to know, you'll tell us. If not, that's okay. Anyway, it's probably none of my business."

"It is your business," he said.

Walt leaned forward from the backseat and said, "Okay, I'll ask if my sister won't. Where are we going?"

"I'm going to visit with Rex," he said.

"Where is he?"

"That's a problem. I had to promise his mother that I wouldn't tell anyone before she would give it to me. The sheriff, though I have his blessing on what I'm doing, doesn't even know where they are."

"You know we won't tell," Sage said.

"How about if I drop you off at a mall? I'll go talk to Rex, and then I'll pick you up again, and we'll have some lunch and head out on the long part of our trip."

"You mean we have farther to go?" Sage asked.

"A lot farther," he said.

Sage studied Zach's face for a moment, and he was aware of her eyes on him. Finally, she asked, "What about the other two?"

"Janie's mom treated me like dirt," he said with a scowl. "She wouldn't give me the time of day. So I guess she's out, but yes, I am going to be talking to Jay. He's out of state."

Sage rolled her eyes. Zach winked at her, bringing a crimson tide across her face. A few minutes later, after dropping Sage and Walt off at a nearby mall, Zach pulled up to an address in Sandy. He parked in front of the house and shut his truck off. He stared at the door for a moment. Then he shut his eyes and offered a short prayer. He needed the Lord's help if he was to come away from here with any knowledge that would help solve the mystery of the murder.

When he'd finished, he took a deep breath, opened the door of his truck, stepped out, and walked briskly to the door, trying to shake off the case of nerves he was experiencing.

The man who opened the door was someone Zach had never seen before.

"Zach," he said. "They're in the family room. Come on in."

Zach followed him, wondering who was there with Rex, hoping it wasn't his attorney. "Bet you didn't expect to see me," Janie said as he walked into the room.

Zach couldn't help staring as she grinned at him from the big armchair where she was sitting. "I sure didn't," he said. "But I'm glad you're here. It's good to see you guys."

Rex was standing beside the window. "Hi, Zach. Good to see you too. I hope it's okay that I asked Janie to come."

"It's great," he said. "I'm just surprised."

"After the way my mom treated you, I'm not surprised that you're surprised. She told me all about it. I'm sorry," Janie said, "She can be a real bear." Unless Zach was reading her face wrong, she meant it.

"I really am glad you're here," he said. "We've got to figure this thing out if we can."

Rex and Janie asked him why he'd left and where he had gone. "I'm sorry, guys, but I can't say." They looked skeptical, so Zach added, "I know you'd like to know what I was doing and exactly where I was, and I promise that once we clear this whole mess up, I'll tell you. But right now I can't."

Janie studied him for a moment. Then she asked, "Where is Bria? I know you know."

"I have no idea where Bria is," he said, even as that truth made his heart ache. "Honestly, I wish I knew."

"But, I thought that you—" Rex began.

"It doesn't matter what you thought. I don't know where she is," he said. "I'm sorry that I got you guys into this mess. If I'd had any idea what a jerk Caden was, I'd have canceled the hunt rather than let him come."

For the next few minutes, they talked about Caden and all the possibilities that might have led up to his death. Janie told Zach that she'd suspected him when he'd run off like he had.

"But then after I got banished and was by myself for hours at a time, I did a lot of thinking," Janie said. "Zach, I still can't help but wonder if Bria did it." As she spoke, she looked to the side. It was like she didn't trust herself to look Zach in the eye when she spoke—lied. He felt she was hiding something from him.

He turned to Rex. "Is that what you think, too?" he asked.

"Well, yes, but then I've been wondering about Sage and Walt."

"What about them?" Zach asked.

"I know it seems unlikely, but it's possible," he said. "I mean, we've got to face it—one of us killed the idiot."

"Do you really believe that?" Zach asked.

"Well, yes," he said. A look passed between Rex and Janie that raised Zach's suspicions to a higher level. "I know there's that mystery guy whose body was found. But everybody's saying that he's just a hunter who fell off a cliff," he added. "I suppose it could have been him."

Zach wasn't getting anywhere. He decided to throw in the bit about the harmonica. "One of the searchers found a harmonica not too far from our camp."

They both stared at him.

"Uh-uh," Janie said. "That would be too weird,"

Rex looked at her. "You have to admit that it did sound like a harmonica," he said.

She slowly nodded. "So there was someone else close by, if that's true."

Rex spoke next. "We know that some guy took Bria out of there. I suppose it could have been him." He glanced at Janie.

"That is possible," she admitted as she stared at something on the floor near her feet.

"So did either of you see or hear anything or anyone?" he asked.

They both shook their heads.

Rex said, "Have you talked to Jay or to Sage or Walt?"

"Not to Jay," he said. "Should I?"

"Maybe," Janie said, finally looking at Rex as she spoke.

"Yeah, talk to him," Rex agreed. "Maybe he saw some stranger up there."

Zach was discouraged. He was getting nowhere. They talked for a few more minutes, but Zach didn't learn anything more. "Let me give you guys my cell phone number," Zach said. "If you think of anything that might help us bring this thing to an end, you are welcome to call me."

When Zach left a few minutes later, he was firmly convinced that Walt and Sage were right—Rex and Janie knew something that they weren't telling. But he had no idea what that something was and he wasn't sure he would ever know.

When he met Sage and Walt a few minutes later, they both looked at him hopefully. He shook his head and said, "They weren't any help."

"They?" Sage asked.

"Oh, yeah, sorry. Janie was with Rex when I got there. They both talked to me, and they were real nice, but they were not any help. You guys are right. Those two are hiding something."

Sage looked downcast as she climbed into the truck through the door Zach held open for her. Then he and Walt both got in.

"Where to now?" Sage asked as Zach started the engine.

"How about some lunch?" he asked. "Then we'll head for Idaho. Jay's up there. Maybe he'll be of some help."

Chapter Twenty-Four

Agents with the FBI and the CIA had been looking nonstop for Kerry Sunger but with no success. When Rich Phillips rejoined the search after taking the days off to be with and resettle his family under new identities in Portland, the search was stepped up a notch. Rich had the advantage of knowing some of the surviving members of the terrorist group and the locations of some of their favorite hangouts.

The cold trail turned hot that Monday morning. What Rich learned had turned his stomach to lead. A member of the group that Rich had known well was arrested that morning. Pressure was applied, and the man had leaked a lot of information. As Rich had feared, Kerry's self-appointed mission had changed from one of convincing the nation to quit destroying the earth to one of personal revenge.

It seemed that Kerry was convinced that both GR Roper and Rich Phillips were dead. However, they had learned that Kerry was now more intent than ever on finding and destroying anyone Agent Rich Phillips had ever been connected with.

Even though Sunger had never seen Rich before his disappearance, he knew about Rich's work, and it had been the threats Sunger had made that had forced Rich to fake his drowning. Rich was convinced now that Sunger did not suspect Rich was GR Roper.

Sunger's anger against the agent who had made the first inroads into his organization following the successful bombings in Pennsylvania, West Virginia, and Nevada had turned to hatred. He'd told the man they'd arrested that day that he was determined to find Mrs. Phillips and her children and anyone else Rich might have been close to.

"I've got to go back to Portland right now," Rich told his friend and supervisor, Jim Crooney, as they met with several other agents in an FBI office in Dallas, Texas, shortly after noon. "They've suffered enough already. They need me with them."

"Rich, I understand your feelings," Jim told him, "but no one can track this man like you can. The FBI has helped us a lot. I'll ask them to send someone to protect them and, if need be, to move them again. But I think that you need to stay on the case. You are our best chance of catching Sunger."

Agitated, Rich stood and pushed his chair away from the conference table. "Then get someone there now," he said. "Keep someone with my family. If you promise to keep them moving, to keep them safe, I will go back to work."

"Thank you, Rich. You have my word," Jim said as he too got up, signaling an end to the meeting. "What do you plan to do now?"

"There are a couple of people who I need to talk to," he said. "I'll let you know how it goes." He walked toward the door and then stopped. Every agent in the room focused on Rich. "One more thing. The sheriff in Duchesne and those kids, the ones who were on the hunt, could be targets of this madman. Zach Barlow went home, and so did the Hinshaws. I don't know about the rest. But they are all in danger. Protect them."

* * *

Sheriff Rutger was feeling well enough that he limped into his office, planning to spend a couple of hours there that Monday afternoon. He hadn't been at his desk more than ten minutes, plowing through a ton of paperwork that had accumulated, when he was told that Jim Crooney was on the phone.

They talked for a while. What he heard was disturbing in one respect and shocking in another. He thanked Jim for calling, hung up the phone, and then sat for several minutes, pondering what he'd just learned. Finally, he asked his secretary to locate Chief Deputy Sessions and Detective Wakefield. "I need them in here as soon as they can come."

"Sheriff, you need to go home. You look like you don't feel well at all," Marlon said when he walked in ten minutes later.

The sheriff shook his head. "I'd rather be home in bed, but I can't do that. We've got problems again."

"What kind of problems?" Andrew asked as he too stepped into the sheriff's office.

"Shut the door, Andrew," Lee said, his face grave and his hands shaking.

"The name of the man behind all the acts of terror and the violence we've been experiencing is Kerry Sunger," Lee began. "This guy is about thirty-five years old, stands just taller than six feet, and weighs around 190 pounds. He keeps his head shaved and usually has three or four days' growth of black facial hair. He has a dark complexion, dark brown eyes, and thick, black eyebrows. A picture of him will be sent to us shortly. I just learned that this thug has become more unhinged than he already was. He is bent on revenge.

"A CIA agent warned me right after the casino bombing that we might be targets. They caught one of the Earth Militia members, who has confirmed that. Rich Phillips's wife and kids are also targets. And Zach and the others from the hunting party are targets too."

Both deputies appeared shaken by the news. "What about our families?" Andrew asked as the color drained from his face.

"We must assume that they are in danger as well," the sheriff said. "I think we've already learned that these people are ruthless. However, on a positive note, some of the most dangerous terrorists are now either dead or in custody. The feds feel that if they can arrest Sunger, the organization will fall apart. And right now it seems that Sunger is working on his own, or pretty much on his own, with a personal vendetta."

"Do the feds have any idea where he is?" Marlon asked.

"No, but Crooney tells me that they have one of their best agents on the case."

"Do we know him?" Marlon asked.

The sheriff chuckled. "You do. Rich Phillips."

There was complete silence in the room.

Finally, Marlon spoke. "Duchesne's Rich Phillips? The international businessman?" he asked.

"The same," Lee agreed. "Only he isn't a businessman; he's an experienced and extremely capable CIA operative." He went on to explain how Rich had faked his death and why. "I guess Zach Barlow saw him recently, but he was told to mention it to no one. Rich himself told me, but again, I promised to keep it secret—until now."

"Why are the feds telling us this now? They've kept it from us so far," Andrew said in disgust.

"I've known for a while, but I promised not to say anything. Sorry, but I guess they figure that this is a last-ditch effort to get this Sunger guy. Phillips is one agent who can do it if anyone can. After that, Rich will be living elsewhere," Lee told his deputies. "I was also told that his family won't be coming back here again."

"This explains a lot," Andrew said.

"Yes, it does," the sheriff agreed. "Now we've got to work on our immediate problem—providing for the safety of our families and the young hunters."

* * *

Zach's cell phone vibrated. He pulled it out of one of the front pockets of his western shirt. "Where are you, Zach?" Sheriff Rutger asked.

"I'm in Idaho," he said.

"Good. And you have Walt with you?"

Zach glanced over at Sage, She was leaning against the window, asleep. "Yes, and so is Sage." He wasn't sure how the sheriff would react to that news.

"That's good, Zach. Don't come back here until I tell you it is safe."

A chill settled over Zach. "What's happened now?" he asked.

"The leader of the Earth Militia, Kerry Sunger, is bent on revenge. You kids are in danger. Do you have a gun with you?" Lee asked.

"My rifle is beneath the backseat," Zach responded.

"Keep it handy. Are you having any success with your friends?" the sheriff asked.

"Not yet, but I still hope to."

"Okay, keep Walt and Sage safe, and keep in touch with me. I'll let you know when it is safe to come home," the sheriff said.

"I'll do it," Zach answered. "And I'll tell them right now what's going on."

* * *

Bria was upset. She, along with her mother and brother, were packing up again. In a few minutes, two FBI agents would be there to pick them up and move them again. They were still in danger, and she was scared. Her fright turned to anger, and she glanced over at their new laptop computer. She wasn't thinking as much about Zach as she had been, but she was suddenly upset that he wasn't here now, when she needed him.

She impulsively opened the computer, turned it on, and checked her e-mail. She had received and deleted several messages from Zach. She half expected to see one now. But when she didn't, it made her even more angry. She began to type a new message to him.

Zach, I am so angry. Why did you leave me? I'm afraid and I'm hurting and I'm alone. It would be better if you don't ever try to e-mail me again. It's best if we never see each other again.

She didn't type her name or read the message over again. She just hit send and shut down her computer.

Chapter Twenty-Five

It was dark and cold when Zach parked in front of the address Jay's father had given him. "If you need us, we'll be waiting here," Sage said.

"Are you sure you guys will be okay in the truck while I'm in there talking to Jay?"

Walt grinned and patted Zach's rifle. "We'll be fine," he said.

"If you get cold, turn on the truck and let the heater run." Zach's eyes met Sage's and he winked. "Are you sure you don't want to come in? I'll bet Jay would be glad to see you."

Sage rolled her eyes. "I'll pass," she said.

Jay seemed nervous, more nervous than Zach had ever seen him. But he also seemed friendly. "Life's kind of changed, hasn't it?" he said, trying to chuckle but coming up short. His eyes looked down.

Zach decided to get right to the point. "Jay, somebody killed Caden. Until we get to the bottom of it, none of us will have any peace. We are all suspect."

"That's the cops' job," Jay said, his eyes drilling a hole in the carpet.

"But they need help. Listen, I'm going to tell you something no one else knows," Zach said, coming to a decision that he'd been toying with for the past hour. "As you know, I left town, but I wasn't just running away."

Jay dragged his eyes up and looked from the chair where he was sitting across the five feet that separated him from Zach. "What were you doing then?"

"Think about it, Jay. What do you think I was doing?"

"I dunno," Jay said. "Maybe you were trying to keep from getting killed, like I am. How could we know that Caden was such a . . . a dangerous guy with such . . . such horrible friends?"

"I was in danger, that's true. I still am and so are you."

"Yeah, I know. My attorney called me and told me what the sheriff said."

"Well, this thing's going to go on for a while. But it will go on a lot longer if we don't figure out what happened to Caden," Zach said. "I didn't leave town because I was running. I managed to make contact with Bria, and she was scared to death. I told her I'd come help her if I could," Zach said, watching Jay closely.

Jay's eyes sprang wide open and his jaw dropped.

"That's right. I went to meet Bria. A man I knew only as Frank picked me up and took me to where she was hiding. And that's what had happened in the mountains that day too, Jay. She was hiding," Zach said. "She didn't kill anybody, but she was afraid of Caden and was hiding from him in the forest, but she got lost."

Jay was rubbing his jaw, his eyes puzzled. "Zach," he said, "how did you get in touch with her?"

"I e-mailed her, and after a couple of days she answered me. Frank, the guy that took me to where she and her mother and brother were hiding under his protection, told her to answer me. She did," Zach said. "And I told her I'd come and help her. She said it was okay, and so I went."

"But how did she get away from whoever the guy was who took her out of the mountains—you know, the guy that kidnapped her?" Jay asked.

"She wasn't kidnapped. Frank was a federal agent. He knew that Caden was dangerous and that he might hurt Bria, so he simply found her and took her to a safe place."

Jay's eyes brightened. "So she's safe? She's okay?"

"The last time I saw her she was. But Caden had friends more dangerous than you can even imagine, Jay. I don't know where she is now, but I do know that she's still in danger," Zach said.

Jay was slowly shaking his head. He didn't offer to say anything else, so Zach said, "Frank was murdered by some of Caden's friends, some of the same people that are after Bria and me and you and the other guys." Jay looked up again when Zach quit speaking. But he still didn't say anything, and pretty soon, his head dropped once more. Zach went on. "Jay, I was with Frank right after he was shot. He knew who killed Caden. He saw it. He talked to me just before he died."

Zach was bluffing now, and Jay jumped like he'd been stung. But he still didn't say anything. "Jay, why don't you tell me what you know? If you will, I'll tell you exactly what Frank told me. If you don't, I'll tell the sheriff."

Jay's jaw began to work. Zach waited. It was Jay's turn to talk. Zach was nearly certain that he knew something, and he hoped that he would finally reveal whatever it was. But when Jay finally spoke, all he did was ask a question. "Have you talked to Rex and Janie?"

"Yes, I have. They know I was coming to see you."

"Did they say anything?' Jay asked.

"They did," Zach said. "But they told me to talk to you. It's time you guys told the truth. You can tell me, or you can tell the sheriff. You can't keep hiding behind your attorneys."

Jay finally looked up. "Bria didn't do it," he said softly.

"I know that, Jay. Remember, I was with her for several days. By the way, she knows about the guy with the harmonica—the second guy that was up there—the one that wasn't Frank."

Jay got up from his chair and walked across the room and then back again. "Frank talked to you and then died?" Jay asked.

"That's right. And I can testify to what he said in court if I have to. I think they call it a dying declaration or something like that," Zach said. He was bluffing more than ever now, but he was certain that Jay was about ready to talk. So he waited while Jay paced the floor, wringing his hands and rubbing his face.

Finally, he stopped and faced Zach. "Janie and Rex will be mad if I say anything."

"Then I guess they'll just have to be mad. Remember, there was a witness."

"Okay, Zach. I'll tell you what happened since you already know."

* * *

As the big jetliner drifted down through a thin layer of clouds, the glowing lights of the Salt Lake Valley came into view. Rich peered below, anxious to be on the ground and on his way to Duchesne, a place he'd come to love but hadn't been sure he'd ever see again.

It had all changed that afternoon in Dallas. A second interview with the man they'd arrested that morning led Rich to another member of the Earth Militia. At the address they'd been given, Rich and a pair of FBI agents found not just that man, but a woman also. While the FBI agents waited just up the street, Rich entered the home, outfitted with a wig and beard almost identical to what he'd worn recently. The man and woman almost fainted when he stepped through the door.

They had believed Roper to be dead. Rich said, "That's what Kerry wanted you to think. But then I learned that there are a lot of things Kerry wanted all of us to believe. He lost sight of our mission. He cares only about himself. He's a traitor."

Before the FBI agents had come in to make the arrests, the two had spilled their guts to Rich. He was now acting on what they had told him—Kerry was headed for the little town in Utah where Calvin Portman had been living when he was murdered. At least that's what they believed. He hoped they were right, because if he was, it would be the last act in Sunger's reign of terror and death.

* * *

The sheriff was lying on a cot in his office. His wife was with friends in the ward. The families of Marlon and Andrew were out of town. This evening was feeling like a repeat of the night Lee had been shot. Every deputy was on duty and dozens of other officers—state, federal, and local—had gathered. But most of them were not in sight. Marlon was running the actual operation. Lee was too weak after an exhausting afternoon to do anything but consult from the cot. Rich Phillips had called a few minutes earlier to let the sheriff know that he was on his way. Everyone knew what Sunger looked like. No one knew what he was driving.

Lee's cell phone rang. He picked it up from the chair next to the head of his cot. "This is Sheriff Rutger," he said.

"Hello, Sheriff," he heard Zach Barlow say. "I know what happened to Caden Pendleton."

The sheriff stiffened, gripping the phone tightly. "Are you sure?"

"I'm sure," Zach told him confidently.

"Would you like to tell me?" Lee asked

"Yes, but not on the phone. I'll head home in the morning. Can I meet with you when I get there?"

Thinking about the threat they were under, Lee said wearily, "Zach, call me when you get to Salt Lake City. Things are kind of tense here again. There is a direct threat we are dealing with, and it's not safe for you to come here until we get things taken care of."

"Are my parent's okay?" Zach asked urgently.

"Yes. In fact, you can let Walt and Sage know that we are providing security for their family as well as yours. And if you are still close enough or have a phone number, let Jay know that we are also taking care of his family. We'll keep them all safe here."

"Jay's with us," Zach said. "So I'll tell him right now."

The sheriff was slow in responding. If Jay was with Zach and the Hinshaws, then he must have held the key to the mystery. But he didn't comment on that. He simply said, "You be careful, Zach. I've got to go now." He was having a difficult time keeping his emotions in check. He cleared his throat before saying, "I look forward to hearing from you tomorrow."

* * *

Zach slowly closed his phone and put it in his pocket as he stared straight ahead. His three friends watched him closely. Sage was the first to speak. "What's happening in Duchesne?" she asked. He turned his head toward her. Her eyes were wide with alarm, and she was again torturing a strand of her blonde hair.

"Our families are safe," he said. "All of them. I don't know exactly what's happening there, but the sheriff said we are to call him when we get back to Salt Lake tomorrow."

The four of them were sitting in Zach's truck, Sage next to him and the boys in the back. The luggage was now in the bed of the truck. Sage reached over and touched Zach gently on the shoulder. "Thanks, Zach."

"I didn't do anything," he said.

She slid close and put an arm around him. "Hey, neighbor," she said, clearly trying to sound lighthearted, "you've done everything. You are the best friend anyone could have."

"Thanks, Sage," he said. "How about if we find a place to stay for the night and get some dinner? Does that sound okay?"

"Sure," Sage said softly as she withdrew her hand and slid over to put her seat belt on.

It was also okay with Walt and Jay. Zach went to check them into a couple of rooms in a hotel. Sage was looking nervous as she stood a short way away, watching him. He caught her eye and signaled her over. "Something's on your mind," he said.

"I don't mean to be a problem, but is it okay if Walt and I share a room? I don't know if I dare stay in a room by myself. I'm such a wimp," she said as she stood swaying nervously.

"Of course, you and your brother will be together. But I also talked them into giving us a connecting room. That way Jay and I will be only a tap or two away."

Her facial features relaxed. "Thanks," she said. "You are so thoughtful. I'm just sorry I'm such a bother."

He reached out and put a hand on her cheek. "Hey, you are not a bother," he said. "I'm really glad you're here. Let's get our bags up to the rooms, and then we'll go get some dinner."

She touched his hand, and even as he moved his from her face, her fingers lingered. He swallowed and then, looking beyond her, he said, "Hey, you guys, let's go get our bags."

Zach felt uncomfortable as he kept glancing at Sage only to find her looking at him. Even though he had no commitment to Bria, he had been fond of her, and the feelings that he found rummaging around inside him every time his eyes met Sage's made him feel guilty. Other than that, the dinner went well. Jay and Walt seemed to be getting along, and Zach was glad. He hadn't forgotten the tension that the two of them had exhibited on the hunt.

As they were walking back to their rooms later, Sage and Zach were walking side by side, and the guys were behind them. He and Sage stopped beside the hotel's souvenir shop so she could get some gum and a book. While she looked around, Zach waited near the entrance. He was startled when he overheard Jay and Walt talking outside the shop. Jay said in a low voice. "So Walt, what's with Zach and your sister? I thought she couldn't see past me. It used to bug me."

"She likes him, but it'll never be. Zach's got a thing for Bria," Walt said.

"No," Jay said. "I thought that you and I were going to get to fight for her affection."

"I'm going on a mission," Walt said. "She'd never have waited for me anyway."

"I don't know if I can go or not, but if I do, I'd be back first because I'm older. Maybe if we try to boost this thing with Zach and Sage along, Bria will be available when I get back." He chuckled.

Walt said, "I don't think it's going to happen. I don't know if you noticed it or not, but Bria was looking at Zach a lot up there on the hunt. I'm guessing that once we get this mess over with, he'll be going to get her from wherever she's hiding."

"Guess we'll have to see," Jay said. "Maybe I ought to ask your sister out again. I know you can't see it because you're her brother, but she's cute. She really is. Maybe I shouldn't let her bug me. You know, Walt, sometimes us guys can't see what's right under our noses."

"That's what I've been told," Walt said.

Just then, Sage approached the checkout stand, and Zach joined her. She smiled up at him, and he felt a flutter in his stomach, an unsettling flutter.

When they were in their rooms, Sage joined the boys as they watched a little TV, then she went to the other room to read, leaving the connecting doors ajar. After she was gone, Zach got his laptop out and turned it on. He didn't really expect to hear from Bria but he still hoped he would.

To his surprise, there was a message from her, but it wasn't a reply to any of the ones that he'd sent to her. Nervously he opened it. The words he read burned like a hot branding iron. The message was full of anger and hurt. *And he'd done it to her*. When would he ever stop hurting others? Despite himself, he read it again. He'd never read anything that hurt like Bria's e-mail. But he knew it wasn't her, it was the terrible things she'd had to endure. He wished he could suddenly be with her. If he could, surely he could calm her down and soothe her hurt.

He deleted the message and shut off his computer. "Hey, guys," he said. "I'll be right back. I need to go out and get some air."

Walt and Jay both looked at him with furrowed brows. "Are you okay, Zach?" Walt asked.

"I'm okay," he fibbed. "I'll be back in a few minutes."

As he shut the door behind him, he felt his emotions flood to the surface. He headed down the hallway, passed the elevator, and took the stairs down to the first floor and fled from the hotel. After he got outside, he rushed to his truck, leaned up against it with his head between his hands, and stood there, trying to sort through his feelings and thoughts.

A few moments later, still feeling as confused as ever, he walked away from the truck and onto the street. He had only gone about a half block when he heard running steps behind him. Remembering the threats, he spun around. But it wasn't an enemy.

Sage slowed to a walk, and Zach waited for her. When she got to him, she said, "Are you okay?"

He shook his head, felt his shoulders slump, and fought with his emotions. "I've been better," he admitted.

"Could you use some company?"

"That's up to you," he said grimly. "I'm not exactly good company. In fact, I'm dangerous. Every time I try to help someone, I only make them miserable."

"I'll take that chance," she said.

Neither of them said anything for three or four blocks. It was late, but Zach knew he couldn't sleep if he went back to the hotel now. So he continued on. The girl from next door never missed a step. She was beside him continually. He felt strength from her presence. He didn't know how that was possible, but it was real.

Finally, he stopped and turned back. "I guess we better not get too far," he said.

She smiled shyly, the glow from a streetlight overhead making her features seem even more beautiful. "If you want to talk, I'd be glad to listen," she said softly.

"Thanks," he said, but he didn't have anything to share right now. "I just need a little time."

A block later, as they waited for a light to change, Sage asked, "I know you and Jay worked something out. He seems relieved, but can you tell me what it is?"

He looked over at her. "I'd like to, but I promised him I wouldn't. But I can say this much, Sage. I now know what happened, and as soon as we can meet with the sheriff, he'll know too. He will have to decide what to do, but it will no longer be my worry . . . or yours . . . or Bria's."

"If it's not my worry, does that mean Jay's not blaming you or me?" she pressed.

"Jay's okay." Zach smiled. "He's not such a bad guy."

She didn't respond to that but seemed instead to withdraw into her own thoughts. Another block passed in silence. Zach's mind drifted back to the stinging e-mail he'd received from Bria. He felt the pain all over again and put both his hands over his eyes and rubbed. Sage reached over and touched his elbow. He dropped his hands.

"Are you ready to tell me what happened? I'd be happy to just listen," she said.

Zach looked at her. Her face was serious, even sympathetic. Suddenly, he plunged into it, saying, "I got an e-mail from Bria. It was terrible." He suddenly couldn't go on.

Sage walked silently beside him for a couple of minutes. Finally, he said, "Bria says she never wants to hear from me again. How could she say that?"

"Zach, I know how girls think. She didn't mean it," Sage said. "What else did she say?"

"She's angry because I left, but Sage, I had to. My folks needed me. And this thing with Caden and all of us was weighing me down. You are all my friends. I had to know the truth. You all have the right to know the truth." He looked at Sage, feeling totally miserable.

"Of course she's angry. She had you almost to herself for all that time, didn't she?"

"Well, sort of, but before I left, it was getting hard. We were arguing some, and she needed time with her family. I was trying not to be a burden on them," he said, shaking his head sadly. "I had to get away."

"She may not see it that way," Sage said. "Think about it, Zach. Think about what she's already lost. She lost her father. And then to lose you, someone so strong and so decent, someone dependable."

"But her . . ." Zach stopped himself in time. He'd almost mentioned the fact that her father was alive, that he was there when he left. He couldn't do that.

Sage took hold of his arm. "Her what?" she asked. "You were starting to say something."

It was lame, but Zach did the best he could to get out of his slipup. "Her mother is strong, Sage. She's hurting too, but she's a strong woman."

"But she's not a man. It's not the same," Sage argued.

"You're right. But I put my life on the line for Bria, and yet she can just write me off?" His voice broke. "I . . . I saved . . ." He couldn't say it.

"What did you save?" Sage asked gently.

Zach turned and faced her. "I don't want to say it."

Sage's face became determined. The light on the street was dim, but he could see her face well enough. She tugged on his arm until he was facing her. "What did you save?" she asked. "Say it, and it will be easier."

"I don't know that it will, Sage. But I'll say it. I saved her life. It wasn't anything heroic that I did. I was saving mine, too, and her mother's and little brother's," he said, his eyes avoiding hers now, looking down at the toes of his black cowboy boots.

Sage reached up and touched him beneath the chin and lifted his head. Their eyes finally met, and then she asked. "Will you tell me about it? If you do, maybe I can help you understand how she's feeling."

"I shot a man," he said. "He was a bad man. He broke into the safe house where we were staying. I shot him with Frank's 9mm pistol."

Sage trembled and pulled her arms back, hugging her chest. "And he died?"

"No, at least the last I knew he hadn't, but he was injured critically. There were others there, but FBI agents had come to help. They got the others," he said, turning away from her and starting to walk again.

She caught up with him. He walked quickly now, like he could somehow escape the horror of that night. "Are we in a race?" she asked gently. He looked over at her and realized she was almost jogging to keep up.

"Sorry." He slowed down but kept walking.

"Zach, I'm trying to think how I'd feel if a guy I liked a lot had done that for me and then left a few days later. It would hurt," she confessed.

"She said that, Sage—in her e-mail, I mean. She said she was hurting and that she was alone. But she's not alone," he insisted stubbornly.

"You're not there. That makes her feel alone. Zach, don't count her out," Sage said. "I think I know how she feels. She's been through a lot of pain, but this is just too much. So she strikes out at the one person she has come to care deeply for. Don't blame her, Zach. Forgive her."

"I can forgive her, but I want her to know that I do."

"Then write and tell her so," Sage suggested.

"I can't," he said helplessly. "She told me not to. She basically told me that it would be better if we didn't contact each other again."

"Give it a couple of days," she suggested. "Then try writing to her."

They had stopped at another intersection across the street from their hotel. He was staring across the street, seeing in his mind the horror he'd gone through and trying to imagine how much worse Bria had it. Sage stepped around to the front and stood close to him.

"Need a hug?" she asked with the slightest hint of a smile.

"Sure," he said.

"It'll be okay," she said and slipped into his arms. "She'll come around," she predicted softly.

* * *

"They're hugging, Walt," Jay said as he stood beside a parted blind.

Walt stepped over to the window. "Sure are. She hugs me, too. She hugs our cousins. Sage is a hugger. Remember, Jay, we grew up real close to Zach's family. He's like a brother to me. He's like a brother to Sage."

"I guess you're right. She's hugged me before. Look, they didn't kiss and they're crossing the street now." He stepped back from the window. "If I asked her out, you know, in a few weeks . . ."

He stopped. Walt looked at him with a cocked eyebrow. Jay turned away and took a step back. "Who am I kidding? I can't ask her out. I can't even go on a mission."

There was bitterness in his voice. Walt fumbled over what to say. He finally said, "Sure you can. Just because you haven't been coming to church much—you have the right to change."

"Sure I do," he said, but he added nothing more. Walt made up his mind right then and there to speak with Zach about Jay. Zach would help him see that he could change. If he did, maybe his sister would fall for him. Only time would tell.

Chapter Twenty-Six

It was after midnight when a lone car, a black van with no windows, drove into town on the Indian Canyon Highway. It turned west and drove clear to the edge of town. Rich, who was watching it, thought that it was going to keep going. But when it turned and drove slowly back toward his position beside the high school, he lifted his night-vision binoculars and trained them on the windshield of the van.

It was hard to tell what he was seeing until the van was almost to him. He shrunk back into the shadows without lowering his glasses. The face of the driver was looking to the south, and then it turned toward Rich. He'd know that face anywhere. He took a deep breath. Then he spoke into the mic of his radio. "The subject is eastbound on Highway 40 in a black van. I'm heading for my car. Use caution; he's probably carrying explosives. But don't let him get away."

A dozen patrol cars converged on the van as it drove toward the river on the east end of town. "Now," Rich said. The air was instantly filled with red and blue flashing lights. The van accelerated and rammed one of the patrol cars head-on. Then it backed up, hitting another to the rear. "Hold your fire," Rich said into his radio. The patrol cars, as per previous instructions from Rich, moved in in a double circle until there was no place for the van to go. Then every officer got out, guns at the ready, and moved to the back of their cars and then to the second layer of cars. Rich didn't want anybody too close in case the van blew up.

Rich moved up to Chief Deputy Sessions's side and took a bullhorn that Marlon offered him. He spoke into it. "Sunger, there is no place to run now. Get out of the car with your hands held high. And move slowly. Do it now!"

"I ain't coming out, copper. You gotta come and get me. But I don't think you got guts enough."

"You don't know who you're talking to, Sunger. This is Roper," Rich said.

From where he was standing at a ninety-degree angle to the van's driver's-side window, Rich could see Sunger's head snap around. But Sunger made no move to exit the vehicle. Rich spoke again. "You were right, Kerry. I was the mole. But your men didn't kill me. Harrison tried, but he died in the attempt. Now get out before we take you out."

Sunger's head was facing out the window of the car. Slowly, a hand came up, holding a pistol in it. "Don't be a fool, Kerry. You'll be dead before you can pull the trigger."

"Show yourself, Roper. I'll show you who will be dead, you coward."

"Don't call me Roper," Rich said. Then he whispered to Marlon, "Get on our radio. Tell everyone to stay down. I know this guy. He'll shoot at me if he thinks he can pinpoint where my voice is coming from."

Marlon relayed the message, and then Rich asked, "Is the FBI marksman ready?" Marlon spoke briefly into his radio before he nodded to Rich. "Okay, I'm going to give him another chance. If he shoots, tell the agent to take him out. I don't want this man adding to his body count."

Marlon once more spoke quietly into his mic. "All's ready," he whispered to Rich.

Rich raised the bullhorn again. But before he could speak, Sunger shouted, "So if I don't call you Roper what do I call you?"

Rich spoke. "Special Agent Rich Phillips."

Sunger's head jerked. "He's dead!" he shouted.

"Wrong," Rich said. "Get out real quietlike now, and I'll prove it."

"You ruined my life, Phillips. People like you are ignorant of the grief you cause the rest of us! You are dead *now,* Phillips!" Sunger suddenly shrieked, and the gun in his hand fired. The bullet struck the car that Rich was crouched behind at the same moment a sharp-shooter's rifle spoke the final word. Kerry Sunger had made his last mistake.

* * *

Bria's mother burst into the room where she was sleeping in still another safe house, this one in Spokane, Washington. "Bria, it's your dad," she cried. "He's on the phone."

Bria sat up abruptly, rubbing her eyes. "What's he calling about?"

"I'll let him tell us both together." Patty put the phone to her ear and said, "Rich, I'm going to put this on speaker so your daughter can hear too."

A moment later, Rich's voice came on the phone. "Kerry Sunger is dead," he said. "And right now, there are officers across the country arresting more of his supporters that I've got evidence against. But with Kerry gone, the movement is pretty well finished."

Bria squealed in delight. "Dad, that's great!"

"Yes, it is. I didn't think there was any chance that we could get this wrapped up so quickly."

"Where did you get him?" Patty asked. "Was he in Portland?"

"No, he went to Duchesne with a car full of explosives. We were ready for him."

Bria's face clouded over. "Were you in Duchesne, Dad?" she asked.

"I still am, but I'll be leaving later today."

"Did you see . . ." Bria began, but she stopped.

"Zach's out of the area," he said. "But I'm sure he's fine."

Patty then began to talk to Rich, and Bria flopped facedown on her pillow, soaking it with her tears.

* * *

Expansive fields passed by the windows of the truck as it rolled down the freeway. Zach was anxious to get back to Duchesne and get Jay and the sheriff together. There were some painful times ahead, but at least, after what Jay had told him, the case would soon be resolved.

He looked over at Sage. She was dressed in a yellow blouse and blue jeans. She reminded him of a sunflower on a sunny summer morning. Zach had gained a new appreciation for Sage. She had been a real help to him the night before. She had given him a different perspective on things, a woman's perspective, and he was grateful for that.

She glanced his way and caught him looking at her. She smiled and lowered her eyes. Zach looked back at the road. Jay and Walt were talking in the back. Jay had admitted to Zach that morning that he was apprehensive about speaking to the sheriff. But he had also thanked Zach for keeping what he'd told him a secret for now. It made it easier, he said, to talk to Walt.

"I wonder how things went last night in Duchesne," Walt suddenly called from the backseat. "I hope we don't have to stay in Salt Lake tonight."

"The sheriff said he'd let us know when we get to Salt Lake if it's safe for us to go on home. I'm with you on that, though. I want to get home," Zach said.

The tires continued to hum on the pavement, and country music played on the radio. The guys in the back both became quiet, and when Zach glanced over his shoulder a moment later, he realized that they were asleep. Sage also looked back there. When she turned forward again, she said, "I don't think they slept much last night."

"Did you?" Zach asked her.

"Sort of," she said. "How about you?"

"I slept better than I would have if you hadn't calmed me down," he admitted, briefly glancing over at her.

"I'm glad I could help," she said, turning her face away from him. "After all, isn't that what friends are for?"

"Yeah, it is, I guess," Zach said, glancing over again and studying her profile for a moment. "Seriously. Thanks, Sage. I mean it."

"So are you going to e-mail Bria again?"

"I think so. But I'll probably give it a day or so like you suggested," he said. "Then I guess I'll just see what happens."

"Hey, I love this song," Sage said, leaning forward and turning the volume on the radio up a bit.

As she sat back a second later, Zach was surprised when she wiped at her eyes then stared out her window at the passing fields.

A half hour passed, and not a word was said by anyone in the truck. Zach's phone began to vibrate in his shirt pocket. He pulled it out and looked at it before answering. It was the sheriff who greeted him with, "Hey, Zach, how are you this morning? This is Sheriff Rutger."

"Good morning, Sheriff," he said. "How are things in Duchesne this morning?"

Sage straightened up and looked over at Zach. "A whole lot better," he said. "I wasn't able to do much last night but wait in my office, but things came to a head. The father of that little gal of yours came through."

"What are you talking about?" Zach asked, grimacing at the reference to Bria being his girl.

"Rich Phillips called me yesterday and said that he had good information that Kerry Sunger was coming to Duchesne and that he'd get here as soon as he could. He drove into town about eleven. By then, my deputies had rounded up a lot of help from around the state and the FBI and CIA had sent several agents to town," he said.

"So did Sunger come or not?" he asked.

"He did, and thanks to Phillips's warning, we were ready."

"Great. So are you saying he's been arrested?" Zach asked anxiously.

Sage was leaning toward Zach, and he tipped the phone so she could hear. "No, not exactly. He tried to shoot your little gal's dad, but he didn't ever really have a chance. An FBI sharpshooter took him out."

Zach breathed a huge sigh of relief. He pulled over so that he could give the sheriff his full attention.

The sheriff was still talking. "Rich says that arrests are being made across the country this morning, arrests on the bulk of the remaining eco-terrorists. Essentially, they are out of business. You can come on back to town now. And if Jay knows as much as you say he does, maybe we can get this whole thing wrapped up."

It wasn't until the sheriff had disconnected that Zach noticed Sage staring out her window again. He thought that was strange considering the good news they had just received. The guys in the back were awake now. "What's going on?" Walt asked.

Zach shut his truck off, took a long, deep breath, and exhaled before saying, "It's safe to go home. Sunger is dead."

Walt cheered. Jay smiled, but he didn't look too excited. Zach didn't blame him; he had a tough day ahead of him. Sage didn't say a word, but when Zach got out of the truck, she and the guys in the backseat did the same. They walked around for a few minutes. Zach was so relieved, he could hardly stand it. Sage smiled some, but mostly she seemed withdrawn. She glanced occasionally at Jay, who was doing the same with her. Zach wondered if, when this nightmare was finally over, there was a future for Sage and Jay. The thing he wanted the most right now was for all of his friends to be happy again—including Bria.

After a few minutes, they got back in the truck and headed for home, to the peaceful little country town that had been badly rattled.

Chapter Twenty-Seven

Late in the afternoon, the sheriff, chief deputy, and Detective Wakefield were in Lee's office awaiting the arrival of Zach and his three friends. Jay's attorney was expected soon. He arrived before the young people and was accompanied by Jay's parents. The officers had all met him before, but he addressed the sheriff and said, "I'm Alvin Eagler, attorney at law. My client is not going to say a word to you until I've had a chance to talk to him and approve what he wants to tell you." He looked to the Kilpatricks for approval. They simply nodded. They were both tense and looked about nervously, but they sat down when the sheriff waved a hand at a leather sofa at one side of his large office.

Ten minutes later, Zach, Sage, Jay, and Walt walked into the reception area. Lee's secretary buzzed him and advised him of their arrival. "Marlon, I'd like to meet with just Jay and Mr. Eagler. Would you take everyone else into the squad room?" Lee asked. "But have Jay step in here." Lee was in a lot of pain this morning, and he hoped that whatever Jay Kilpatrick had to say wouldn't cause him a lot more. He stayed sitting at his desk. It hurt to get up and down.

Marlon got to his feet and exited the room. Andrew followed him. A moment later, Jay was ushered in, and Andrew shut the door, leaving the sheriff alone with Jay and his attorney. "I'd stand, Jay, but it was a long night, and I'm not feeling too perky," Lee said.

Jay walked over to the sheriff's desk and extended his hand, saying, "That's okay, Sheriff. So what happens now?"

"I guess your attorney wants to meet with you for a minute. But before he does, I'd like to say a couple of things," Lee told him.

"Where did Zach go?" Jay asked, looking about him, his eyes wide. "I want him with us."

"We don't need him," Alvin Eagler said sternly. "What did you want to say, Sheriff, before Jay and I go out?"

"I'm not going out," Jay said. "And I want my dad and mom and Zach here when I talk to the sheriff."

"I forbid that," Alvin said.

Jay looked at him with surprise. "Why?" he asked. "You don't even know what I'm going to say."

"So you haven't been totally candid with me?" the attorney asked, looking offended.

"No, I haven't. And you're only here because Janie's and Rex's parents convinced my parents that I needed an attorney," Jay told him, a stubborn set to his jaw.

"We'll step out right now," the attorney said, grabbing Jay by the arm and tugging on him.

Jay shook his arm free. "Sheriff, please have my parents and Zach come in, and I'd also like Marlon Sessions and Andrew Wakefield here."

"Jay, you aren't listening," Alvin said angrily.

Jay ignored him. "I think I'd like Walt and Sage to hear what I have to say too. Is that okay?"

"It's okay with me, Jay," Sheriff Rutger said. "But you do need to listen to your attorney."

Jay stubbornly shook his head.

"Then should we go to the squad room?" Lee asked.

"No, this is fine," Jay said. "It won't take long. Anyway, you don't look like standing up would feel very good."

Lee smiled. "You're right there," he said as he reached for his phone to buzz the squad room. He kept his eye on Alvin Eagler, who clearly wasn't happy. However, Alvin made no move to stop the sheriff, so he made the call.

Marlon and Andrew brought in a couple of extra chairs, and as soon as everyone was seated, Lee said, "Okay, Jay, let me just remind you that anything you say can be held against you."

Jay waved a hand dismissively. "I know my rights. Let's get on with it."

"Jay, I forbid you to say another word," Alvin said from the chair beside him.

Lee noticed how Mr. Kilpatrick raised his eyebrows. But he didn't speak. Jay did. "You can't make me stay quiet. I already told Zach, and now I want to tell everyone else."

"Don't!" Alvin thundered.

Jay looked at his parents. His dad shrugged his shoulders, while his mother dropped her eyes. He faced the sheriff. "I killed Caden Pendleton," he said with a sober face.

Alvin Eagler looked like he was going to have a stroke. He jumped to his feet and grabbed Jay's arm. Jay jerked it back, freeing himself. "Dad," he said. "Do you want to fire this guy, or should I?"

Both of his parents, however, were shocked beyond speech. Jay looked at them for a moment, and then he decisively turned to Alvin again as the attorney made a second attempt to grab his arm, and said, "You are fired. You can go now."

Zach was sitting at the back of the room. He was the only one not in shock. All the color had drained from Sage's face. She looked like she was about to faint. "I think you should explain, Jay," Zach said quickly. "We don't want anyone thinking you murdered anyone, because you didn't."

Lee gave his full attention to Jay. Andrew opened a notebook. Marlon also listened intently. A little color came back to Sage's face. Alvin made one last attempt. "Jay, let's you and I go talk for a moment. You are making a terrible mistake."

Jay didn't even acknowledge that the attorney had spoken. He faced the sheriff and said, "Like I was trying to say, I killed Caden, but I did it to save Janie's life. When I led my horse into the camp, Caden was talking to Janie and jabbing his hunting knife toward her. He looked angry, and she kept backing up." He paused, and Lee noticed that his eyes glanced toward Zach. Zach nodded, and Jay spoke again. "He told Janie he was going to kill her and that if he had to he'd kill the rest of us. I was leading my horse into camp, but I let go of it and stepped closer to them. Caden looked at me then and told me I shouldn't have returned when I did."

He stopped speaking, and the sheriff urged him to continue. After a moment, he began again. "Janie was really scared. She told me later that Caden had told her he was part of a national organization that was going to change the country. She'd laughed at him, and that was when he pulled out his hunting knife and said he would kill her. I told him to drop the knife. He lunged at Janie. She jumped and he missed her. There was a rifle lying on the ground. I didn't realize that it was Bria's at the time. Anyway, I grabbed it, jacked a shell in, and told Caden to drop the knife. He lunged at Janie again, and I fired." The sheriff raised a finger, and Jay stopped. "Did you know any of this, Mr. Eagler?" he asked.

The attorney shook his head. "He said he didn't know what happened."

"I was scared," Jay said. "I shot the guy. I figured I was going to prison. But sitting up there in Idaho, I got to feeling bad about being such a coward. Rex and Janie and I had agreed to not say anything if we didn't have to. We all figured I was in a lot of trouble. Then Bria was gone, and after that Zach disappeared too. The more that happened, the more scared I got. I told Mr. Eagler that I didn't know what happened, but I could tell that he didn't believe me. He told me to not say anything to anybody. So I didn't, not until Zach came up to Idaho and talked to me. I'm glad now that I did."

Lee said, "I'm sorry, I interrupted your story. What happened after you shot him?"

"Rex rode into the camp. He told Janie and me that he'd seen what happened. He also said that he'd seen another hunter a little way from the camp shortly before he'd gotten back, and it might look like the guy had shot Caden. Anyway, we checked Caden. He was dead. We were all scared then, especially me."

The sheriff's intercom buzzed. He picked it up, listened for a second, and then said, "Have him come in."

He put the receiver down and said, "Rich Phillips is here."

"Who is Rich Phillips?" Alvin asked as Lee noted the looks of shock on the faces of many of those in the room.

"Do you remember when that man from Duchesne fell overboard in Strawberry Reservoir and never came up back in May?"

"Yes," Alvin said. "The one who drowned. Bria Phillips's fa—" He stopped as a puzzled look came over his face.

"That's right. Rich Phillips is Bria's father. He's here," the sheriff said. Then, looking at Jay again, he said, "Is it okay if Mr. Phillips comes in?"

"Yeah, that'd be great," Jay said. "But I need to tell him how sorry I am that I let it look like Bria might have done it."

Detective Wakefield opened the door, and Rich stepped in. "I'll get a chair," Andrew said.

Rich waved him off. "I can stand. Thanks for letting me join you."

"I think most of you know Rich," Lee said. "He works for the CIA." He smiled. "He's recently returned from the great deep." Then Lee gave Rich a quick review of what Jay had told them. Rich simply nodded an acknowledgment and said, "Go ahead, Jay."

Jay was facing the back of the office where Rich was leaning against the wall. "I'm sorry, Mr. Phillips. I know I caused your daughter a lot of problems—the other guys, too."

"Her problems weren't your fault. They were mine, mine and a group of extremists," Rich said. "She's doing okay now."

"Thanks," Jay said and turned back.

Rich said, "Sheriff, if I may?" The sheriff nodded at him. "The man Rex saw was one of two CIA agents we sent up there to keep an eye on Bria and Caden. His name was Boyd Swift. He's the man whose body was found at the bottom of a cliff. It appears to have been an unfortunate accident that probably happened in the dark as the agent wandered away from your camp. I believe you have his harmonica. I know it sounds strange, but he used the harmonica to communicate with the other agent—the one who took Bria to safety. We knew we couldn't get cell-phone coverage up there, and we didn't want to use radios that the terrorists could track, so the harmonica was a way for the two agents to communicate on the mountain."

Lee noticed how Zach first looked in surprise at Rich and then nodded as understanding seemed to pass over him. "That explains what Frank was trying to tell me just before he died."

"Boyd was keeping an eye on Bria."

"Thanks, Rich," the sheriff said and turned back to Jay. "So what did you and the others do next?"

"We decided that if we pulled him into the bushes and put the rifle there, and, like I said, we figured we could blame the whole thing on this other guy, the agent. We figured that I would go to prison if I admitted shooting him. It was stupid and selfish. I can see that now, but that's what we decided. So we moved Caden. I laid the gun and his knife by him, and then we left. Zach was the one who found him. You know the rest."

"Jay," the sheriff said. "Your fingerprints were not on the rifle."

"I was wearing gloves," he said, and the sheriff nodded.

"That makes sense."

The sheriff sat back then, holding his side and grimacing. "I'll need to talk to Janie and Rex, but it looks to me like this thing is over. Jay, go home and get some sleep. And thanks for finally clearing this up for us."

"Will I have to go to jail?" Jay asked. "I know I did a terrible thing by not admitting what I'd done right at the first. I owe everyone an apology."

"So do Janie and Rex. As far as going to jail, if Janie and Rex back your story, you'll be okay."

Zach spoke up. "I'm pretty sure they will. They both encouraged me to go talk to Jay. I could tell that they wanted to tell the truth but that it was like they thought it should come from Jay. We are all glad to have this over."

* * *

The next evening, Zach was in his room trying to work up his courage to respond to Bria's e-mail. He'd hoped, after talking with Rich Phillips, that she would contact him. Rich thought she would, but she hadn't. He went down to dinner. When he came back, he again checked his e-mail account. To his surprise, there was a message from Bria.

He opened it eagerly and yet with a certain amount of dread. He didn't know what he felt anymore. He was afraid of what she was feeling. He opened her message and read.

Zach, if you open this, please read it all the way through. I'm sorry that I was so awful to you. You saved my life, and I appreciate it. Some of the best days of my life were when you were with us. I've never known anyone as unselfish as you. I had no right to get so angry when you left. And I had no right to lean on you so much when you were with me. I'm all mixed up right now. Dad says we won't be coming back to Duchesne to live. I guess that's just as well. We'll be living in Portland. Dad will be here in a few days, and then we are going to go house hunting.

He tells me that everything is cleared up there. Tell Jay I'm sorry about what happened to him. Jay's a great guy. I wasn't very fair to him. And tell him I hope he goes on a mission. Tell him to write to me. And please tell the others how sorry I am about what happened.

Zach, I'm sorry if I've made you miserable. I'm sorry if I made you hate me. I've never liked a guy so much in my life. But after having a little distance between us, I've realized that it was circumstance that made us lean on one another. Plus, with me living so far away now, it's just not going to work for us. Please don't think badly of me. Bria.

Zach stood up and walked around his room. He felt rejected and at the same time relieved. He wasn't angry with her, and he certainly didn't hate her. He could never hate her; in time he might be able to love her. He was confused. He needed to talk to someone. Maybe his folks, he thought, but then he decided against that. There was someone else who could help more. He pulled his cell phone from his pocket and dialed the Hinshaws' home number.

"Hello," Walt said.

"Hey, Walt, how's it going?" Zach said.

"Great. I just got an e-mail from Bria. She says that she won't be coming to live in Duchesne, but she does want to visit. She said she'd look me up, that she wanted to be my friend. She also said to tell you that she wasn't mad at you anymore. I told her to tell you herself," Walt said. "Have you heard from her?"

"Yes, I read an e-mail from her just a few minutes ago. You're right, she's not mad at me."

"Hey, that's good news," he said.

"Yes, it is," Zach agreed. "Is your sister there?"

"Sure is. Just a second, and I'll get her."

"Hi, Zach," Sage said a minute later. "Walt tells me that you heard from Bria."

"I did. Now I need some advice," he said.

"Okay, what?" she asked.

"Are you busy? I thought I'd come over."

"I'll be here. In fact, I'll wait outside for you," she said.

It was snowing lightly when Zach drove up the lane to the Hinshaws' yard. Sage was standing beside the gate, snow lighting on her golden hair. She had a coat on but also had her arms folded tightly against her chest. She smiled at him when he pulled up and stopped. He got out and walked over to her. "Thanks for letting me lean on you," he said.

"It's getting a little chilly. Can we walk while we talk?" Sage asked.

"I'm sorry to bother you," he said. "But, well, you just have a way of making me feel better and putting things in perspective. Do you mind?"

"Not at all," she said as they started back up the lane where Zach had just driven in. "So what did Bria say?"

Zach told her as clearly as he could remember it. He looked at Sage as he finished. They stopped and faced each other. The huge yard light reflected off her face in a gentle glow. She looked at him with a kind of strange look on her face. "So what do you want to know?" she asked.

"I want to know what to do."

"And you're asking me?" she asked with a mysterious smile.

"Yep, I couldn't think of anyone else who would understand like you do," he said, as he watched the light reflecting in her eyes. "I don't know what to say when I write her back."

For a moment, she seemed deep in thought, and then she smiled and said, "If it were me up there in Portland, I'd be hoping you'd just get on a plane and come."

"Really?" he said.

"You asked my advice. That's it. Go find her, Zach, and don't wait. Go in the morning. When you get there, tell her how you feel. Don't beat around the bush. Just find her and tell her."

He could have sworn she wiped at her eyes as she turned away. "Thanks, Sage," he said. "I knew I could count on you."

* * *

Two evenings later, there was a knock on the Hinshaws' front door. Sage answered it and was surprised to see Zach standing there. She swallowed the lump that formed in her throat and said, "Back already?"

"Yep," he said with grin.

"How did it go?"

"It went well," he said.

She tried to keep her face from showing her true feelings. He said, "Get your coat, and I'll tell you about it."

She left him standing there as she opened the coat closet. She started to put the coat on. Zach said, "Here, let me help you with that."

The snow from two nights ago was gleaming now beneath a full moon. The yard light shined brightly. Sage walked with Zach down the driveway and out the gate. They walked for a minute or two in silence. Finally, Zach stopped and faced her. She looked at him and had to fight back the tears. This was so hard.

"The other night when I was here, you gave me some advice. You said that if it were you in Portland that you wouldn't want me to write, that you'd want me to come. And you also said that when I did, I should say exactly how I felt."

"Yeah, I told you that," she agreed as she felt like her heart was about to burst. "Was I right?"

"I don't know yet."

"But I thought you went to Portland. That was my advice," she said, having to force every word. "Do I have to tell you again?"

"No, I got the message," he said. "I'm hoping that your advice is good."

Sage looked away, toward the glistening snow in her father's fields and then up at the full moon. She didn't say anything. She felt Zach's hand as it touched her chin and gently pulled her face toward him. He looked at her with an intensity she'd never seen in his eyes before. She tried to pull hers away, but she didn't have the willpower or the strength.

A subtle change came over his face. "We'll see how good your advice is."

"You should," she said, her body trembling.

"Sage, you've been next door to me for most of my life." Her heart was pounding so hard that it hurt. Unable to move, she watched him. His hand was still on her chin. He released it. "Sage, I've been a fool. I love you. I just couldn't see it. But these past two days, it finally hit me. I love you. You said—"

She reached up and put a cold finger on his warm lips and said, "I know what I said. And I meant it. Thanks for following my advice. I love you, too, Zach Barlow. I've loved you since I was just a little girl, but you've always been just out of my reach."

"I'm not out of reach now," he said as his strong arms encircled her and pulled her close.

When their lips touched, it was like an electric shock. She melted into his arms, the kiss deep and lingering. Never had Sage felt as secure anywhere as she felt here with this man tonight.

The bright moon shined around them, and on them, blessing their love.

ABOUT THE AUTHOR

Clair M. Poulson retired after twenty years in law enforcement. During his career, he served in the U.S. Army Military Police, the Utah Highway Patrol, and the Duchesne County Sheriff's Department, first as a deputy, then as the Duchesne County sheriff. He currently serves as a justice court judge for Duchesne County, a position he has held for about twenty years. His forty-year career working in the criminal justice system has provided a wealth of information from which he draws in writing his books.

Clair has served on numerous boards and committees over the years. Among them are the Utah Judicial Council, an FBI advisory board, the Peace Officer Standards and Training Council, the Utah Justice Court Board of Directors, and the Utah Commission on Criminal and Juvenile Justice.

Other interests include activity in the LDS church, assisting his son in the operation of their grocery store, ranching with his oldest son and other family members, and raising registered Missouri Fox Trotter horses and other farm animals.

With his latest book, Clair has published eighteen novels, many of them bestsellers.

Clair and his wife, Ruth, live in Duchesne, Utah, and they are the parents of five children and have twenty-one grandchildren.

You can visit Clair at www.clairmpoulson.com.